RAINE ENGLISH

Tin Angel

Elusive Dreams Press

Tin Angel

Published by Elusive Dreams Press

Excerpt from *Date with a Vampire* by Raine English copyright © by Raine English

Print ISBN: 978-1-62935-000-4

Digital ISBN: 978-1-62935-001-1

Edited by Linda Ingmanson

Cover by Char Adlesperger

www.RaineEnglish.com

First electronic publication: November 2012

First print publication: September 2013

The Romance Reborn Series

Book One: Tin Angel

DEDICATION

To my family. Thank you for all your support.
Mom, you never stopped believing.
Nikki, live life with no regrets.

ACKNOWLEDGMENTS

Many thanks to Linda Ingmanson for her editing and encouragement, and for being such a good friend.

CHAPTER ONE

"*H*ow's this look?"

Alice Hart leaned forward in the overstuffed armchair, squinting her tired eyes to get a better look at the tin angel Jack Billings had set atop the Christmas tree. Wrapped with faded gold foil and netting, the angel was almost as old as she.

"The tree looks wonderful, Jack. Whatever would I do without you?" She smiled at the handsome young man who'd come to her rescue countless times over the five months he'd been renting her upstairs apartment. A tumble of black hair fell across the bluest eyes she'd ever seen. He brushed it back and flashed her a Cary Grant grin.

"Aw, you're such a charmer, you'd have no trouble rounding up one of your other admirers." He stepped down off the stool and stood next to her chair.

Alice swooshed a wrinkled, liver-spotted hand through the air. "Go on, it's Saturday night. You mustn't waste your time with an old woman. Go on, before you're late for your date."

Jack's deep, throaty laughter filled the parlor. Alice liked the sound of it. She didn't get many visitors. Pastor Riley and Doc

Brooks didn't count. They came weekly out of obligation, but Jack came because he wanted to. She tucked the wool blanket on her lap snugly around her legs. If only she were young again, she just might pursue a man like Jack.

"What makes you think I have a date?" He got down on one knee and rested an elbow on the arm of her chair. With his chin in his hand, he stared deeply into her eyes. "There's no one I'd rather be with than you," he teased, but there was a kindness in his voice that touched her.

"Careful or you'll make me blush." She plucked at the blanket with long, spindly fingers—fingers that had once been beautiful and able to fly gracefully over ivory piano keys. But that was years ago, before the arthritis had set in. "The tree looks beautiful," she said, shifting her gaze.

"Beautiful, indeed. I'll be back tomorrow to check on you." He leaned over and gently kissed her cheek.

His finely sculpted lips were warm. A tingle ran down her spine, burning a trail of shame. She was ninety years old. She shouldn't still have these feelings. Yet she realized that was one of old age's cruelest tricks. While on the outside she had grayed and withered, inside she still felt twenty-five.

Alice squeezed his large, strong hands and bid him good night. After Jack left, she leaned back in the chair and stared at the Christmas tree. The glass ornaments twinkled against the multicolored lights. A deep, hollow feeling filled her chest. This could very well be her last Christmas. At her age, how many more could she expect to have? Tears pricked at her lids. She never imagined her life would turn out as it had, but then does anyone ever imagine they'll wind up alone? Even now, after more than sixty years, she could still picture Thomas Long's face—his lopsided smile that sent her heart pitter-pattering every time he flashed it her way, and those deep chocolate eyes that looked straight into her soul.

A tear trickled down her cheek. The war had taken Tom before they could marry. But he wasn't the only one who'd died that awful day in 1942. She'd died along with him. At least in spirit. If it hadn't been for Hart Theater, the family business where she played the piano each night, she'd have had no reason to ever leave her parents' rambling Victorian home.

Jasper, a sleek black cat with piercing gold eyes, jumped onto her lap. He curled into a ball and let out a raspy, contented purr. "At least I've got you," Alice whispered, stroking his back.

She shouldn't have let life slip by. Surely there could've been someone, somewhere who'd have found her attractive. If only she'd put herself out in the world, perhaps she'd have met someone...someone like Jack. He was just the type of man she would love to have met when she was young. The kind of man Tom had been—gentle and considerate. A lump formed in her throat. Nothing about life was fair.

She stared past the gleaming Christmas tree, through the leaded glass windows, out to the snow-lined street. She'd lived in Silvercreek her entire life. She'd watched the small Connecticut farming community become a bustling industrial town, but she'd never truly been a part of it—just a bystander looking in from the outside. She sighed and closed her eyes. What she wouldn't give to be able to live life over, if only for a few weeks. To be twenty-five again and in love...

Something sharp scratched Alice's arm. She opened her heavy-lidded eyes to find Jasper stretching contentedly on her lap. The grandfather clock ticking softly in the room's shadowed corner showed midnight. She'd fallen asleep in the parlor again. She pushed out her bottom lip and shook her head sadly. Pretty soon she'd be sleeping through the night in the chair.

Nudging the cat off her lap, Alice reached for her cane. Even with support, her legs were wobbly, and her joints ached from rheumatism. Slowly, she made her way to the bedroom. She slipped into a nightgown and then took the hairpins from the bun at the top of her head. Long silver strands cascaded down her back, falling just below her waist. She'd always worn her hair long, even as a child. It covered her like a blanket, hiding her imperfect features—the thin straight nose, the overly full lips, the dark wide-set eyes, and the square jaw. Not to mention her tall, lanky frame. Yes, she was far from beautiful, but her hair was exquisite.

Despite the twinge of pain in her gnarled fingers, she plaited her hair expertly from years of practice. She pulled back the down comforter and climbed in between the flannel sheets. Her stomach rumbled angrily. She'd not eaten dinner again. The only time she remembered was when she ate with Jack. Thank goodness for Jack. Without him, she'd most likely starve. Ignoring hunger's grumbling, she closed her eyes and let sleep take hold.

She slipped into a world where her body no longer ached and her heart wasn't broken. She floated on a cloud, and in her dreams, she became whatever she wanted—a beautiful young girl in love. As she drifted deeper into sleep's abyss, the years melted away.

"Dance with me." Tom's eyes sparkled. The pale light cast glints of gold on his sleekly combed hair. His fine, black tuxedo, tailored to perfection, accentuated his muscular build. She'd never seen him more handsome.

He took her hand and brought it to his lips, then led her through huge double doors into a candlelit ballroom. The orchestra began to play a waltz. She placed her hand on his shoulder, and he swept her across the polished floor. Their steps matched perfectly. He pulled her closer, holding her tight, as they twirled. His warm breath tickled her ear, and she relaxed against him, content to be in his arms. They danced round and round through cotton-candy clouds, but suddenly, he was ripped from her, disappearing in a swirl of mist and fog.

"Don't go. Don't leave me," she cried.

ℰᏩℭ

Alice awakened to find dawn's purple glow beaming in through her window, but her tired eyes burned as if she hadn't slept a wink. That dream! So vivid, almost as if it were real… Why, she could still feel the warmth of Tom's hand in hers, the scent of roses and beeswax candles lingering in the air, the effortless sway of their bodies moving in rhythm. She tried to drift back to the dream so that she might summon Tom again, but the moment was gone. She sighed and blinked the sleep from her eyes.

Jasper prowled onto her pillow and let out a series of loud meows. Food was a priority for the cat, if not for herself. She stepped into a pair of warm, fuzzy slippers and reached for her cane. Jasper led the way into the kitchen, where Alice poured a cup of cat food, then put the kettle on for tea. The cold, drafty room made her shiver, and she went into the parlor for a throw.

The Christmas tree sparkled in the morning light. She glanced up at the tin angel on top. Tom had given it to her before he left for war as a token of his love. Every time she looked at it, she felt as if the angel wrapped her in its golden wings, replacing her loneliness with serenity. "Forgive me," she whispered. "I know it's served no purpose to have mourned you my entire life, Tom. I should have tried to live…to love again. Not that anyone could have taken your place, but to waste my life…well, I realize now that was wrong."

The room went black. She blinked quickly, trying to make out anything: a piece of furniture, the Christmas tree, something…but it was as if she'd fallen into a cavern so deep that not even a pinpoint of light could penetrate. Had she gone blind? Perhaps she'd had a stroke. Oh Lord, was she about to die? She reached for her cane, but her hand froze on the brass handle. A piercing blue light illuminated the parlor. Oh no, it was too late. Death had claimed her.

At her feet lay the tin angel. When she reached for it, a gust of wind more powerful than a February Nor'easter blew her into an overstuffed armchair. The angel rocketed into the air and spun like a top, then burst into tiny glittering particles that fell around her in a shower of gold dust. An exquisite figure emerged—pixie-like in appearance, its gossamer wings fluttering like a butterfly's.

"What's happening?" Alice whispered, gripping the chair.

A tinkle of laughter more melodious than church bells spilled from the angel's bow-shaped lips. "Don't be frightened, Alice. I've granted your wish."

"Wish? I haven't wished for anything."

The angel floated nearer. "But you did. You wished for youth and love."

"A feeble dream."

"But a wish, nonetheless."

Alice frowned. "Maybe, but I know better than most, wishes don't come true."

The angel lifted an iridescent brow, her gaze leveled at Alice. "Really?"

With the angel's stare fixed on her, Alice glanced down over her body. Her eyes widened in disbelief. What had happened to her wrinkles and liver spots? She held out her hand. Whose smooth, supple skin was this? Next she flexed her arthritic fingers, then waggled them when no familiar stiffness stopped her. "Oh my, there's no pain," she said in disbelief.

Alice rose from the chair and, like a child filled with joy, twirled on her toes, then hurried across the room without the use of her cane and with a spring in her step that she hadn't had in years. She stopped in front of a large gilt-framed wall mirror. "It can't be true." The reflection that greeted her was one she hadn't seen in decades. Luminous smoky-gray eyes. A radiant rosy complexion accentuated by high cheekbones and a wide sensuous mouth, shiny chestnut hair… She ran her index finger over her bottom lip, down her chin and along her firm jaw.

"I don't believe it. I'm gorgeous. And young!" Tears streamed down her cheeks. This was how she'd looked in her youth, only the ugly duckling had become a swan. Times had changed and so had the standard of beauty. For the first time in her life, she liked the way she looked. But how could this be? She was ninety years old, far from young and beautiful.

Alice didn't know what to do. Part of her wanted to dash into the streets and dance: another part of her wanted to run back to bed, hide under the covers and wake up again. She looked at her agile, young hands and shook her head. She pressed her palms together and took a long look around the room. The same antique rose throw lay across the sofa. And there on the end table stood her favorite photograph of Tom in his uniform, yellowed now with age. Only she had changed.

Alice shook her head slowly, took a deep breath, and looked back at the angel. "Well, okay, maybe every once in a while miracles do happen. But why now? Why this?" She waved a smooth, wrinkle-free hand in front of herself.

"Because you've been given a second chance at life."

"A second chance? I don't understand."

"You're in limbo, Alice."

The blood drained from her face, and the room seemed to tilt. "You mean I'm dead?" Her voice came out as little more than a squeak.

Golden curls danced around the angel's face as she laughed. "Let's not call it that. Let's just say you've had a transformation."

Alice leaned against the wall to steady herself. "All right, then, this…transformation, how long will it last?"

"Till New Year's Day. Unless you find true love before then."

"What! If I haven't found love in over sixty years, how in the world can I find it in ten days?"

"It will do you no good to be negative. Besides, Tom is rooting for you."

"Tom sent you?"

The angel nodded. "A soul plagued by guilt can't rest. He wants you to love again."

"But what if I don't find love?"

The angel's radiant complexion darkened. "Then you'll forfeit this second chance—"

"And I really will be dead," Alice said glumly, finishing the tin angel's sentence. A moment later, blackness enveloped her. "Wait," she cried. "Don't leave, there's so much I need to ask you." But the darkness swallowed her useless plea. The tin angel had disappeared.

Maybe this was just another dream? She scratched the side of her leg with her fingernail. The ensuing sting confirmed she was indeed awake. She glanced at the top of the Christmas tree. The tin angel was gone. Great. She'd been given a second chance at life, but she had no idea how she was going to find love.

The piercing wail of the teakettle sent Alice sprinting to the kitchen. Steam shot from its spout, and water bubbled from its rattling lid like a science experiment gone awry. She grabbed a potholder, then lifted the copper kettle from the burner, setting it on a hot plate next to the stove.

Jasper sat on the counter, cleaning his face with his paw. If a cat could frown, that was the look he shot her between licks. Large golden eyes glared at her, and a low growl rumbled in his throat when she reached out to stroke his head.

"What's the matter, Jasp? Don't you recognize me?"

The cat inched back. "It's me," she said with a laugh, "only a new-and-improved model." She held her hand out for Jasper to sniff until he seemed satisfied she was indeed his owner.

"I've got so much I want to do. I don't know where to begin." She looked down at the fuzzy pink slippers too large for her feet and the floral nightgown barely skimming her ankles. "First off, I'd better find some clothes that fit."

She left Jasper to finish his grooming and headed toward the bedroom. Inside, she opened her closet and groaned at the stack of cardigan sweaters and stretch pants. They might be all right for an old lady, but they'd never do for a young woman about to have the time of her life. She took a moment to say a prayer of thanks for this miracle, then rummaged through a row of blouses until she came to a coral silk—the one she liked to wear when Pastor Riley came to call. He said it complemented her eyes. Yanking it off the hanger, she tossed it on the bed, then found the pair of black trousers she always wore with it.

She slipped out of her nightgown and noticed the cotton briefs about to fall down around her knees. She hadn't realized how much her waist had thickened over the years, leaving her to wonder about the changes that might have occurred to the rest of her body. She already knew her feet were smaller and she'd gained an inch or so in height. She averted her gaze to her breasts. And she knew something else—she no longer sagged.

Shopping was definitely at the top of her to-do list.

၈၁၈

Jack slid the mustard jar next to last week's leftovers, then reached for the milk. He let the refrigerator door slam shut behind him as he moved over to the kitchen table. From the corner of his eye, he saw the answering machine's flashing red light. He didn't need to play the message to know who'd left it. Bethany Snow. A long-legged blonde beauty and the daughter of Dr. Eugene Snow, dean of Chesterfield

Hall and Jack's former employer.

At one time he'd been convinced he loved Bethany, but after three years with her he'd felt more like her puppet than her fiancé. When he'd learned Silvercreek Elementary School needed a music teacher, he'd had no problem leaving Boston for the peaceful lifestyle of a small town. He was through with high-maintenance women. He'd take a simple girl any day—someone like Alice must have been. He imagined what she must have looked like in her youth, a fresh-faced beauty with an understated style. Since he'd moved in, he'd gotten pretty close to her. She needed someone to catch up on odd jobs around the old house, and he was happy to help her out. At first he'd thought of her like a grandma, but she'd become a good friend, entertaining him with stories from simpler days when life—and love—wasn't so complicated. If he could only find a woman like her, an old-fashioned girl...

He poured the milk into his coffee, then took a sip as he walked over to the answering machine. Sure enough, Bethany's smooth, silky voice filled the kitchen.

"Jack, love, I have fabulous news, and if I don't tell you now, I'll just burst. Randolph agreed to give me a few days off over the holiday. That means I can spend New Year's with you. Isn't that fabulous? It'll be like old times. Call me, love."

He took a gulp of his coffee, forgetting how hot it was. Bethany never asked for time off from her news position at WWCO Radio. Could her mission be to have him put a ring back on her finger? The thought left a queasy feeling in his stomach, similar to how he felt after eating day-old pepperoni pizza. He'd have to deal with Bethany, though, like it or not. Just not now. He was already running late. His students at school might enjoy his tardiness, but he doubted the neighboring classrooms would look favorably upon the chaos coming from his music room. Besides, he still had to drop off breakfast to

Alice.

He set his coffee cup down and grabbed the still-hot cinnamon buns he'd purchased earlier that morning from the little bakery around the corner. Renting Alice's upstairs apartment made it easy for him to check in on her and provide her with a meal. He let the door slam shut behind him and raced down the back stairs whistling "Deck the Halls."

Jack hopped up the steps to Alice's front porch and knocked on the thick wood door, listening for the tapping of her cane on the foyer floor. A few moments later, the door opened a mere six inches. An unexpected beauty with gleaming chestnut hair, full sensuous lips, and mesmerizing gray eyes peered out at him. "I-I'm here to see Alice." He felt ridiculous for his stutter, but this girl knocked the breath out of him.

"She's not here."

"Well, where is she? When will she be back?"

"I don't know. I'll tell her you came by." She snatched the cinnamon buns out of his hands, then slammed the door.

"Wait a minute. I didn't even tell you my name." He spoke to the thick mahogany door. What in the world was that all about? Something wasn't right. Alice never went anywhere. Who was that rude woman, and why was she so eager to get rid of him? And where the heck had his buns gone? She sure snatched those away quick enough. He needed some answers, and he was going to get them. Only he'd have to wait until later, as his watch showed 8:35 a.m. Just barely enough time to slip into school before the bell rang.

ଚୈଙ୍କ

Alice's hand shook as she set the cinnamon buns down on the kitchen table. In all the excitement, she'd forgotten about Jack. In her mind, his face flashed—dark brows rising over surprised blue eyes, mouth open about to protest—just before she'd snatched the hot rolls from his long, musician's fingers and shut him out. He would want to know what happened to Alice. To the *old* Alice… What a pickle! Jack would be back. And then what? She couldn't keep slamming the door in his face. Well, one thing was certain. She couldn't tell him the truth about her miracle transformation. But the thought of deceiving him didn't sit well with her either.

Jack was a good friend, and she didn't have many of those. She thought back to the countless times he'd come to her rescue. Like the time the pipe burst in her bathroom, and he turned off the water before the whole first floor flooded. Yes, he'd proven to be a good friend all right, but, even still, she knew he wouldn't believe her if she told him the truth. Who would? No, she had to come up with a story, and a good one at that. Thankfully, with Jack at work, she had plenty of time to think of something. Besides, she wasn't about to let this put a damper on her day. She was a young woman with lots to do!

Shaking off the doldrums, she reached for the telephone and dialed Silvercreek Cab Company. While waiting for the cab's arrival, she went into the bedroom and pulled down a shoebox from the closet shelf. She set the box on the bed and removed the lid. Inside were stacks of fifty and one-hundred-dollar bills. Alice liked to keep her money at home. She didn't trust banks, after witnessing her parent's despair at losing much of their savings in the Great Depression's run on banks.

She counted out one thousand dollars, then tucked the money into her wallet. As she returned the shoebox to the closet, she heard the honking of the cab's horn. She grabbed her purse and raced out the front door.

When she arrived at Lorelle, a high-end boutique, she selected an armful of outfits and proceeded to try each one on. With her shyness still an issue, she peeked out from the dressing room curtain to make sure the communal area with the large three-way mirror was empty before going out there to view the gorgeous evening ensemble she'd slipped into.

Alice had always avoided mirrors, yet she admired her reflection like some shallow debutante. The black ankle-length skirt she wore swirled around her legs as she moved, showing off her calves, and the matching lace blouse revealed just the right amount of skin. She'd never owned anything so beautiful—and she wouldn't now, she told herself sternly. Where in the world would she wear it? With a sigh, she turned away from the mirror and headed back toward the dressing room.

A cute young woman with a short sassy haircut and a face full of freckles rushed over to her. "Oh, miss, that outfit has your name on it. Here, let me accessorize it for you." The sales clerk took hold of her arm and led her across the store.

"I was just about to change," Alice sputtered.

"This won't take but a minute. I'm sure you'll love the result. Look." The clerk pulled a delicate gold chain from a jewelry display. She slipped it around Alice's neck, then reached for the matching earrings. "You look stunning," she cooed, holding the earrings next to Alice's face. "But you need to do something with this." She grabbed a strand of Alice's waist-length hair, tucked it inside the black lace blouse, and grinned. "Yes, that's it. I knew it." The clerk tucked in the rest of Alice's hair, then led her over to a mirror. "Now don't get me wrong. You've got beautiful hair—just too much of it. It hides your pretty face. But now, well, take a look." She stepped away so Alice could see herself.

Alice gasped. The clerk was right. She didn't need to hide behind her hair. With a shoulder-length style, it would still be long, but it wouldn't overpower her.

"You like?"

Speechless, Alice could only nod.

The clerk pulled a business card from her pocket and placed it in Alice's palm. "This is Frederick. He's a fabulous hairdresser. Tell him Kendra sent you. He'll take extra-good care of you. Now, will you be putting today's purchases on your credit card?"

"No, cash." Alice entered the dressing room with her head awhirl. She had less than two weeks to find true love, and she was about to buy an outfit she didn't need and cut twelve inches off her hair. Had she gone mad? Or maybe she was doing exactly what she needed to do in order to attract the man of her dreams.

ℰᏆᏟᏚ

At the salon, true to Kendra's word, Alice was given the royal treatment, beginning with a lengthy shampoo and fabulous scalp massage. She listened to the steady *snip, snip, snip* of Frederick's shears as he cut her hair. Her eyes were squeezed shut and her heart was pounding, yet it wasn't fear she felt but excitement. As each section of hair dropped to the floor, a weight lifted. Old insecurities disappeared, and, like a butterfly emerging from its cocoon, she too was free.

With the final click of the shears, she snuck a glance.

"No, no," Frederick shrieked, spinning her chair away from the mirror. He stood with hands on hips, tapping the toe of his heavily studded cowboy boot. "You mustn't peek till I'm ready for the reveal." He spoke with a heavy European accent that she thought he used more for effect than from living abroad.

"Sorry," she murmured, sinking into the chair. The sleeve of his polyester shirt—the likes of which she hadn't seen for decades— brushed her cheek as he worked mousse through her hair.

He grabbed the blow dryer as if he were drawing a pistol and held it beside his leather-clad thigh. "Now, tip your head down to your knees, and let me finish this masterpiece."

Alice bent down and studied the veins in the marble floor while

Frederick worked his magic on her hair.

"Here we go, Miss Alice. Sit up and toss your head back." When she obliged, he turned her toward the mirror. "Voila."

His smile reminded her of the Cheshire cat's, and she definitely felt like Alice in Wonderland, but her hairstyle was a work of art.

Mountains of glossy chestnut hair skimmed her shoulders. Not too short. Not too long. Perfect. Just perfect. "I don't know what to say."

"Ahh, no need for words. Your eyes say it all, and with the right shadow, they could seduce a man with a glance." Frederick snapped his fingers. A pretty young girl with flawless skin came running. "Take Miss Alice to the makeup counter and make her siz-z-le."

By the time Alice left the salon, she barely recognized herself—glossed lips, sultry eyes and cheekbones a cover model would die for. Too bad she didn't have anyone to show off her new look to.

At home, she dropped her armful of packages on the sofa. Jasper jumped off the windowsill and strolled around her feet. He didn't rub against her legs as usual but kept his distance, as if trying to make out this latest change in her appearance.

"It's all right. It's me. Get used to it, my friend, this new look is here to stay. At least for ten days or so," she said glumly. A chilly bolt lanced through her. The reality of her limited time dimmed the glow of the tin angel's miracle. If she didn't find true love by New Year's...

To rid herself of her melancholy, Alice waltzed over to her old record player and put on Frank Sinatra. As she swayed to the music, she opened her packages. She pulled out outfit after outfit, holding each one up, then tossing it toward the sofa. Some made it to the cushions, but many landed on the floor.

Alice undid the buttons on her coral blouse, then unzipped her trousers. "Away with the old," she sang, slipping out of her clothes and tossing them into the air, "and in with the new." She picked up an animal-print shirt, held it up to her chest, then twirled around the parlor in her underwear.

A knock on the front door froze her. Every muscle tensed. For a moment, she was taken back to the night her world shattered—the night Tom had been taken from her. She'd been about the same age, but this was a new day, and it wouldn't be a solemn-faced sergeant bringing bad news. Oh Lord, it must be Jack. She dropped the shirt and raced to the bedroom for her robe. She wasn't prepared for a visitor. And she still didn't know what she was going to tell him.

CHAPTER TWO

*J*ack shoved his hands in the pockets of his jeans while he waited for Alice to open the door. The sun had set, giving way to evening's bitter cold. He shivered inside his coat and prayed that nothing was wrong with the old gal. He'd spent most of the day wondering where she could have gone and who that strange woman was who'd answered her door.

He was just about to knock again when that very same woman opened the door a crack, making no attempt to conceal her annoyance or her nervousness. "What?"

His stomach soured. Something wasn't right. He could feel it. "Where's Alice?"

"She's still not here, and I don't know when she'll be back."

His gaze traveled down, and he caught a glimpse of a long slender leg peeking out from Alice's favorite robe. "It's freezing out here. I have some questions I need to ask you, so may I please come inside? I'm Jack Billings. I live upstairs."

"I know."

He raised his brows in surprise. "You do?"

"You're Alice's tenant. She told me a good-looking man was

renting her upstairs apartment."

The way she stared at him made him think she also found him attractive. Although flattered, he knew her type only too well—the type who piled on makeup and had every hair in place before she'd leave the house. A high-maintenance woman out to land any eligible man. He'd sworn off her type when he called off his engagement with Bethany. Three years was more than enough time with a woman who took longer putting on her makeup than he took to shower, shave, and dress.

She flung the door open. "You can't stay long."

"Why would I? I'd just like to know where Alice is and what you're doing in her house." He sidestepped her into the foyer, then strolled toward the parlor.

When he reached the doorway, his jaw dropped. The room looked like a cyclone had gone through it. Clothes were strewn everywhere. The girl might be beautiful, but she was a slob. "No time to pick up?"

A rosy flush glowed beneath her porcelain complexion. "I went shopping." She pushed past him and began to gather up her clothes.

"I prefer to hang my wardrobe," he said.

She shot him an icy look as she scooped up a sheer pink bra dangling from the Christmas tree. Her cheeks reddened again, and she tucked the garment under her arm. He wouldn't have thought her to be modest. After all, she'd let him in while wearing a robe that did little to conceal her figure, and an unusually curvaceous one at that for a woman so slender.

As if reading his mind, she adjusted the clothes in her arms so that they covered her ample cleavage. "Please excuse me while I put these things away."

"Of course." He watched her leave the room. There was something familiar about her. Was it possible he'd met her somewhere before? Not likely. He'd never forget a woman that attractive. Yet, the way she held herself…the slight tilt to her head when she spoke… His brow furrowed in frustration. Who was she, and what was she doing here? He'd seen Alice only yesterday. She never mentioned going anywhere. Something odd was definitely going on.

A few minutes later, the girl returned, wearing stone-washed jeans and a lavender sweater. A price tag hung from her sleeve. "You forgot one," he said, pointing to her arm.

She looked down and laughed. The sound was lovely…and familiar.

"Who are you?" he asked.

Her back stiffened. "I'm Ali—Ally. Alice's niece." Her gaze didn't quite meet his.

"Niece? That's strange, she never mentioned a niece. As a matter of fact, she never mentioned any relatives at all."

She plopped down on the sofa, crossed her long legs at the ankles, and peered up at him with huge innocent eyes. "I'm not surprised. My dad was always the black sheep. Aunt Alice hasn't seen or spoken to him in years. So why would she mention me? I barely know her."

"Back to my original question, what are you doing in her house?" Jack moved closer, resting his hand on the arm of the sofa. He wrinkled his nose. She smelled like a perfume factory. Had she put the whole bottle on?

"My dad's ill. He wanted to see her. To make amends. They're both up there in years."

"Go on," he demanded.

She took a deep breath, then folded her hands in her lap. "Alice is visiting my dad, and I'm here. That's it. What else is there?"

Jack gritted his teeth. What else is there? A lot, he thought angrily. His gaze scanned the room. Alice's favorite fuzzy slippers peeked out from the bottom of an old chair. Something wasn't right. Not right at all. He didn't believe a word this girl said, but he forced a smile. "I still don't understand why you're here."

The way she nibbled her lower lip gave him the distinct impression she was either nervous or making up her story as she went along. "A guy... I needed some time away from him, and Aunt Alice said I could stay at her place."

A guilty heat traveled up his neck. Perhaps he'd misjudged her. Her story made some sense. He understood the need to get away from someone who was driving you crazy. He'd been through those days. "Let's say I believe you. Alice doesn't drive—"

"My dad had his driver drop me off and take Aunt Alice back to upstate New York," she said quickly. "Now if your grilling is over, please leave." She stood and walked to the door.

Jack followed her into the foyer. She was smooth, he'd give her that much. And her story did make sense. And there was a strong resemblance to Alice. He could see it in her bone structure and her almond-shaped eyes. They were the same color too, only brighter. But something still bothered him.

Ally swung the door open.

"Thank you. I appreciate your honesty." He studied her face for a moment, trying to read her, but the only thing he saw was her desire for him to leave. Stepping off the porch, he headed around back to his apartment. She couldn't get rid of him that easily. He'd keep an eye on her, that's for sure.

ↄↃ

Alice's stomach was in a knot as she closed the door. Somehow she'd managed to pull off the story of the brother from upstate New York. A huge feat, especially for someone who'd never been able to lie— and to think she'd lied to Jack, of all people—but what else was she to do? He'd never believe the truth. A wave of anxiety swept through her. Relax, she told herself. You did no harm. Jack's appeased, and you've nothing to fear.

She slumped back to the parlor and stared at the top of the Christmas tree, where the tin angel used to sit. "What now? Jack must think I'm some kind of nut." With a sigh, she turned out the lights and padded toward the bedroom, her shoulders hunched and her mood grim. A mountain of clothes covered the bed. She held up the black blouse and matching skirt and shook her head sadly. "I might be young and beautiful, but I'm still alone, and the loneliness has never been so great." It didn't seem fair to look like a college co-ed on the outside and feel like a reclusive old woman on the inside.

With little joy, she put away her new clothes, then slipped into the soft blue nightshirt she'd purchased at Lorelle. After turning down the bed, she slid between the flannel sheets and closed her eyes. Jack's image filtered behind her eyelids. He wore his straight, jet-black hair fingered back from his classically handsome face. With his striking blue eyes—the color of the sky on a perfect spring day— and sensuous lips, he was a man few women could resist. And she was no exception. Hormones she hadn't had in decades now raged.

Not only was Jack something to look at, but he was exactly the type of man Tom would approve of. Suddenly, a thought occurred to her. Could Jack be the one? Could he be her true love? Nah, he seemed completely unaware of how he made her pulse race. And when he looked at her, for some reason his eyes reflected nothing but scorn. Why? When she was an old woman, he'd never looked at her that way.

As she drifted off to sleep, her dreams endowed him with an entirely different emotion. His desire for her was obvious by the way his lips pressed hot and hard against hers, and his strong muscular arms held her firmly against his broad chest.

Through the fogginess of her dream, she heard a bell ring. Was that the telephone? She forced her eyes open and grabbed for the receiver. "Hello." Her voice was husky from sleep.

"Ally? I'm sorry, did I wake you?" Jack sounded almost friendly. Quite a change from earlier, when suspicion had laced his words.

"Have another question for me?"

He chuckled smoothly. "Yes. Have dinner with me tomorrow."

Alice sat up and switched the phone to her other ear. Had she heard him correctly? Perhaps she was still asleep.

"I'll take your silence for yes. Be ready by eight."

The phone went dead. It took Alice a few seconds to hang up the receiver. When she finally did, she flopped back in bed, closed her eyes and fell asleep with a smile. Maybe her golden opportunity would shine after all.

ഇൗരു

Jack stared at the phone long after he ended his call to Ally. It wasn't like him to intentionally deceive someone, and he didn't feel good about doing it now. He knew Ally assumed he'd asked her to dinner because he was attracted to her, which wasn't untrue, but that wasn't his reason for wanting to spend time with her. He knew her type only too well. He'd been surrounded by them his entire life. Memories of his mother's country club friends sprang to mind—women who were obsessed with their looks and a fear of growing old. All were gorgeous and used to men vying for their attention, catering to their every need. Not that he wouldn't mind catering just a little to Ally.

He had to admit he'd wondered what it would feel like to kiss those delicious lips, but he wasn't fool enough to actually carry it out. He'd been trounced on enough in his last relationship. He'd never let that happen again. Though Bethany might have convinced herself that she loved him, women like that never truly loved. They didn't even know the meaning of the word. Thankfully, he wasn't so naïve to think Ally was any different.

Propping the pillows up behind him, he lay back on the bed. In the corner, where the wall met the ceiling, an intricate spider web glistened. In its center, a fly struggled to break free. If Jack wasn't careful, he could find himself in the same situation—the victim of a cunning adversary. His forehead furrowed. He didn't want to hurt Ally, but he was going to have to make her think he was interested in her in order to find out what happened to Alice.

It took him a while to fall asleep, and when he did, he tossed and turned all night, tormented by weird dreams of Alice needing his help.

The next day at school, he had trouble concentrating on his students' lessons. His mind kept drifting to Ally. There was a lot more to her story than she'd told him. He was sure of it, and that made him even more determined to get the truth out of her at dinner.

80C3

Alice ran her hand over the black lace outfit lying across her bed. If it hadn't been for that sweet little sales clerk, she never would've bought it. Thank goodness she had, because here she was getting ready for a date with Jack. Jack Billings—her friend, and an extremely attractive man. A tremor of fear soured her excitement. She had to be careful tonight. What if he recognized her? How could she possibly explain that she was really Alice? Would he believe her if she told him an angel had granted her wish to be young again? Of course not. He'd think she was insane.

Many times throughout the day, she'd come close to canceling their date. Even now, she was tempted to tell him she couldn't make it, but she'd waited so long to look into a man's eyes and see desire…to hear her name whispered like a caress… No, she wasn't about to risk losing that chance, even if it meant she had to be on guard. She might have little time to live life, but she intended to do just that. Maybe…just maybe…she'd fall in love. And this date would be good practice. Lord knew she needed the practice in case Mr. Right did appear.

She glanced in her dresser mirror. Surprisingly, she'd done a good job with her hair and makeup. She'd even managed a straight line with her eyeliner. She dressed quickly, sprayed some eau de parfum, then gave her hair a fluff. At eight o'clock on the dot, she heard a knock at her door. Jack never failed to be punctual. It was one of the many things she liked about him. She grabbed the little black bag the girl at Lorelle had insisted she buy to go with her outfit and rushed to the front door.

Alice tried not to gasp when she saw Jack, but was there ever a more beautiful man? His jet hair skimmed the collar of his camel-colored overcoat. Beneath it she caught a glimpse of a charcoal suit. She breathed a sigh of relief. She'd been afraid she might be over dressed; after all there weren't many fine restaurants in Silvercreek, and, for all she knew, he could have been planning to take her to Mac's Diner.

He seemed pleased with the way she looked as well. His gaze traveled slowly over her, stopping briefly at the curve of her hip, then again at the top of her scooped-neck blouse. Her skin grew warm, as if he'd touched her. His eyes locked with hers, and what she saw caused her heart to thunder. There it was. The look she'd been waiting for. Desire. And he made no attempt to disguise it.

"You look gorgeous," he murmured.

She smiled shyly. "So do you."

Grabbing a black velvet coat—another purchase from her shopping spree—from the hall closet, she let Jack help her into it. He took hold of her hand, wrapping his fingers around hers, and led her outside to his car. She sank into the soft leather seat. Her knees quivered. She hadn't been on date in…well, she hated to even think about how long. Calm down, she told herself. *You're out with Jack, not some stranger.* But that only made her legs shake more.

She watched as over six feet of hard-bodied man slid behind the driver's seat. A shadow of stubble, which she found very sexy, covered his chin and upper lip. She had a strong urge to run her fingertip across his face, but common sense took over, and she turned her attention to the road. Jack wound his Acura around the streets of Silvercreek as if he'd lived there his entire life.

"Where are we going?" she asked, unable to suppress her curiosity.

He flashed her a smile as bright as one in any toothpaste ad. "It'll be more fun if it's a surprise."

Alice wanted to say, *I don't care where we eat. I'm happy just to be with you.* Instead, she stared silently through the window into the dark. The moon's silvery light danced over snow-covered trees, making her feel like they were driving through an enchanted forest. "Thank you," she whispered, hoping the tin angel could hear her. If she had only this one night with Jack, it would be enough. A tear threatened to spill onto her cheek, but she blinked it back.

They drove in silence, leaving Silvercreek behind, and headed toward Hartford. She was glad Jack wasn't one for idle conversation. She didn't want anything to break the spell she was under. When she stole a glance at his handsome profile, her skin prickled into gooseflesh. She was on a date…a date with Jack. She needed the reminder it was real and not a dream. Up ahead, the lights of the city gleamed brightly. A few minutes later, Jack pulled into a parking lot. Overhead, a huge neon sign with Mario's Restaurante spelled in purple and pink fluorescent letters lit up the sky. Alice waited for Jack to come around and open her door. He offered his arm, and she stepped gracefully onto the pavement.

"Ah, old-fashioned values?" He smiled down at her. "I like

that."

If only he knew *just* how old-fashioned, she thought.

With his hand on the small of her back, they crossed the parking lot. Upon entering the restaurant, a tingle of excitement coursed through her. She never imagined she'd dine in a restaurant with Jack. Large, exotic-looking plants lined the entrance. Dimly lit, with dark wood paneling, the atmosphere inside was rustic and homey. Not at all what she'd expected.

They were given an intimate table in the back. After listening to the maître de recite the specials, she opened her menu. Her brow wrinkled at the many choices offered. How would she ever decide? Dinner at home was zapping something frozen—usually macaroni and cheese—in the microwave.

When she looked up, Jack was studying her. "Shall I order for you?"

She sighed, appreciative of his insight. "Yes, please. That would be wonderful."

"You take after her," he said softly.

"Who?"

"Your aunt." He reached across the table and lifted her hands, studying them. "They're slender and graceful, just like hers. It's amazing. And to think you barely know her."

Alice pulled her hands back and stuck them under the table. "Some things can't be helped."

"Such a shame. She's a wonderful woman."

Alice noticed the sparkle in Jack's eyes. He obviously admired her.

"And your father. Is he like her too?"

She dropped her gaze from his intense blue eyes. She hadn't expected him to bring up her imaginary father. "No, he wasn't. He's not...much like her. Tell me about yourself. What is it you do for work?" she asked, quickly changing the subject.

His face lit up as she'd expected. Jack loved his work—especially the children—and she knew it was a subject he could talk about for hours. Many nights after he'd had dinner at her place, he'd stay past midnight, talking about school and the children.

"I teach music over at the elementary school. Music is my passion," he said.

"M—" Alice bit back her words. She'd been about to say, *Mine too*, then realized her mistake. She couldn't appear too similar to a woman she was supposed to barely know.

"Merchandising," she spouted, looking down at her skirt. "Fashion merchandising. That's what I do."

The sparkle left Jack's eyes. "And I'll bet you're quite good at it too." From his tone, she knew he hadn't meant it as a compliment. She'd better be careful, or Jack would become more suspicious of her than he already was.

Thankfully, the waiter arrived. "Are you ready to order?" he asked, putting an end to that uncomfortable conversation.

"Yes, we'll each have the braised beef short rib," Jack said, "and bring us a bottle of your best red wine."

She watched him over the rim of her water glass. The copper lamp in the center of the table cast a warm glow over his swarthy complexion. His raven hair glistened. Oh no! Her thoughts were beginning to wander to places they shouldn't. She'd best control her reaction to him, at least until they were through with dinner. She lowered her lashes and studied the tablecloth's red-and-white-checked pattern.

"Is something wrong?"

When she looked up, worry shadowed his expression. He was a compassionate man, one who didn't deserve to be deceived, but it was impossible for her to ignore the powerful feelings churning inside. "I was just thinking how happy I am to be here with you." At least that wasn't a lie.

The lines creasing his forehead disappeared. He rested his elbows on the edge of the table and leaned in toward her. "I'm enjoying your company too."

Although she didn't doubt his sincerity, she couldn't help but wonder if, given a choice, he wouldn't rather be with Alice. How odd that she should feel that way. After all, she was young and beautiful—the object of every man's desire. So why in the world would she think he'd prefer the company of an old woman? Deciding to ignore such crazy musings, she accepted his compliment with a wide smile.

"That boyfriend, the one you left back in New York, must be crazy to have let you go."

A heated blush stole up her neck. He did desire her. For a sinful moment, she wondered what it would feel like to spend the night wrapped in his arms.

With impeccable timing, the waiter interrupted with the wine. He popped the cork, poured Jack a glass, and waited silently while Jack swirled, sniffed, and sipped. When Jack nodded his approval, the waiter poured a glass for Alice.

She brought the goblet to her lips, then quickly set it back down, nearly splattering wine over her lap. Doc Brooks was headed toward their table. In his mid-sixties with a mop of white hair swept to one side and slicked down with hair spray, the short, heavy-set man moved with amazing agility.

"Charlie, great to see you," Jack said, springing to his feet and shaking the doctor's hand.

"My wife and I love this place. We don't miss a week." He glanced at Alice through thick bifocal lenses. "Pleasure to meet you…"

"I'm sorry, this is Ally, Alice's niece," Jack said.

Doc Brooks frowned. "That's funny. I've known Alice for years, and she never mentioned a niece."

Both men stared at her. Her knees began to shake. "I hadn't seen my aunt since I was a child." She hoped her nervousness wasn't taken as a sign she was lying.

"I see. How's Alice doing?" the doctor asked, his tone anxious.

"She's spending the holiday with my dad." Alice prayed Doc Brooks would hurry up and leave.

"That's odd. She never said a word."

"Not to me either," Jack chimed in. "Ally's father took sick. She left suddenly, isn't that right?"

Her fingers trembled in her lap. "Yes."

"I hope she's careful. Alice has such trouble getting around." Doc Brooks' small, round eyes focused on her face. "It's nice to have met you, Ally is it? Quite a striking resemblance." He scratched his ear as he walked back to his table.

When Alice turned to Jack, he was still staring at her. "What?" she asked, her defenses on high alert.

His sensuous mouth turned up into a smile. "You look amazing tonight."

A nerve twittered at the side of her cheek. "Thank you."

He took hold of her hand and rubbed his thumb over her skin. Electricity seemed to arc through her. A man hadn't touched her that way since Tom. She'd forgotten how wonderful it felt. She closed her eyes, and her nervousness evaporated. She was beautiful, and Jack desired her. All the feelings she'd kept bottled up inside were dangerously close to erupting. She wondered what his kiss would feel like. Would it be soft or deep and sensual? The all too vivid image of him pressed hard against her made her mouth go dry. She moistened her lips with the tip of her tongue. What had happened to her common sense? She mustn't have these kinds of daydreams.

Alice opened her eyes. The look on Jack's face brought back all her worries. Was that suspicion she saw? But when he realized she was watching him, his expression changed to one of warmth.

The waiter set a plate in front of her. She lifted her fork and took a bite.

Jack filled her wineglass to the rim. "Tell me, what do you think of Silvercreek?"

She set down her fork and looked over at him. His eyes were friendly, not probing as they had been a few moments ago. "I haven't seen much of it, but the people I've met are charming." She held his gaze.

He smiled, and she liked the way his eyes crinkled at the corners. "Allow me to remedy that by becoming your tour guide."

She took a quick drink of wine to calm her rapidly beating heart. "I'd like that."

The delicious dinner and glass of wine combined with Jack's charm put Alice at ease. By the time they'd polished off a wonderful dessert and were sipping coffee, she was getting the hang of being her alter-ego, Ally. She'd produced an answer to each of Jack's politely probing questions.

"How long have you been teaching?" she asked, directing the conversation away from herself.

He took a drink of coffee, then set down the cup. "This is my first year at Silvercreek Elementary. I taught at a school in Boston for nearly four years but began my career at the school I attended as a child. I was there for a while, then got the itch to try big-city life."

"How did you like it?" she asked.

Jack leaned back in the chair. "Shock and awe about sums it up. Boston's only an hour from my hometown, but they're worlds apart."

Alice sipped her coffee. Although she knew his feelings about the city, she enjoyed listening to him talk.

"Growing up, I knew most everyone in town," he continued. "When you're young, you don't necessarily see that as a good thing. I sure didn't. Having the whole town know my business made me long to be anonymous. I'm sure you can relate to that."

She arched a brow in surprise.

"To the anonymous part," he explained. "You're just visiting here. You can do whatever you want, and no one will know or care. That's got to be appealing."

She shifted her gaze away from him and stared into her drink. Being so shy, she'd never had many friends. She didn't socialize— never had until she met Tom, but then her whole world collapsed when he died. Her fingers tightened around the cup.

"I'm sorry. Have I upset you?"

Beneath his concern, she thought there was a slight change in tone, maybe even a faint hint of sarcasm, but she couldn't be sure. Had his suspicion of her resurfaced? Why?

Alice looked over at him and forced a smile. "No, no. I'm fine." To keep him talking about himself she asked, "How did you end up here?"

Jack shrugged and waited while the waiter refilled their cups before answering. "The nightlife wasn't for me, neither was the traffic or the stress that went along with it. I longed for a small town—one like where my Aunt Stacy lives. As a boy, I spent my summers with her. She's the complete opposite of my mother." He raked his hair off his forehead. Alice knew this was a difficult subject for him. "My parents liked to travel…without a child to cramp their style. So I want what Stacy has…a life where family comes first."

Alice poured some cream in her coffee, then stirred it with a spoon. "She sounds wonderful."

"Indeed," he answered. His eyes darkened, and she knew he was missing her.

A few moments later, his mood seemed to brighten. "Alice keeps me from getting too homesick," he said with a smile. "She reminds me of my aunt. There've been many nights I'd sit in Alice's parlor, listening to music and playing gin rummy with her."

She remembered those nights fondly. Jack was almost as good at the game as she.

"Do you play cards?" There was no misreading the hopeful gleam in his eyes.

She ran her hands over the napkin on her lap and tried to rid herself of the ridiculous thought that he might be able to read her mind. "A little."

"We should play sometime. But I have to warn you, although I'm not a sore loser, I like to win."

"Do you always?" she asked.

The waiter brought over the check, and Jack handed it back along with his credit card. "What? Win?"

"Yes."

He laughed. "It seems only when Alice lets me."

Her mouth twitched. She fought hard to hold back a smile. How did he know she would sometimes throw a game? And she'd thought she'd done such a good job keeping it from him. "It seems like you've settled in here."

Jack slipped the credit card the waiter returned to him into his wallet, then scribbled his name on the receipt. "I love this town. I could see myself spending my life here. Now, all I need is to find that special someone." His gaze locked with hers.

The warmth in his eyes grew to a steady heat that echoed through her and made her wonder where this night might end.

"We should probably get going," she said softly.

Jack rose and stepped around the table to pull out her chair. His hand brushed her arm, and a tingle ran up the back of her neck. She hurried through the restaurant, suddenly feeling the need for fresh air, but before she could reach the door, her heel caught on something. She started to fall forward. Grasping for anything to keep her balance, her fingers locked on to one of the decorative trees flanking the entrance. As she careened headfirst into the plant, strong arms encircled her waist, putting her back on her feet.

"Darn these shoes," she muttered under her breath. She should've known better than to try to wear three-inch heels. She'd nearly lived in slippers for decades. A little practice at home before venturing out in public would've been smart.

"Are you hurt?" Jack held her firmly, his vivid blue eyes flicking over the cleavage showing from the top of her scoop-neck blouse, then up to her face.

"I'm fine, thank you." But that wasn't true. She thought she might die right there of embarrassment.

His breath tickled her neck. He was holding her a little too close. She began to tremble and didn't know whether it was from the accident or his nearness. Either way, she needed air. "Please, may we go now?"

His eyes glistened dangerously, and he tilted his head in toward her. Oh Lord. He was about to kiss her. She parted her lips slightly and waited. With his arm still wrapped around her waist, he spun her around and led her out the door. If she'd been embarrassed before, it was nothing compared to how she felt now.

She kept her gaze on the pavement as he guided her to his car. There was no way she could look at him. Maybe he hadn't noticed how desperately she wanted him. Wishful thinking. She couldn't have been more obvious if she'd kissed him herself.

Jack opened the car door and helped her in. She slid down into the seat, wishing she could disappear. She watched him walk around the front of the car but turned her head to look out the side window when he climbed into the driver's seat. He started the engine, and they were heading back to Silvercreek. An uneasy silence loomed between them, so different from the comfortable quiet they'd shared when driving to dinner. Alice wrung her hands in her lap. He was probably regretting this date.

She watched as they left the lights of the city far behind. The scenery changed as they entered her small hometown. Hartford's large gray buildings were gone, replaced with charming old homes billowing smoke from their chimneys. She imagined families sitting before roaring fires, telling stories. A sense of loneliness washed over her. She'd missed out on so much.

As they wound down Main Street, she spotted her old Victorian. Its blue paint was cracked and peeling, but the house was still magnificent despite showing its age. She was glad to be home.

Jack pulled the car in the driveway. After he turned off the engine, he placed his large strong hand over hers. She risked a glance at him, and what she saw in his eyes set her heart pounding. With a look more intimate than she'd ever seen, he leaned over, and this time, he kissed her.

Soft at first, his kiss deepened into a passionate expression of feeling Alice hadn't expected. The tips of her toes tingled. She curled her arms around his neck, despite her inner voice warning her to be careful. His lips seared a fire over her skin, moving from her trembling mouth to the curve of her neck.

She pressed him close. Her doubts were lost in a deep pool of desire. A soft moan of delight escaped her. He caressed her throat, then moved his tongue along her ear. While her pulse raced, tiny pangs of guilt began to take root, forming a knot in her stomach. What if Jack's feelings matched hers? What then? How could she be so selfish? She knew her fate, but Jack had no idea what was going to happen come New Year's Day if she hadn't found true love. And how in the world could she hope to build any kind of relationship with him based on secrets and lies?

Alice pulled back and ran a finger over her lips. "I'm sorry. I can't do this." She swung the door open and bolted toward the house without looking back.

Once inside, she headed straight to the parlor and sank wearily into the overstuffed armchair. She stared at the top of the Christmas tree where the tin angel used to sit and said, "I'm such a fool. I can't imagine what Jack must be thinking. All he did was kiss me, and I ran away. He has no idea of the guilt I'm feeling. He must think I'm an idiot, or worse, that I'm not interested in him." She covered her face with her hands.

"And rightly so."

She fanned open her fingers. "What?" Her startled gaze scanned the parlor, but the voice seemed to come out of nowhere. "Who said that?"

"Open the door. I'm in the closet."

Alice flew across the room, then into the hall and yanked open the coat closet. Inside, the tin angel fluttered like a moth trapped in a jar.

"What are you doing in there?" she asked with surprise.

"I don't always land exactly where I plan to."

"Great. I've got an angel who can't tell direction for my guide. I hope when my time's up, you take me to the right place."

The angel's melodious laughter chimed. "Don't worry, heaven and hell are far enough apart that even if I'm off a bit, the worst that can happen is you'll wind up in purgatory, and they don't keep you there very long."

"Well now, that's reassuring."

The angel giggled again. "I'm glad to see you've kept your sense of humor."

"I never knew I had one of those," she said glumly.

The angel floated nearer. "Don't put yourself down like that. You're a wonderful person; however, you're doing a fine job of confusing Jack."

"I know," Alice moaned. "But I don't know what to do."

"Tell him the truth. You've never been one to lie."

She opened her eyes wide. "How can I? He'll never believe it."

The angel's brow furrowed. "How do you know that?"

"Because he doesn't trust me." She began to pace the floor. "Sometimes he looks at me with such scorn…"

"And why do you think that is?"

Alice shrugged.

"Use your intuition." The angel studied her intently. "What is your heart telling you?"

Alice hesitated a moment before answering. "I don't know. At times I don't think he likes me much, and at others, well… Maybe I'm wasting my time on Jack. I'm not even sure if he's the one."

"You won't know if you keep running away. Remember, you only have until New Year's Day to find true love. Time is slipping away. Use what's left wisely. Take chances and enjoy yourself."

She stopped pacing and stood in front of the angel. "You make it sound so easy. I've been alone so long I don't know how to let my guard down. How to let a man get close to me."

"Just be yourself, and everything else will come."

"Thank you," Alice said softly. She reached out to touch the angel, but the gossamer wings fluttered, and an instant later, the tin angel was gone.

CHAPTER THREE

*D*aryn Cramer touched the gas pedal and watched the speedometer rise. The BMW handled like a breeze. He liked fast cars, fast women, and fast money. Living on the edge was his way of life. Always had been. He was his mother's son, after all. He pressed harder on the accelerator, and the car raced through the sleepy town of Silvercreek. He could almost hear her raspy voice nagging at him. *"Slow down, son. We sure don't need a ticket. Remember the rules of the game. Whatever you do, don't bring attention to yourself. You can drive your fancy cars and wear your designer clothes, but do not tangle with the law."* Damn, he missed her. She'd been gone nearly two years, and not a day went by that he didn't think of her.

He glanced over at the passenger seat to the beauty beside him. She had long, sleek red hair, a small upturned nose with a sprinkling of freckles, and gorgeous hazel eyes. She was a hot, sexy diversion. That was for sure. And she was good at the game. Almost as good as he.

Cassandra Black looked at him, her lovely mouth turned down in a pout. "I'm hungry. I need some food."

He knew there was only one answer that would suffice. If he

said no, he'd never have a moment's peace. "Sure, babe. Let's just get out of this town, though. We'll be on the highway in no time, and I promise to stop at the first rest area."

She snorted. It was a sound you wouldn't expect to hear out of a woman whose goal in life was to appear refined. "Fast food? You've got to be kidding."

His instinct was to ignore her, jump on the interstate, and get as far away from this hick town as possible. They'd been here too long as it was. Exhausted all prospects. Hadn't his mother taught him not to linger? Once the job was done, move on. It wasn't wise to stay in one place for too long. That was how you got caught. Besides, he longed for Atlantic City. Jersey was only a little more than four hours away, and there were bound to be plenty of targets there. But the way Cassie tapped her foot and clicked her long nails on the dash made him think twice. "Oh, come on, sweetie. It's only one meal." He reached over and squeezed her hand.

She snatched it away and ran her fingers along her shapely thigh. "You like the way I look, don't you?"

He chuckled. "You know I do."

"Then you know better than to try to get me to eat junk food," she hissed.

They were on the outskirts of town and nearing the entrance to I-91. He took his foot off the gas pedal, and the car began to slow. Daryn debated what to do. It had begun to snow. December weather in New England was unpredictable. What started as a few fluffy flakes could quickly become a blizzard. They really should be on their way now.

As if reading his thoughts, Cassie ran her hand over the side of his cheek and said softly, "Honey pie, my stomach is growling. Come on, let's get some food. I'll make it up to you later in a way I know you'll enjoy." She smiled at him seductively.

He took hold of her hand and kissed it. Oh, what the hell? It was only dinner, and Cassie could be dessert later in the backseat of the Beemer.

He spun the car around, doing a U-turn in the middle of the road. "Okay, you win. I don't have the energy to argue with you right now. But know this, if something goes wrong, it'll be your fault."

"Don't be so dramatic. What could go wrong? We're only stopping to eat."

"With you, something simple can become a nightmare in no time."

"Nice, hon. Real nice." She jabbed her finger into his side.

Daryn shot her a look that said he'd had enough. Thankfully, Cassie got the message and turned her attention out the window. When they reached the center of town, it was snowing heavily; exactly what Daryn had feared.

"Looks like we might be here longer than just dinner," he said dryly.

Cassie shrugged. "That's fine with me. Give me a bottle of wine, some good food, and a soft bed."

He smiled to himself. If they were going to spend another night in Silvercreek, he was going to enjoy it. Cassie would make sure of it.

Without much trouble, they found a place to stay—the Wayside Inn, a quaint hotel across from the town green. He parked the car, then reached in back and pulled his briefcase off the seat. After placing it on his lap, he snapped it open. Inside was a mountain of fake IDs, birth certificates, and various other falsified documents. He took a moment to rifle through them, careful not to send them sliding onto the floor, before selecting two driver's licenses.

For their last swindle, they'd pretended to be husband and wife and wore disguises, so Daryn wasn't too worried about being recognized by anyone, but it never hurt to be cautious. For all he knew, the police could be looking for them right now. He was a pro, though. An expert at covering his tracks. This time, they'd pose as brother and sister—Ross and Taryn Saunders.

They checked into two connecting rooms. Cassie went into one, and he into the other, not wanting to arouse suspicions. A moment later, he unlocked the adjoining door.

Cassie sat on the edge of the bed, her short skirt hiked up across her thighs. He walked over to her and ran his hands over her smooth satiny skin. "Why don't we get comfortable and just order room service?"

"Um, we could do that," she said and began to unbutton his shirt. "What do you feel like having?"

"You." He brought his mouth down on hers. She responded to him instantly. As they kissed, he pushed her back onto the bed and straddled her. Soon he had her panties off, his jeans undone, and was ready to enter her. There were times to make love, and there were times for just pure, raw sex.

This was one of those times.

ॐ

Cassandra tucked the sheet around her naked body and studied the man asleep beside her. Daryn was Hollywood handsome and knew it. But that arrogance was one of the things she loved about him. When he entered a room, every woman took notice. She was the lucky one, though. He belonged to her. The others could look and drool all they wanted, as long as they didn't touch.

She was fully aware of her own sex appeal—attracting men had never been a problem. They made a smoldering couple…in every way. To call their relationship tumultuous was an understatement. They were like oil and vinegar, yet, when shaken, a delicious mix.

She listened to the quiet rhythm of his breathing. He was the only man she'd ever known who didn't snore. Daryn was damn near perfect. She didn't even mind the fact that he always fell asleep right after they made love. So much for ordering room service. As if on cue, her stomach let out a loud rumble.

She needed to eat something. Now. Cassandra pushed back the sheet and climbed out of bed. Before she walked over to her suitcase to get her clothes, she scrutinized her flawless body. Her breasts were large and firm, exactly as Daryn liked. Her stomach flat. Her hips generously rounded. She was the image of womanly perfection, and she needed to be sure to retain that so Daryn never got the urge to trade her in for a younger model.

Cassandra dressed quickly, took a twenty-dollar bill from Daryn's wallet, and slipped quietly from the room. A minute later, she perused the hotel gift shop. She found a fashion magazine, a can of herbal iced tea, and a bag of SunChips. As she strolled toward the checkout line, she passed an aisle with a large display of cereal bars. She ran her hand across the wrappers, and her fingers curled around an oatmeal-raisin cluster. Without hesitation, she dropped it into her handbag. The rush that followed was exhilarating. It happened every time. And this was no exception.

†‡

Jack flipped through the Christmas cards he'd received from his students, then tossed them in a pile on his desk. He leaned back in the swivel chair, glad he didn't have to return to school until after the New Year. He stared out the bedroom window at the falling snow. The flakes coming down were the big, fluffy kind that stuck easily. The oak tree at the side of the house was covered in white. Its branches sagged. A few thin ones blew back and forth in the wind, scraping along the windowsill.

His thoughts drifted to Ally, as they'd done most of the day. He'd worked on his strategy—to make her fall for him so she'd open up—like a general planning for war, but last night had failed miserably. He went over the evening again in his mind. Dinner went well. He chuckled while he thought of that little episode where she almost wound up headfirst in the plants. She acted a little peculiar after that, making the ride home a bit uncomfortable, but his kiss seemed to put things back on track, until she took off like a scared rabbit. He didn't doubt in the least she'd enjoyed his kiss. He could tell right off when a woman was into him and, boy, was she ever. So what had happened? She'd said something about how she couldn't do this. Do what? Kiss him? It wasn't as if he was about to seduce her in the front seat of his car. So what was it that terrified her?

Jack stood up and strolled over to the window, resting his palms on the sill. If he wasn't careful, she might not be the only one falling. No matter how many times he told himself women like her were nothing but trouble, he was still drawn to her. Keeping to his plan might take all his willpower.

He watched the snow pile up on the ground. At the base of the oak tree, Jasper rubbed his back against the rough silvery bark. Off to the right, a yellow streak tore down the driveway, heading toward the cat. In a flash, Jasper raced up the tree and clung to a branch outside his window. The cat stared through the glass at him with wide, fearful ochre eyes, then let out a wail as if crying, *Save me.*

Down below, the yellow streak—a rambunctious Labrador retriever—barked and clawed at the tree. Jasper inched farther down the branch.

"Don't try it," Jack warned, fearful the cat would attempt to leap onto the slippery windowsill. Two floors up was a long way to fall, even for a cat. "Stay put. I'll see what I can do." It had been years since he'd climbed a tree, but how hard could it be? While putting on his leather jacket, he headed out the door and down the back stairs.

Outside, the walkway was slick from the snow, and Jack stepped carefully. By the time he reached the base of the tree, the yellow lab was gone. Ally stood in its place. Wearing only a sweater and tight-fitting jeans that hugged every curve, she shivered as she looked up at Jasper.

"He's too afraid to come down," she said.

"Give him time. When he's cold enough, he'll find a way."

Ally glared at him. "Animals can get frostbite, you know."

"Relax," he said, placing his foot in the crook of the tree and hoisting himself up. "I came out here to rescue the cat, if I don't break my neck first."

With relative ease, Jack shimmied up the tree. When he reached the branch where Jasper perched, the cat eyed him suspiciously.

"It's okay," he said, "I don't want to be up here any more than you, so don't give me trouble."

As if realizing this was his only option, the cat inched his way along the branch, coming close enough so that Jack could reach out and grab him. He tucked Jasper inside his jacket and started the climb down.

"Thank you. I don't know what I would have done without you," Ally called up.

"If you really want to thank me, how about offering me something to drink?"

"Hot chocolate, with or without marshmallows?"

"I'm an old-fashioned guy; I always take mine with."

"Somehow I knew that," she said with a laugh.

Jack slid down the trunk until he came to the crook. He swung his leg over, trying to find a footing, but his boot slipped on the ice and snow, throwing him off balance. As he grappled for a branch, Jasper leapt out of his jacket and crawled up the back of his neck, clinging to the top of his head. The cat's sharp claws dug into his scalp.

"This is the thanks I get for saving you?" he muttered, holding back a painful groan. Scalped by a cat. So much for his knight-in-shining-armor act. He grabbed for Jasper, then landed spread-eagle in the snow.

"Oh no! Are you all right?" Ally knelt beside him, her warm breath brushing his cheek.

For a moment, he considered playing up the situation, but he wasn't that cruel. Besides his wounded pride, he didn't think he suffered from anything more than a few bruises. "I've survived a lot worse than this," he said, sitting up and brushing the snow from his clothes. "If that cat hadn't stuck its claws in my head..."

"You did a fine job rescuing Jasper." The corners of her mouth trembled slightly, and he knew she was trying hard to contain her laughter.

He followed her gaze to the front porch. The cat sat on the top step, cleaning snow from his paws. "You think this is funny, don't you?"

"How could you say that? Laugh at you?" She stared at him with wide innocent gray eyes, but her lips still quivered.

"How about that hot chocolate?"

"Of course. Here, let me help you up," she said, holding out her hand.

He wrapped his fingers securely around hers, then attempted to stand. A stabbing pain shot through his ankle, and he tumbled back in the snow, dragging Ally down with him.

"Very funny," she quipped, but his pained expression must have told her it was no act. Her brow quickly wrinkled, and a worried expression lined her beautiful face. "Oh Lord. You're hurt. Is it your foot, your leg, what?"

Jack bit back a groan. "My ankle. I must've sprained it."

"Well, I've got to get you inside where it's warm; then I can have a look at it. Wait here, I'll be right back." She raced up the porch stairs.

"I don't think I'll be going anywhere." He knew she'd missed his sarcasm, being too preoccupied with whatever it was she was doing. He watched her enter the house with Jasper on her heels. Less than a minute later, she returned carrying a cane. Alice's cane! What kind of monster lay beneath Ally's perfect facade? Alice couldn't go anywhere without her cane. He kept a tight lid on his simmering anger. This wasn't the time to question her, but once they were inside, she'd better have a good explanation or else...

"Here," she said, handing him the cane. "Put your weight on this while I pull you up."

With Alice's cane wedged in the snow and Ally's hand in his, Jack was able to stand without too much difficulty. He hobbled into the house and collapsed on the sofa in the parlor.

Ally grabbed a throw and tucked it around him. "Let me get those boots off you," she said, leaning over him to untie his laces.

Her hair swept across his legs, and the fresh aroma of cucumber mint wafted up. He leaned back against the cushions, his eyes closed, and waited for the spasm of pain that was sure to come when she pulled off his boot, but her touch was so gentle he barely felt any discomfort. With nimble fingers, she rolled down his sock, then slid it carefully from his foot.

"Oh my," she said softly. "You have quite a bit of swelling already. I think you should see a doctor."

Jack opened his eyes and looked down at his injury. His ankle was nearly twice its normal size, and the top of his foot was a purplish color. He glanced at the clock on the wall. 5:15 p.m. Charlie Brooks would've already left his office for the day. "I hate hospitals," he said flatly. "I'll ice it, and if I don't feel better in the morning, I'll call the doctor."

Ally sprang to her feet. "I can call Doc Brooks right now. He doesn't mind making house calls."

"How do you know that?" He grabbed hold of her arm before she could reach for the phone.

She hesitated a moment before answering. "Just an assumption. He must have come to the house when he had to treat Aunt Alice. Unless, of course, you drove her to the office?" One shapely brow rose, and he knew she'd tried to turn the tables on him.

"Doc Brooks, as Alice…and now you…call him, came to the house weekly." He tried to keep his tone light, while his mind scrambled for an explanation of what this girl could possibly be up to. "I don't want to bother him tonight. There's probably nothing more he could do other than ice it anyway."

"Okay, then let me go get you an ice pack."

He sensed her relief at not having to make that call after all. When he released his grip on her arm, she hurried from the room as if her shoes were on fire. What the heck was her story? She sure was an odd one. He didn't doubt she was related to Alice, but the more time he spent with her, the more he distrusted her. He glanced at the cane propped up against the sofa. How could Alice go anywhere without it? He'd get some answers from Ally if he had to grill her like the criminal she might very well be. It surprised him when his stomach turned at the thought. She seemed like a genuinely nice person…

A few minutes later, her footsteps warned of her return. He pasted a smile on his face and prepared to act again as the curtain went up for another scene in a play he wasn't sure would have a happy ending.

"How's my patient?" she asked, toting a tray with two cups of hot chocolate, a bag of mini-marshmallows, and a large ice pack. Her face was still flushed from the cold, and a lock of chestnut hair fell haphazardly across her brow. She smiled at him with an innocent charm that made her look about twelve.

After setting the tray on the coffee table, she gently placed the ice pack on his ankle. A shock wave raced up the back of his spine, not only from the cold but also from the touch of her warm fingers against his skin. "Thank you. I'm feeling better now that you're here."

She bit her lip, and he knew she was wondering if he was flirting with her. She reached for one of the delicate china cups, then handed him a hot chocolate. "How many would you like?" she asked, opening the bag of marshmallows.

"Surprise me."

Using silver tongs, something he would have expected Alice to do, she dropped five mini-marshmallows into his cup, then filled her own till cocoa nearly spilled over the side. She never ceased to amaze him. He'd thought for sure she'd use her fingers.

"I have a sweet tooth," she said as if revealing a secret.

Another similarity with Alice, although she'd recently developed diabetes and had to refrain from such treats. It seemed these two women had an awful lot in common.

Jack sipped his cocoa and watched her over the rim of his cup. She sank into the armchair across from him, tucking one long, lean leg up under her, then, like a contented child, began to eat the marshmallows with a spoon. He reached down next to the side of the sofa and grabbed Alice's cane. "Where did you get this?"

She drew her brows together into a frown. "From the closet. Why? Is there something wrong with it?"

"It belongs to Alice." His voice rose a bit, despite his trying to control it.

"Of course it does."

"She can't get around without it."

"I know that, Jack. What's the problem? She used a different cane when she left."

He gulped his chocolate, embarrassment burning hotter than his steaming drink. What in the world was wrong with him? Alice probably had a closet full of canes. He was becoming suspicious of everything. If he wasn't careful, he'd scare Ally away. "I'm sorry," he apologized. "I think my injury has affected my thinking."

A smile curved her full lips. "I understand you're concerned about my aunt, but believe me, she's fine."

"I'm very fond of her," he said, trying to excuse his paranoid behavior.

"And I'm sure she is of you too."

"We have so much in common."

"The music?" Ally was looking at him as if trying to read his mind.

He'd said too much already. "She's a fine woman," he said quickly. "They don't make them like that anymore."

"Men either. Except for you." She said it under her breath, but there was no denying he'd heard her correctly.

"You're a puzzle, Ally Hart. You look one way, yet act another."

She lowered her lashes so he couldn't see her eyes. "I don't know what you mean."

"Most beautiful women are superficial…"

"Things aren't always as they seem."

He couldn't have said it better himself. His gaze flicked over her perfect exterior, and he wondered what secrets were hidden beneath.

Ally drank the last of her cocoa, then set the cup down on the table. She unfolded her legs from under her and stood. "You're so young to have formed such an attitude about women."

Jack raised a brow. That sounded odd coming from her lips, as if she were so much older and wiser. "Not all women, just a certain type."

Ally strolled over to the old Wurlitzer piano at the far end of the room. Her fingers grazed the keys almost lovingly.

"Do you play?" he asked.

"No," she said, turning her back to him. "You?"

Using the cane, he hobbled over to her and slid his fingers over the keys. "I do, but nowhere near as well as your aunt." He sat down at the piano and played Rachmaninoff. "Alice's talent is rare. Music is a part of her soul. It's a shame her fingers are so stiff now. Her bad days outweigh her good, but when she does play, it's flawless."

Ally watched his hands glide effortlessly over the keys, and he thought he saw the same look in her eyes that Alice would have had for a piece done well. "This is one of your aunt's favorites," he said quietly.

"Yes, it is."

His fingers slowed, and he studied Ally's face.

"I-I meant, I could see why. It's lovely."

"Very." His gaze lingered on her lips, and she looked away. He liked that about her—that shyness, that unexpected innocence. "It's getting late. I should go," he said, ending the piece on a crescendo.

"No." Ally moved across the room and stood by the window. "You'll never get up all the stairs to your apartment with that ankle. Stay here. You can sleep on the sofa."

"I don't want to put you out. I'm sure I can make it." Suddenly, a thought occurred to him. Spending the night here with Ally just might get her to open up and tell him the truth about Alice.

"No, I insist. It's no bother, really. Besides, I'd feel terrible if you hurt yourself trying to climb those stairs."

"All right, if you insist." Jack tried hard to keep from smiling at his good fortune.

ℴℴ

"Are you hungry?" Jack called from the parlor.

Ally shook her head, returning from the kitchen with a freshly filled ice pack. She set it on his ankle.

"Feel like pizza?"

Pizza. Just the thought of it made her stomach growl. She couldn't remember the last time she'd had it. "With the works?"

"That's the only way to go." Jack reached for the phone on the table beside the sofa and dialed. "Hey, Louie," he said into the receiver, "Jack Billings. Send over my usual." After he hung up, he said to Alice, "Louie's on Center Street; nobody makes a better pie. You'll love it."

She didn't doubt it. Anything would be better than what she could prepare. "I don't cook much," Alice said wryly.

Jack chuckled. "Your aunt doesn't either. Although she can use her age as an excuse."

The way he looked at her made her think he thought she was just too lazy to learn. "I would cook if I had the time," she said, trying to explain her lack of domestic talent.

Jack leaned forward, reaching for the picture on the coffee table. Anxiety shot through her. Inside the polished silver frame was a photograph of Tom in uniform. It has been taken the day he left for war. That was the last time she'd seen him.

"What was he like?" Jack asked, running his finger over the glass.

"Who?" Alice's voice came out like a squeak.

He set the picture back on the table. "The boyfriend you're hiding from."

Relief swept over her that he hadn't been referring to Tom, but oh Lord, another story. She hadn't anticipated having to make up tales, and she didn't like it. Not one bit. What else was she to do, though? Her mind scrambled, trying to think of something to tell him. She thought of Bethany and the little bit Jack had told her of their relationship. "He was controlling," she said. "Self-absorbed. I don't think he knew me at all."

Jack's fabulous blue eyes were tender as he watched her. "I know exactly how you must feel. I left a long-term relationship for those very reasons. I had to get away. That's why I moved to Silvercreek."

Of course she knew that already, but had to pretend this was the first time hearing it. "I'm sorry. It's difficult when love doesn't work."

He shrugged. "Some things weren't meant to be." His gaze locked onto the picture of Tom. "But that's a tragedy. Alice never got over her loss."

Battling poignant memories left her close to tears. She swallowed hard, then cleared her throat. "Do you regret falling in love?"

Jack leaned back against the sofa and took a moment to answer, as if choosing his words carefully. "I cared for Bethany, but I wasn't head over heels in love. I discovered that when I met Alice. She'd found her true love and even though they weren't destined to be together, she never settled for less. Tom lived inside her…"

His voice was wistful. He understood her so well, and it was as if he felt her pain. Alice wanted to touch him…to run her fingers over his skin…to lay her head on his shoulder and feel the silky softness of his hair against her cheek. She'd waited a lifetime for these feelings, and now they were blossoming for this beautiful man who seemed to know her better than she knew herself. Yet, she was deceiving him… Everything she'd told him was a lie. She turned her head so he couldn't see the guilt in her eyes.

"What are your plans for the holiday?"

She'd forgotten tomorrow was Christmas Eve. "I don't have any plans. I guess I'll wear my sweats and watch old movies." She tried hard to sound upbeat.

"Spend it with me."

Although there was nothing more she'd rather do than spend the evening with Jack, she wasn't sure that would be such a good idea.

Her feelings for him were growing stronger by the minute, and if he found out she was a fraud, he'd hate her—and rightly so. "Oh, I don't know."

"Well, just think about it. Please."

She twirled a strand of hair around her finger. "I doubt if I'll change my mind." The loud peal of the doorbell saved her, at least temporarily.

Jack handed her a twenty-dollar bill. She left the parlor to answer the front door, paid the pizza deliveryman, and returned carrying their dinner. After setting the box on the coffee table, she went into the kitchen for something to drink. She came back with two glasses of ice water and a stack of napkins tucked under her arm.

She sat down on the edge of the sofa and reached for a slice of pizza. "I'm afraid I'm not being a very good hostess," she said. "I forgot to bring plates."

Jack had his pizza slice folded in half. "I'm fine. Just surprised."

"Surprised?" She took a bite and used her thumb to wipe a bit of sauce from her chin.

"I guess after seeing you use tongs for the marshmallows, I expected you to use a fork with your pizza."

She rolled her eyes and smiled. "I'm not afraid to get my fingers dirty."

"I'm glad. I thought women like you were all the same, afraid to enjoy life because they might break a nail or smudge their makeup."

"What?" She nearly choked on her pizza. "That's a horrible thing to say."

He looked at her sheepishly. "Hey, I'm sorry. I didn't mean to offend you. I was just being honest."

"If insulting me is being honest, then I can do without that kind of honesty." She ripped a piece of crust from her pizza and bit down hard.

"That wasn't my intention. My last relationship was a disaster. Forgive me? Friends again?"

Friends? A friend's not what I need. I need you to fall in love with me. But she couldn't tell him that. Instead, she said, "Sure. Your comment is long forgotten."

Jack pushed the pizza box away, then clasped his hand over hers. "Really?" He stared at her, and she knew he was trying to see if she was telling the truth.

"Really." She squeezed his hand.

He pulled her closer until her leg brushed his thigh. A tingle of excitement coursed through her. He pressed his mouth against hers and with his tongue, he parted her lips. She didn't resist. Instead, she wrapped her arms around his neck and leaned against him. She could feel the beating of his heart. If this was how he treated his friends, then she wanted to be his best friend. His lips moved down her throat to the base of her neck, stopping at the spot where her pulse thrummed. She had to bite back a sigh. This was heaven.

The sound of the doorbell jarred her back to reality. Jack looked at her, and the disappointment on his face matched her own.

"Expecting someone?" he asked.

"No." She tugged on her sweater to adjust the one shoulder that had slipped down, revealing her pink bra strap, then ran her hands over her mussed hair. "I've no idea who it could be." She hoped Jack didn't pick up on her reluctance to answer the door. Whoever waited outside couldn't be anyone she wanted to see. "I'm sorry. I'll be right back and then maybe we could pick up where we left off?"

His brilliant smile was all the answer she needed. As she walked into the foyer, she prayed she'd be able to send this caller away quickly. When she opened the door, a rush of cold air mixed with wet snow stung her face, but that wasn't what froze her. The sight of Pastor Riley did!

He stared at her in much the same way Doc Brooks had the other night, as if trying to figure out who she was and why she bore such a striking resemblance to Alice.

"I'm Ally. Alice's niece." She knew her voice sounded flat, almost annoyed, but she couldn't help it. She hated to have to lie to another one of her closest friends.

He continued to stare at her, disbelief written all over his wrinkled face.

"My aunt's away for the holidays. She's visiting with my dad in upstate New York. She'll be back after the first of the year." Alice attempted to close the door, but he stopped it with his hand.

"Not so fast, young lady. I've never heard mention of a niece before, and I've known Alice for over forty years. If you're who you say you are, then you won't mind showing me some identification."

Part of her wanted to laugh. Part of her wanted to cry. And part of her wanted to hug Pastor Riley because of his concern for her welfare. But she couldn't do any of those things. What she had to do was get rid of him quickly.

"I'm sorry, but who do you think you are? The police?" she said. "I'm not in the habit of showing anything to strangers."

"I'm Pastor Riley. Alice is a member of my congregation." He pushed past her so that he stood in the foyer. "I don't mean to be rude, miss, but I'm sure you can understand my wanting to be sure Alice is fine. After all, an elderly woman living—"

"Ally? Is everything all right out there?" Jack called from the parlor.

Pastor Riley's face brightened. "Good. Jack Billings is here. Just the man I need to see." In a few quick steps, he crossed the foyer and headed toward the parlor.

Alice quickly closed the door, then hurried after him. Her mind was a whirl as she tried to figure out how to handle this situation.

ॐ

Jack heard Ally's light footsteps nearing the parlor. He sat up straight when he heard the familiar voice that could belong to none other than Pastor Riley. His native New Hampshire accent was a dead giveaway. When they appeared in the doorway, he was surprised to see Ally so shaken. Her usually bright complexion had turned pasty as if she'd swallowed something awful. Dots of perspiration beaded her brow line, and she clasped her hands together so tightly her fingers had turned red.

The pastor didn't look much better. His usual jovial demeanor was uncharacteristically subdued. His bushy white brows were drawn together so that deep furrows lined his forehead. What on earth had happened? He grabbed the cane and sprang to his feet as quickly as his injured ankle would allow. His gaze darted from one to the other, when a thought occurred to him that sent his heart into his throat. Alice! Something terrible had happened to her. His hold on the cane tightened. "What's going on?" He could barely believe that hollow voice was his own.

"Jack, you must know Pastor Riley. He's come to call on my aunt." He waited for Ally to go on, but she paused for what seemed like an eternity.

Finally the pastor spoke. "Jack, Ally here tells me Alice is visiting her brother. Is that true?"

His gaze flicked over Ally, traveling up to her face and holding steady on her gray eyes, imploring him to back her up. "Yes, I believe it is," he said, but his words were clipped.

The pastor turned to Ally. "Would you mind giving us a minute alone?"

"Of course." A tiny spot of red marred her lovely mouth from where she must have bitten her lip. She turned on her heel and left them, her footsteps disappearing down the hall.

"Something's not right, Jack. I can feel it. Did Alice tell you she was going somewhere?" the pastor asked.

He averted his eyes, studying the oriental carpet beneath his feet. "Well, no, not exactly."

Pastor Riley ran a hand through his salt-and-pepper hair. "The girl's stunning and probably charming as heck too, but I can tell she's lying. The story she fed me, and obviously you, stinks."

"Now wait a minute, we don't know that she hasn't told us the truth." Jack spoke with conviction, surprised he was defending her.

The pastor shook his head. "Just the other day, a parishioner came to me for advice. Seems a pair of grifters claiming to be long-lost relatives had bamboozled her grandmother. Before she was on to them, they stole most of her money and quite a few items from her home. I wouldn't be surprised if this young woman here doesn't have a partner waiting off in the wings. I think the police should be notified. This could be more serious than just petty theft. Alice could be in danger."

Jack sank onto the sofa, his stomach clenched tight. This was worse than he'd thought. But he didn't believe Ally was capable of hurting anyone. "Don't worry. I'll handle this." He patted the older man's arm. "I'll find Alice; you can be sure of that."

"Yes, I'm sure you will." But his faded eyes were sad.

Jack knew what he was thinking and refused to let his mind wander to such a dark place. "I will find her. And I will bring her back safe and sound."

"I know you'll do everything you can. Let me give you a bit of advice, though. Be careful of that girl."

He wasn't the kind of man who let his feelings override common sense. "Don't worry about me. I'll be fine."

The pastor let himself out, insisting Jack stay off his ankle. But the only pain he felt now was in his chest. He needed to think this through thoroughly. Sort out the facts from hearsay. What he did next was of the utmost importance. A wrong move could prove disastrous.

He was glad when Ally didn't come racing back into the parlor. He needed time alone. Leaning back against the sofa, he clasped his hands behind his head and stared at the Christmas lights twinkling on the tree. His gaze traveled up to the top. The tin angel was missing! Could Ally have taken it? Why? It wasn't worth much, but its sentimental value was priceless. Alice had told him the tin angel story many times.

His thoughts whirled… Ally… Grifters… He squeezed his eyes shut, trying to erase her exquisite face. "You almost had me fooled," he whispered. "I will get to the bottom of this, even if it means involving the police."

೫೦೧೫

Alice watched as Pastor Riley stepped carefully through the snow. She waited until she heard the low rumble of his car's engine before letting the thin lace curtain slip through her trembling fingers to fall softly across her bedroom window. She tried to keep control of her emotions, but this miracle transformation had become a nightmare. Pastor Riley didn't buy one word of her story. She could tell by the way his usually friendly eyes had frosted over when she started to tell her tale of Alice's trip to upstate New York, and by the time she'd finished, the frown lines on his forehead were so deep they had to be permanent.

A small groan escaped her at the thought of the pastor and Jack discussing her as if she were a criminal. She'd wanted to tiptoe down the hall and listen in on their conversation, but her upbringing wouldn't allow that, even now, even though her future might very well depend upon it.

She stole a glance in her dresser mirror. Her skin was grayish, and beneath her eyes, purple shadows of worry stood out like an admission of guilt. How had this happened? She wasn't a dishonest person. This transformation was supposed to bring happiness. She took a deep breath, then let it out slowly. No matter what Pastor Riley said to Jack, there was no proof her story was a lie, and there was no proof she'd done anything wrong.

She pinched her cheeks, bringing a pink glow to them, then, after running her hands over her hair, she took a quivering step toward the parlor. As she neared the doorway, she cleared her throat, alerting Jack to her arrival.

He looked over at her. Distrust burned in his eyes, and she knew Pastor Riley had gotten him to doubt her story.

Gathering up all her courage, she sat down next to him on the sofa and smiled. "Pastor Riley seems like a very nice man," she said softly, trying hard to keep her voice steady.

"Very nice. An honest and caring man too."

The way he said it cut deep into her soul. He thought her a liar, and he was right. Her heart sank. He deserved better. He deserved the truth…but the truth would make her far worse than a liar. Jack would think her insane.

"Pastor Riley cares deeply for Alice," he continued, "and would do anything to keep her from harm."

Alice slipped her trembling hands under her knees. "She's fine, Jack. What's it going to take to convince you of that? Do you think I'm a criminal? Do you think I've done something horrible to her?" The thought that he could actually believe that filled her with anger.

"Of course not, but it does seem odd that she didn't tell anyone she was taking a trip."

Alice shot him a fiery look. "Would you like me to call her, so you can talk to her? Would that convince you?" She didn't know why she'd said that. The words seemed to slip from her tongue as if they had a mind of their own. It must be her anger that fueled her stupidity, because if Jack took her up on her offer, her masquerade was over.

She challenged him with an unwavering stare. "Well," she goaded, walking over to the telephone.

As she reached for the receiver, he said, "Don't be silly. I'm not Alice's keeper, just her friend."

"Thank you." She held back a sigh of relief as she joined him on the sofa. However, she kept a reasonable space between them, despite longing to be in his arms as she'd been before Pastor Riley's untimely interruption. But there was no going back. Jack didn't trust her. She would have to work harder to gain his confidence.

CHAPTER FOUR

*J*ack watched as Ally left the room in search of blankets and
pillows. He was tired. Exhausted, in fact. Besides his throbbing
ankle, his head pounded. What was wrong with him? He'd had his
chance to talk to Alice, to make sure she was all right, and he'd blown
it. Why hadn't he taken Ally up on her offer? Only an idiot would
have missed that opportunity! Had it been her steely stare challenging
him to call her a liar that had made him back down? Or was it that he
feared she'd never forgive him for not trusting her if she turned out
to be innocent of any wrongdoing?

He didn't know why he cared what she thought of him. Maybe it
was because she fascinated him with her sophisticated style and
childlike charm. She was unlike any woman he'd ever known, and his
attraction to her was becoming painfully hard to resist.

He closed his eyes, remembering the feel of her petal-soft lips
against his, her velvety skin beneath his hands. Just the thought of
her sent waves of desire flowing through him. If he were reckless,
he'd toss caution aside, but he needed to stay with the game plan—
make her think he was interested while keeping his heart out of it. If
she was indeed one of those grifters, as Pastor Riley seemed to think,

he'd have to get to the bottom of her plan and fast. She'd taken Alice's tin angel and who knew what else.

The sound of her footsteps roused him, and he checked his emotions while he awaited her return.

Ally's arms were full carrying plaid flannel sheets, a wool blanket, and two pillows. His initial reaction was to help her, but he caught himself before he foolishly leapt to his feet and caused more injury to his ankle.

"Thank you," he said with a grin.

She smiled back. "You're welcome."

He sensed the strain between them lessening, and with it, a weight lifted from his chest.

"Do you think you can manage to move over to the chair so I can make up the sofa?"

Jack reached for the cane. "I might need a little help."

Ally plopped the bedding down next to him and placed her hand under his elbow to help him to his feet. Her nearness once again stirred his desire. He fought the temptation to take her in his arms. Instead, he let her lead him to the overstuffed chair.

He watched as she tucked the sheet in around the cushions, offering him an enticing view of her very shapely backside. She cast a glance over her shoulder, as if she knew he was watching her.

"Enjoying the view?"

"I can't help it. I'm male, and you do fill out those jeans very nicely." She shot him a curt look, but he sensed she was glad he found her so attractive.

She unfolded the blanket, laid it across the sheet, then plumped up the pillows. "Ready?" she asked, lending him her arm.

"You bet." With the cane and Ally's help, he hobbled to the makeshift bed.

"Is there anything else you need before I call it a night?"

Just you. "I'm fine. Good night, Ally."

"Good night, Jack." She disappeared down the hall, turning out the lights as she went until only the glow from the Christmas tree remained.

He lay there in the near dark until his lids grew heavy. He'd known Ally only a short while, yet at times he felt as if he'd know her much longer, and for some reason it gave him comfort knowing she slept just down the hall.

෫෭෬

Something sharp scratched at Jack's arm. He forced his tired eyes open and found Jasper sitting beside him on the sofa. The grandfather clock ticking in the parlor's shadowed corner showed 7:00 a.m.—way too early to rise during Christmas vacation. Jack turned on his side and closed his eyes. But Jasper prowled onto his pillow and let out a series of loud meows.

"Go away, cat," Jack moaned, although he knew that was highly unlikely. Food was a priority for Jasper, and there was no doubt he wanted it now. Still groggy from a less than restful night, Jack grappled for the cane propped against the sofa.

Wearing only his boxers, he hobbled toward the kitchen, but a goddess in a pink bathrobe cut him off in the foyer.

"Going somewhere?" Ally's gaze devoured him, widening as it lingered on his naked chest.

He returned her gaze with equal interest. Chestnut hair with glints of gold fell about her shoulders in a wild tumble. Her cheeks were flushed, her lips—rosy and full as if she'd just been kissed. He kept his gaze on her face, trying hard not to lower it to the skin peeking out from her robe, all dewy and soft. Even in a bathrobe, with no makeup on and her hair mussed from sleep, she was one of the most striking women he'd ever seen.

"Looks like you're an early riser too," he said.

62

"Yup. As a matter of fact, I'm usually up even earlier than this."

Maybe he'd misjudged her. Maybe she wasn't as high maintenance as he'd thought. Most of the women he'd known, when given the opportunity, would sleep the morning away, using their need for beauty sleep as an excuse. But Ally sure didn't seem to care about that. And she didn't seem to mind that he saw her with no makeup and mussed hair. And that pink bathrobe! While she looked adorable, the high-maintenance type wouldn't be caught dead in it. Could he be wrong about Ally? He gave himself a mental shake. Ridiculous! So what if she didn't care what she looked like in the morning, she could still be a criminal...a grifter. The thought disturbed him, not only because that could mean she was lying about Alice, but because he genuinely liked her. The vision of her behind bars didn't sit well with him.

Jasper let out a long wail, then sat in front of Jack, staring up at him with large golden eyes. "Well, I guess I better feed the beast."

Ally planted her hands firmly on her hips. "My ca—my aunt's cat is not a beast."

He quirked a brow at her. She'd almost called Jasper her cat. She looked away but not before he caught a glimpse of the heated flush that stole up her face. Why would she think of the cat as hers? She sure was a mystery.

Jack skirted around her, following the cat into the kitchen. "Care for some breakfast? I make a mean omelet," he called over his shoulder.

"No thanks. I don't usually eat first thing in the morning. But you go ahead. I'm going to take a shower."

He studied her back as she padded down the hall. He wasn't so sure of her reason for not wanting breakfast. More likely she wanted some time away from him so he wouldn't question her about the cat slip-up. Though little did she know, he wasn't about to forget. Oh no, he'd simply put it on his list of things that didn't add up.

Alice let the hot water pummel the back of her neck, hoping the shower's pulsating spray would loosen her stress-tightened muscles. Jack had to be wondering why she'd almost called Jasper her cat. Even though he didn't acknowledge her mistake, his expression told her what she needed to know. He still didn't trust her. And this flub only confirmed that he had good reason not to. She had to be more careful. She couldn't afford any more slips of the tongue. Jack was no dummy. For all she knew, he could be pretending to be interested in her just to gather information to use against her. What she didn't need was for him to contact the police because he suspected she was some sort of criminal. That thought made her shudder.

She wanted so badly to tell Jack the truth, but she couldn't until she was sure he had real feelings for her. Lord knew she was falling for him. Only then did she have a small chance that he might believe her story. But if she kept messing up… She slathered her body with soap, trying to wash away her anger and stupidity. She'd best hurry and join Jack, lest he think she was avoiding him.

When Alice entered the parlor, Jack was standing by the window staring out at the snow-covered lawn, seemingly deep in thought. He'd gotten dressed, had even managed to get his boots on.

She crossed the room to stand beside him. "How's your ankle?"

He shifted his weight onto his injury and gritted his teeth. "It'll be fine."

"You really should have Doc Brooks check it out," Alice advised.

"A couple more days and I'll be good as new." But he leaned against the cane for support. "I suppose I should get going. Don't want to outstay my welcome."

"Don't be silly. You're not." Her mind scrambled for a reason to

keep him from leaving. When would she see him again? "The stairs…
I don't think you're ready to climb—"

"Nonsense," he interrupted. "You're acting like a nervous
mother hen. I'll be fine, but do you mind if I use the cane for a bit
longer?"

She shook her head. "Of course not. Use it as long as you need."
Her palms started to sweat. This wasn't working. He was leaving.
What to do now? *Think…think of something…don't let him leave without
plans to see him again.*

"Jack," Alice tried to keep the desperation out of her voice,
"remember that offer you made…the one about spending the
holiday—"

"With me," he said, finishing her sentence. A little grin curved
his lips. "Yes, I remember, but I was beginning to think you'd
forgotten."

A tingle of excitement ran through her. "If the offer's still open,
I'd love to."

There was no mistaking the delight that swept over his face. "I'll
come get you around seven. We'll go see the Christmas lights on the
green."

"Sounds wonderful." She hadn't viewed the lights in years. Her
arthritis had kept her from doing so many things.

It wasn't until after Jack left that she remembered her snow
boots didn't fit. Looked like she'd have to go shopping again.

෴

Daryn sat across from Cassie at a table by the front window of the
Ginger House, the hotel restaurant, and watched her spread butter on
her bagel with precision. He was itching for them to be on their way.
They'd spent way too long in Silvercreek. Not that he'd minded
spending a day and a half in bed with her. "After breakfast, we
should check out," he said. "It finally stopped snowing. The roads

should be clear."

She leaned back in her chair and leveled her gaze at him. "I need to do a little shopping first."

A muscle flicked angrily at his jaw. "Do what? Why? What could you possibly need?"

She narrowed her eyes to slits. "Don't talk to me like that, as if I'm some kind of shallow, empty-headed nitwit."

He took a long sip of coffee. Cassie was many things, but a shallow, empty-headed nitwit wasn't one of them. She was sharp-tongued, sly as a fox, and an expert at falsifying documents. Why, if she hadn't forged Marie Brenner's will, they wouldn't have been able to steal money from her estate. They were partners. Equal partners. Well, almost. He needed her. Couldn't do what he did without her. When his mother died, he'd thought his days of grifting were over. He'd been a month away from his thirtieth birthday and had nothing to show for his age but a wallet full of hundred-dollar bills. He'd been in some bar in a city somewhere drowning his sorrows in vodka and grapefruit juice when Cassie entered his life by trying to pick his pocket. The memory of that day made him smile as he looked over at her. "You have no idea how much I adore you."

She smiled back at him and reached across the table to squeeze his hand.

"If you need to go shopping, fine, but only if you can keep it to one store and be done by noon. I don't want to miss the hotel's checkout," he said.

"Absolutely. I promise. There's the cutest boutique across the street. See?" She pointed to a brick-front building with a pine-green awning with the name Tres Belle written in gold script across the front. It looked expensive. No doubt Cassie's shopping spree would wind up costing him a pretty penny. "It shouldn't take me long at all," she went on.

He took the last sip of his coffee, then signaled the waitress for the bill. As he waited for her to bring it, he stared out the window. A strikingly beautiful brunette crossed the street. Her gleaming chestnut hair swung in rhythm to her stride. And what a stride! Her faded jeans accentuated the soft curve of her hips and the slender outline of her long legs. Just because he was in a relationship with Cass didn't mean he couldn't appreciate a hot woman. And boy, was she hot. He watched her enter Miller's, a department store next to Tres Belle. He'd love to see her up close and maybe partake in a little harmless flirting.

The waitress plopped down the bill, and he quickly pulled out a fifty from his wallet, but before he could hand it to her, she walked away.

"Whoa, miss" he said, waving the money in the air, but he might as well have saved his breath. The waitress had slipped inside the kitchen.

Cassie looked at him with raised brows. "What's the big hurry?" She checked her watch for the time. "We've got more than two hours before the noon checkout."

"I know. I know." He dropped the fifty on top of the bill, then pushed out his chair and stood. "But knowing you as I do, that's probably not near enough time to shop." He couldn't tell Cassie the real reason for the rush was so he could check out another woman.

He shoved his wallet into his pocket. "Ready?" He took hold of her hand and helped her to her feet.

"What about the change?" She glanced down at the bill. "The total's only twenty-seven dollars."

"Do you think the waitress will complain about such a large tip? It'll make her day."

Cassie stared at him, her lovely eyes searching his face as if seeing him for the first time. "You never cease to amaze me. I hadn't known you to be generous to strangers." She stood on tiptoe and kissed his cheek. "Just one more reason to love you, I guess."

Daryn should have felt some guilt at deceiving her, but he didn't. His lies were a means to an end—attaining whatever he desired. "I love you too, babe."

He draped his arm across her shoulders, then gently led her out of the restaurant and across the street. When they reached Tres Belle, he went back into his wallet and pulled out four hundred dollars. "Here, go buy yourself something nice."

"Aren't you coming with me?" she asked, her brow furrowing into a ridge.

"Don't scowl; you'll make a wrinkle," he joked.

She didn't laugh. Instead, she persisted with her questions. "Where are you going, and why aren't you coming with me?"

He had to come up with what she'd consider an adequate response, or she'd never let up. "Hon, do I really need to?" He pointed next door to Miller's. "I thought I'd wander around the men's section. Maybe find some sexy cologne you'll find irresistible on me."

Her frown turned into a smile. She took the money from him and slipped it into her purse. "Have fun."

"I'll come find you in a bit." He kissed her lightly and sent her on her way.

When Cassie was out of sight, he entered the store. It didn't take him long to search out the statuesque brunette beauty. She browsed the shoe department, totally unaware that he watched her.

∞൚

Alice picked up a pair of brown leather boots with a soft fleece lining and nearly choked when she saw the price tag—two hundred dollars. She'd spent a bundle on her last shopping spree. Although money wasn't a problem since she'd acquired quite a nest egg when she sold the family theater and the block of property that went along with it, she'd always been frugal. Why buy something expensive when more than likely you could find another item close to it for considerably less? She eyed the sale rack in the corner, but the boot's butter-soft calfskin nearly melted between her fingertips as if saying, *Buy me, buy me.*

Oh, what the heck. It was only money, and, besides, she couldn't bring it with her to where she was going in another seven days. As long as there was enough cash after she was gone to keep Jasper comfortable, she might as well have fun with the rest of it.

Alice made her purchase and actually felt good about spending the money. She had a spring in her step as she strolled through Miller's. She'd only been in there once before. When she was a young girl, her mother had insisted they look for a dress for a special holiday performance at the theater. Miller's had been around for generations and was known for its fine-quality merchandise as well as its high price tags.

She stopped at a glass display case filled with leather gloves and spotted a pair that would match perfectly with her new boots.

"Beautiful, aren't they," the sales clerk gushed.

The girl couldn't be more than sixteen or seventeen, even though it was clear she worked hard at trying to appear older. She wore her hair slicked back in a twist. Her lips were painted with a deep red lipstick the color of blood, and her eyes were encircled with smoldering charcoal shadow that instead of making her look grown-up only accentuated her baby face. This must be her first job, Alice thought kindly, remembering the days she'd worked at the theater.

"Those gloves will keep your fingers toasty during an early morning walk," the clerk said.

"Or an evening stroll on the green." Butterflies began to flutter her stomach as she thought of tonight's date with Jack.

"Oh, you're going to see the lights? I went last night." The clerk pulled out a tray and set it on the counter in front of Alice. "It's so romantic. All those twinkling white lights make being in love even more wonderful." A dreamy look came over her face, and Alice knew she was thinking of some young man she was smitten with.

Alice took out the pair of gloves she'd been admiring and ran them over the back of her hand. They were just as soft as she'd expected. "I'll take these," she said, handing them to the clerk.

"Is your husband taking you tonight?" the girl asked.

Alice felt the heat rise up to her cheeks at the thought of Jack as her husband. "Oh no...no, I'm not married."

"Boyfriend, then?" The clerk moved over to the next counter and took out a tray of gleaming key chains. "Have you gotten him anything for Christmas yet? These are gorgeous. Fourteen-karat gold."

"No, no I don't think—" She bit back her words when she spotted the treble clef sign. Jack would love that. She imagined his look of surprise when she gave it to him. "I'll take that one," she said, pointing to the key chain with the beautifully scripted G dangling from it.

The clerk nodded. "Ah, he's a music lover. Good choice." She handed the large chunk of gold to Alice.

It was heavier than she'd expected. Cold, smooth, and expensive. "Very nice," she said, handing it back. "Would you gift wrap it, please?"

"Of course."

The clerk disappeared behind a huge perfume display, returning a few minutes later with an elegant red foil box. "Your total is four hundred fifty-five dollars." She seemed extremely pleased with herself, and Alice wondered if she was being paid on commission.

Alice reached into her purse and pulled out her wallet. She

carefully counted out the cash and handed the clerk five hundred dollars.

"I'll be right back with your change," she said with a smile.

Alice studied Jack's gift. This Christmas—most likely her last Christmas—looked like it was going to be one of the best she'd ever had.

"Excuse me. I believe this is yours."

Alice turned to her right. Beside her stood an extremely handsome man with a fifty-dollar bill in his hand.

"You dropped this," he said and placed it in her palm.

"I did? Thank you. I'm not usually that careless."

"I'm just glad I was here to find it for you." His dark blond hair fell boyishly over one eye, and he brushed it back with obviously manicured fingers.

She studied him without trying to appear rude. He was tall. Over six feet, she guessed, as he stood a good inch above her. He wore jeans and a black leather jacket that fit him perfectly and added to his sexiness.

"You have exquisite taste. Your husband is going to love his gift."

Alice shifted her weight from foot to foot nervously. Why did everyone assume she had a husband? "I'm not married."

"Really? How is that possible? Someone so lovely... Well, I'm sure your boyfriend will be thrilled with it."

Alice couldn't keep from blushing. There was no doubt that this man was flirting with her. And she couldn't help herself. She liked it. "He's not really my boyfriend. Just a good friend."

"Ah, in that case, perhaps we could meet for coffee sometime?"

She didn't know what to say. The old Alice never would have considered such a proposal. She'd never been out alone before with a stranger. But the tin angel's words ran through her mind. She was running out of time. If she didn't find true love soon…well, she never would. She looked at him shyly through her lashes. He was awfully handsome. And what harm could come from meeting him for coffee? Besides, maybe he was the one—her soul mate. Things weren't going well with Jack and his suspicions about her.

"Why not?" she said softly.

"Good." He reached into his jacket pocket and pulled out a small notepad and pen and set them on the counter. "I'm here for the holidays. I'm staying at the Wayside Inn. Would you mind if I give you a call?"

"How can I say no? You did save me fifty dollars." She scribbled her name and number on the paper while he watched her write.

"Thanks, Ally." He put the pad and pen back in his pocket. "I'm Ross Saunders. And you will hear from me soon."

"It was nice to meet you. And thanks again for this." She waved the fifty-dollar bill at his back as he walked away, then took a quick sharp breath in disbelief that she'd made a date with him. When she looked up, she realized the sales clerk had returned with her change. She wondered how long she'd been standing there. By the look of disapproval on her face, it must have been long enough to have witnessed her giving out her name and number.

She stuffed Jack's gift in her handbag and tucked her other purchases snugly under her arm before receiving her change from the clerk. Alice avoided her eyes. Guilt tugged at her heart. Don't be ridiculous, she thought. You've done nothing wrong. Yet, she felt as if she'd deceived Jack. She knew she was being silly. He wasn't her boyfriend, and he probably didn't even like her all that much.

She left the store and hailed a cab. For the entire ride home, she was at odds with herself. Part of her was happy that a new man had entered her life, and part of her thought she might have just made a huge mistake. To ward off those misgivings, she tried to convince herself that Ross most likely would never call, so she had nothing to worry about.

℘℧

Daryn whistled happily as he left Miller's. He may have just hit the jackpot. Ally had to be loaded. After all, she had a wallet full of cash. And she fell easily for his you-dropped-your-money scam. Oh yeah. She would be an easy mark. There was no doubt of that. And boy, would he enjoy playing her. The woman was gorgeous. All he had to do now was convince Cass to spend the holidays in Silvercreek.

He entered the boutique and spotted her right away by a rack of cashmere sweaters. It would have been impossible not to notice her with her fiery red hair. A pain squeezed his chest as he thought of all the times he'd cheated. He wished he knew why. It wasn't because she didn't satisfy him. She did. And it wasn't because he didn't love her. He did. At least as much as he was capable of loving someone. So why wasn't that enough? He'd had these same thoughts many times. Usually after he'd been with another woman. But now it seemed just the anticipation of deceiving Cassie triggered them. Maybe it was because he was terrified of losing her? Yet, if that was the case, wouldn't it make sense that he'd stop these useless affairs with women he could care less about? The problem wasn't common sense, however. It was his libido. Therefore, the only option he had was to remain cunning. Cassie had warned that if she ever caught him with another woman, she would leave him. And he didn't doubt her. He had to make her believe he had no interest in Ally, other than to steal her money.

Cassie's head was tipped down as she fingered through some garments, so she didn't see him approach her. He reached around her waist from behind and squeezed her to him. When she nearly dropped her bags in surprise, he kissed the side of her neck, then whispered, "I hope you bought something with me in mind."

"I guess you'll find out later, won't you?" She wriggled free from his grasp to pull a forest-green sweater off the rack. She held it up to her chest and asked, "What do you think of this color? Does it look good with my eyes?"

"Everything looks good on you, babe." He saw a wrinkle start to form between her brows, so he continued, "But that green makes your eyes look incredible, so buy it, and let's get out of here." Before she could protest, he took hold of her arm and led her to the checkout counter. He paid the cashier, then ushered her out of the store.

"What's the hurry?" she said, looking at her watch. "I'm not late. It's only eleven-thirty. We've plenty of time before the hotel checkout."

He only hesitated for a second before answering. "We're not leaving."

"What? Why?" Her voice rose in pitch. "But we were going to spend the holidays in Jersey."

Daryn had to convince her quickly, before she worked herself into a panic. "I know. I know, babe. But something's come up that's more important than Christmas in Atlantic City."

She rolled her eyes, and he knew she was on to him. It would come as no surprise when he told her it was a scam.

"What's it this time, hon? Another nice elderly couple that we're going to swindle out of their savings?"

Her sarcasm wasn't wasted on him. "Now don't tell me you're going soft on me," he shot back.

"Of course not. I just thought we'd take a little break."

He shook her shopping bags. "A break? How can we take a break when you're always doing this?"

Tears welled in her big eyes. Oh shit. He hadn't wanted to upset her. "Baby, calm down." He draped his arm over her shoulders and walked with her across the street. "Let's not do this out here."

"Do what? Make a spectacle? Attract attention?" Her voice rose at least an octave or two.

"I mean it, Cass," he said icily. "Don't push me."

"Are you threatening me?" She stopped in front of the hotel.

"Damn it, woman. Of course not. I just don't want to wind up in jail." He took her by the elbow and herded her inside. "Now just hold on, at least until we're back in the room," he said under his breath. When they reached the reservation desk, he pasted on a smile. "Hello. My sister and I have decided to extend our stay in town through the holidays. We won't be checking out now after all. We'll be here until the first of the year."

The clerk, a middle-aged balding man, couldn't take his eyes off Cassie. "Of course, sir. We're pleased to have you both continue your stay with us. If there's anything I can do to make your visit more comfortable, please don't hesitate to ask for me." He took a business card from behind the desk and slid it across the counter to Cassie.

She picked it up, and Daryn could tell she gritted her teeth as she did so. He shot her a warning glance, and she forced a half-smile at the clerk before spinning on her heel and marching toward their rooms.

Once inside, he knew all hell would break loose if she had her way, so before she could say a word, he put one hand over her mouth. "Now, just listen to me. Luck is with us, baby. I've stumbled across a great score. And there'll be no forging wills or falsifying documents. This one'll be easy. I promise you." He took his hand off her mouth and replaced it with a kiss.

He was tender at first, but as his need for her grew, his kiss deepened until he thought he'd explode with desire. In a flash, he had her clothes off and his as well. He pushed her back onto the bed and straddled her, then played with her until she screamed with delight.

When she was ready, he mounted her and thrust hard into her. That was the way she liked it. And he had no problem complying.

When they were both spent and covered with sweat, he rolled off her and lit a cigarette. He didn't smoke often, but after sex was the time he enjoyed tobacco the most. The taste of Pall Mall and Cassie on his tongue was intoxicating.

He closed his eyes while he smoked and chose his words with care. "I saw a woman in Miller's this morning pay for her purchase with a wad of cash. I mean she had a lot of it, so I pulled the you-dropped-your-money scam on her to see how easily she'd con, and boy was she simple."

He opened his eyes and directed his gaze at Cassie. The sight of her splendid body sent desire raging through him. He fought the urge to make love to her again. Business came first, and they needed to discuss it. They had to come up with a foolproof plan before he scheduled a date with Ally.

Cassie stared at him as if he'd lost his mind.

"What?" he snapped. He didn't like it when she looked at him that way. It made him feel like she thought she was superior to him.

"Nothing." I'm just wondering why some lady buying stuff with cash would make you think she'd be a good score. I mean, when I see people paying with cash, I don't think that." She shrugged. "Just wondering. That's all."

He tried to hide his annoyance. "I told you; she had a lot of cash. She whipped out five-hundred bucks like it was nothing."

She sat up and covered herself with the sheet. "How old do you think she is?"

Daryn knew where this conversation was headed, and he didn't like it. "I don't know, Cass. Twenties probably. What does it matter?"

"It doesn't. Just curious," she replied.

Although her tone was restrained, her pupils had darkened, and he knew an explosion wasn't far off. Daryn had to tread carefully, or he would regret ever having brought up the subject. He reached over and rubbed her shoulder. "Look, it's no big deal. We don't have to do another scam right now. The idea just came to me when I saw all that money, and I thought I'd be able to get you a really special Christmas present if we did one more quick one."

She turned to face him and ran the back of her hand across the side of his cheek. "Really? You want to do this for me?"

"Of course," he lied. "I know how much you love beautiful things."

"Oh, sweetie." She leaned over and kissed him. "Thank you for thinking of me."

"Hey, I think of you all the time. You should know that by now."

She swung her leg over his as if claiming ownership of him. "I do. It's just sometimes I can't help but worry—"

"Babe," he cut her off before she could finish. He knew what she was going to say, and he didn't want to deal with Cassie's jealousy right now. "You don't have to worry about anything. I promise you, I'm not going anywhere. You're stuck with me." He draped his arm across her shoulders and pulled her close.

"Do you have any idea how you'd like to play this one?" she asked, seemingly pleased with his response.

"I haven't figured it all out yet, but I thought we'd scope out her place."

"You know where she lives?" she asked.

He hesitated a moment before answering. "No, but I have her phone number." Cassie's complexion darkened, as he'd expected. "Before you go and get all worked up over nothing, hear me out."

Her bottom lip quivered ever so slightly. "Okay. This better be good."

"I asked her out for coffee in order to get her name and number."

Cassie moved over to the other side of the bed, leaving a good foot of space between them. "And of course she said yes. What does she look like? Is she pretty?"

"Shit, Cass. Why do you have to do that? What difference does it make what she looks like?"

She folded her arms across her chest. "Do you really want me to answer that question?"

"I'm not gonna lie to you. Yeah, she's good looking. So what? Why would I want hamburger when I have steak at home? Huh?" He flashed her a toothy grin.

A small smile curved her lips. "Daryn Cramer, you sure have a way with words."

He was glad the tension between them was gone. He hated to waste time trying to reassure her everything was okay when he had business to attend to. Daryn took the paper out from his pocket and dialed Ally's phone number.

ॐ

Alice answered the phone on the second ring. It must be Jack calling to cancel their date for this evening. She hesitated, then said, "Hello."

"Ally?"

"Yes." The caller wasn't Jack.

"This is Ross…Saunders. I'd like to buy you that cup of coffee."

This charade was beginning to really wear on her. She hadn't expected him to call and certainly not this soon. She must have made quite an impression on him. "When did you have in mind?"

"I could pick you up in, say, thirty minutes?"

Thirty minutes? No. That was much too soon. Besides, Alice had never done anything spontaneous in her life. She was about to turn him down when a vision of the old Alice—miserable and alone—made her change her mind. Why not see Ross? What did she have to lose?

"I'd prefer to meet somewhere, if you don't mind." Jack had often warned her not to be so trusting. This world was different from the one she'd grown up in. He'd made her promise never to open the door to strangers, and she was sure he'd frown upon her getting into a car with one. As nice as Ross seemed, she needed to get to know him better before she invited him to her home.

"Of course. How about my hotel? The restaurant serves wonderful lattes."

"Fine. I'll see you soon." When Alice hung up the phone, she realized her hands were shaking. She had dates with two very attractive men and on the same day. Who would have thought her simple life could become so complicated? She took a few minutes to freshen up, then called Silvercreek Cab Company to take her to the Wayside Inn.

She hesitated briefly before entering the hotel and wondered if agreeing to meet Ross had been a wise decision. After all, she knew nothing about him. There was a sour feeling in the pit of her stomach, and for a second, she considered leaving, but if she kept running away from her opportunities, life would pass her by again. Hadn't Ross been a complete gentleman? He'd found her fifty dollars, and instead of pocketing the money, he gave it back to her. How many people in this day and age would be honest enough to do that? From the stories Jack had told her, not many.

She scanned the hotel lobby and spotted the restaurant across the way. As soon as she entered the doorway, she saw Ross seated at a table by the window. He saw her at the same time and waved.

She summoned her courage and, with a confident stride, headed toward him. When she arrived at the table, he stood and pulled out a chair for her. He was even more handsome than she remembered.

His features were near perfect, making him almost too beautiful for a man.

"Thank you," she said, as she sat beside him.

There were two lattes on the table. He slid one in front of her and took a sip of the other, then said, "I went ahead and ordered for us. Hope you don't mind?"

She shook her head as she smoothed a napkin on her lap.

He openly studied her, and by his look of approval, he apparently found her attractive too. "I'm so glad you agreed to meet me," he went on. "With all the traveling I do, it can get pretty lonely."

She stared into his extraordinary tawny eyes—flecked and ringed with gold. "What is it you do for a living?"

He took another sip before answering. "I help families get their affairs in order. Mutual funds, life insurance, wills, that sort of thing."

A heaviness centered in her chest, and a melancholy frown tightened her face. She just might need his services.

"What's wrong?" he asked, obviously noticing her mood shift.

"Oh, nothing. I was just thinking of all those elderly people who need your help. They must be so indebted to you."

He leaned back in the chair, stretching out his long legs. "Yeah, I'm sure there are any number who would love to show their gratitude, but once I'm through with a job, I don't look back. Too many more out there to help."

"You must be a very compassionate man," she said softly.

His look was one of faint amusement. "I try to be. I get it from my mom. She was always willing to go the extra mile to get the job done."

Alice blew on her latte before taking a drink. "Is it a family business?"

He paused a moment. "Yeah, I guess you could say that."

"Is your mom stilling working?"

A touch of sadness flitted across his features. "No. She passed on."

Alice dropped her lashes quickly to hide her embarrassment. "Oh, I'm so sorry."

"That's okay. She's right here." He placed his hand over his heart, and she thought she saw a tear glisten his eye. "Enough about me, though. I want to hear about you. Have you lived in Silvercreek long?"

She dreaded having to lie, but she couldn't tell him the truth. She would have to tell another story. "No, actually, I don't live here. I'm staying at my aunt's house for the holidays. I'm from upstate New York."

He raised a brow at her. "Is the rest of your family here too? Parents? Siblings?"

"Um, no. No one. Not my aunt either. She's in New York with my dad." He was looking at her oddly, so she knew she had to elaborate on her story. "They haven't seen each other in years. This was a good time for them to reunite, and, well, I needed some time alone, so that's why I'm here."

"You're spending the holidays alone?" A hopeful gleam brightened his expressive eyes.

"Not exactly. My aunt has a tenant who's become a friend. He rents her upstairs apartment. As a matter of fact, I'm going to be seeing him tonight," she said awkwardly.

Disappointment marred his handsome face. "I guess that means this coffee date won't have a shot of becoming a dinner date?"

She shook her head. "I'm afraid not. Another time perhaps?"

He offered her a wide smile. "Absolutely."

They chatted for a while, mostly about the benefits of small-town life, and after she finished her latte, she checked her watch for the time. "I hate to rush off but—"

"You have to get ready for your date." He finished her sentence for her, and there was no mistaking the regret in his voice. "It was wonderful getting to know you a little."

"I enjoyed it too." She pushed her chair back and stood. A second later, he was at her side. He pulled a twenty-dollar bill out of his wallet and stuck the corner under his cup; then he placed his hand on the small of her back and walked her across the restaurant. When they were outside, he hailed her a cab.

"Thank you," she said.

"My pleasure." He helped her into the taxi, and she gave the driver her address as Ross closed the door.

What a nice man, Alice thought. It really was too bad she couldn't have spent more time with him.

ɞɔ

As Daryn watched the cab speed away, he put the address Ally had given the driver into his BlackBerry; then he sent a text message to Cassie, telling her to meet him in the hotel lobby right away and to bring the car keys. Ally had played right into his lap. He couldn't have wished for a better scenario—an elderly aunt away for the holidays, leaving her young, naïve niece alone in her house. This was going to be the perfect scam. Just perfect.

Cassie arrived a few minutes later, and, before she could bombard him with a million questions, he took the car keys from her hand and ushered her toward the parking garage.

"How did it go?" she asked as they walked.

"Much better than I'd hoped." When they reached the car, he opened the passenger door for her, then walked around to the driver's side. He sank into the Beemer's soft leather seat and thought how much he loved his profession. There wasn't another job on earth he could do that would yield the returns of this one. And with so little effort. Yes, he was a lucky man indeed.

He said a silent prayer of thanks to his mom for her excellent schooling, then, with a grin, he turned to Cassie and said, "We're in the money. The girl, Ally, has an elderly aunt who's in upstate New York, and Ally's staying at her place. Alone. Mostly. There's some tenant who rents an upstairs apartment. The good thing is, she's going out with him tonight, so while she's away, we move in. Couldn't get easier than that."

"Sounds simple enough," she said.

"Yeah, piece of cake." He plugged Ally's address into his phone's GPS and headed toward Main Street.

He spotted the house right away—a big, old Victorian in need of repairs. It must have been quite a place in its day, however. He parked across the street, far enough away so as not to be seen scoping out the place, yet close enough to have a clear view of the front door.

ಬಿಜ

Jack studied his reflection in the bedroom mirror. He'd always been confident of his appearance, not cocky, mind you, but self-assured. Women had always been attracted to him, even from a very young age. It started in elementary school. Must have been fourth grade when Anna Hughs passed him that love note. She'd been a giggly bundle of nerves waiting for him to read her poetry. With her long dark ringlets and rosy cheeks, she was a nine-year-old boy's vision of beauty. Was it any wonder he'd always been attracted to brunettes after that?

Once he saw beyond Ally's makeup and fancy clothes, she fit his image of female perfection to a tee. Watch it, he warned himself. Remember the plan. Charm some information out of her tonight, but whatever you do, make sure your head rules and not your heart.

He glanced over at the bed where the little red foil box glistened in the lamplight. That sales clerk at Miller's had been an angel suggesting he get Ally a gold charm for Christmas. If that didn't get her to open up to him, he didn't know what would. An image of it dangling delicately from a chain around her lovely, statuesque neck sent a heat rising up through him. He'd better control it or else he'd wind up back in the shower…only this time he'd be taking a cold one.

There was something so irresistible about her, if he wasn't careful, he could get hurt. No matter how wonderful she appeared, she could very well be the grifter Pastor Riley had warned him about. He tried to envision her taking advantage of the elderly but couldn't do it. She was so like Alice that she had to be the sweet, charming girl she appeared.

No matter what this night might bring, a touch of romance or not, he was going to find out whether she was what she seemed and whether he could believe her when she said Alice was spending the holiday in upstate New York.

The ringing of the telephone turned his thoughts away from Ally, and he reached for the phone on his bedside table. But his hand froze in midair. Bethany Snow appeared on his caller ID. "Not now," he groaned. There was no doubt she was calling because she wanted to spend New Year's with him. He was going to have to squash that plan and get her to leave him alone, but the last thing he wanted to do right now was argue with Bethany. He was already running late for his date with Ally.

Letting the answering machine pick up Bethany's call, Jack grabbed the teal-blue sweater he'd laid out across his bed and slipped it over his head. With a quick rake of his fingers through his hair, he was ready to go.

CHAPTER FIVE

*A*lice paced the foyer floor. She glanced in the parlor to check the
time on the grandfather clock. 7:05 p.m. Jack had said seven
o'clock. He was never late. Panic chilled her as her thoughts jumped
on. What if he'd changed his mind? What if he wasn't coming?
Maybe he'd tried to call earlier to cancel, when she'd been out with
Ross. She didn't have an answering machine, so there was no way for
him to leave a message. Maybe he was trying to get up the nerve to
call her now and cancel. Maybe she should call him and do it for him.

"Oh, stop it!" she yelled, clamping her hands over her ears in an
attempt to block the doubts clouding her mind.

Her raised voice startled Jasper from his lookout perch on the
windowsill. He jumped down and came to rub against her ankles as if
to tell her to calm down. She stroked his back with trembling hands.

If this is what Jack does to you, you're really in trouble. She looked at the
clock again. Only two minutes had gone by since the last time she'd
checked. If he didn't get here soon, she wouldn't have to worry about
the date. She'd have died from a heart attack before then.

The loud rap on the door took her by surprise. She glanced
nervously at her reflection in the wall mirror. The low-rise black

denim pants were a perfect fit, and her yellow sweater was snug but not so tight as to be vulgar. She'd lightened up on the makeup, using only a hint of peach-toned blush, a whisk of mascara and a clear gloss over her lips. She hoped Jack liked her new image.

She wasn't chic as she'd been the night he'd taken her out to dinner, when she'd worn that lovely black lace outfit she'd gotten at Lorelle. But there was no sense trying to be something she wasn't. Inside this young body, she was still the old Alice.

If Jack preferred the glamorous type, then he'd have to look elsewhere to find it. She'd decided to be herself—the natural girl-next-door type.

She tucked a stray hair behind her ear, drew a deep breath, and opened the door. How come every time she saw Jack he looked better than the last? In faded jeans that hugged his muscular thighs, a worn leather jacket, and a wool scarf wrapped around his neck, he looked rugged and handsome.

"Sorry I'm late. Hope you haven't been waiting long." He smiled at her, exposing his even white teeth.

"No, not at all. I'm only just ready to go myself." She wasn't about to tell him she'd been watching the clock. She slipped on her coat and joined him out on the porch.

He studied her a moment, and she held her breath. His gaze lingered on her face. "You've done something different. Is it your hair?"

"Nope. Hair's the same."

He narrowed his eyes. "I know what it is. You're not all done up, that's it. You look like you. Like you did this morning when you first woke up."

She bit her bottom lip and frowned. "I'm not sure I should take that as a compliment."

He cupped her chin in his hand and turned her face toward the porch light. "Hmmm, nice bone structure, gorgeous eyes, and those lips…"

"Oh, stop it, Jack," she said, slapping his hand away.

He laughed. It was the same laugh she heard when he was winning at gin rummy. It came from deep inside. There was nothing artificial about it. It was the laugh he reserved for friends, and her heart swelled with joy that he was beginning to relax around her.

"All joking aside, Ally, I like you better this way. You're a gorgeous woman. You should let your beauty shine through, not cover it up."

Her eyes widened with surprise. "Do you really think so?" She'd been trying so hard to copy the makeup artist's techniques, thinking Jack would like her better that way.

He caressed her cheek with his fingertip. "I do."

Her skin warmed under his touch, her veiled desire for him dangerously close to the surface. "We should probably get going."

He ran his finger over her bottom lip, then down her chin. "We can take my car or walk, whichever you prefer."

She looked up at the starlit sky and decided in an instant. "I choose the scenic route." To stroll through town on Jack's arm would be heaven on earth.

He smiled at her. "My choice too."

As they stepped off the porch, she noticed his limp. "Oh, Jack, I'm so sorry. I didn't mean to be selfish. I'd forgotten about your ankle." Her feet crunched through the snow as she headed toward the carriage house, where Jack housed his car. "Let's drive."

"No, no," he said, bringing her to a halt. "I want to walk too."

"But you might slip…and you don't have your cane," she cried, just now realizing he stood without support.

"I left it home purposely. I was hoping you'd let me lean on you," he said, tucking her arm in his.

Didn't he know he didn't need a reason to hold her? But she appreciated his attempt at being coy just the same.

As they walked, she found herself glancing through the windows of the elegant old homes they passed. Families were gathered around Christmas trees, sipping eggnog, doing all the things families do together on Christmas Eve, and for the first time, Alice wasn't envious. There was no place she'd rather be than right here…right now…with Jack. She wasn't alone falling asleep in her big overstuffed chair, wishing her life had turned out differently. Her wish had come true, thanks to the tin angel.

She glanced up toward heaven. "Thank you." The words she hadn't meant to speak aloud came out in a soft puff of white. She glanced at Jack from the corner of her eye to see if he'd heard her.

"For what?" he asked, answering her question.

"For spending this evening with me," she said quickly, before nerves kept her from uttering what she felt inside.

"It's my pleasure." His pace slowed to a stop, and he leaned over to bring his mouth down on hers. It was a quick, soft kiss, yet it made her toes tingle.

"I've been waiting all day to do that," he said, draping his arm over her shoulders.

She blinked nervously in stunned silence.

Jack chuckled. "We can walk now," he said, taking a step forward.

Alice fell in stride beside him. Moonlight cast a silvery glow upon his raven hair. She felt the urge to reach up and run her fingers through it. She wanted to run her hands down the back of his neck, over his powerful shoulders, and down his thickly muscled arms. Unnerved at the direction of her thoughts, she shifted her gaze forward.

Up ahead, the lights from the green twinkled, making it look like they were about to enter a winter wonderland. Rows of miniature pear trees were strung with thousands of tiny white lights. As they approached, a choir of carolers sang "Silent Night."

In the center of the spectacle sat a magnificent horse-drawn carriage. The driver, looking like a character straight out of a fairy tale with his top hat and tails, steadied the stomping horses while a couple settled in for a ride. A few minutes later, the carriage rolled past them, then disappeared down the street.

"Reminds you of Cinderella, doesn't it?" Jack asked.

She nodded, breathless from the beauty of it all.

"Care to take a ride?"

She gazed up into his fabulous blue eyes. "I'd love to, but are you sure you don't mind the wait? It's pretty cold out."

"We'll keep each other warm." He turned up the collar on her coat and held it closed, then with the other hand brought her closer to him.

She inhaled the rich, earthy scent of his cologne, a tantalizing collection of spices that left her senses reeling. His hard, muscular thigh pressed against her, and a long-repressed need to have a man hold her surfaced. She wrapped her arms around him and let her desire free as she held him in a heart-pounding embrace.

Snow fell around them like cotton, forming a patchwork pattern on his hair. She brushed a shimmering flake from his brow with the back of her gloved fingers. His arm tightened around her waist; then his mouth brushed hers, hardening into a long, lingering kiss. She opened her lips to his probing tongue.

Consumed with a feverish passion, she lost track of time. It wasn't until the carriage driver tapped Jack on the shoulder that she was brought back to reality.

"I hate to interrupt, but you two are in line, right?"

Jack nodded and, with his arm still around her, led her toward the carriage. He helped her up, then climbed in beside her. The driver handed him a sueded Berber throw, which Jack draped over them, tucking it around her legs.

"Warm enough?" he asked.

She smiled and snuggled closer to him. "I am now."

He rested his arm around her shoulders and kissed her. A large crowd had gathered by the carriage. All were waiting to ride. She didn't care if she and Jack looked like a couple of teenagers out on a first date, because that was exactly how she felt.

The driver chirruped to the horses and turned them onto the road. Jack had been right about her feeling like Cinderella, and he certainly fit the image of Prince Charming, right down to the ends of his shiny black hair. If Alice had been given a magic wand, she couldn't have created a more perfect evening. Only one problem marred her happiness, and it wasn't being turned into a scullery maid at the end of the night. For her when the clock struck midnight on New Year's Eve, signaling the start of a new year, she would become an old woman whose life had come to an end.

She tried to fight back the tears and helplessness that threatened to consume her. Not tonight. You mustn't think about that tonight, she warned herself. Just enjoy the moment. That's all you have.

"What's wrong?" Jack asked, concern etched on his face. "What's made you so sad?"

"I was wishing this night could go on forever."

"Don't worry. I'm sure you'll have many more just as memorable, especially if I have anything to do with it." The sincerity in his voice touched her as much as his words.

After driving through town, the driver pulled the carriage up in front of Gilly's Tavern and rang a set of brass sleigh bells. "There's none better than Sally Gilly's homemade apple cider."

"What do you think, should we go inside and warm up a bit?"

Jack's nose was red from the cold, as were his cheeks.

Alice knew Sally from way back, but she doubted the old woman would recognize her now, some sixty-five years younger than she should be. She gave Jack her approval, and he pulled some money from his wallet to tip the driver.

He jumped down from the carriage, then held his hand out to help her. When she stepped onto the snow-covered road, Jack let her slide into his arms. He held her a moment, then kissed the top of her head. They entered the tavern hand in hand.

A few old-timers sat at the bar drinking whiskey, smoking cigars, and telling tales of how their wives would be furious when they got home smelling of booze and stale smoke.

"It's Christmas Eve," bellowed one old man looking an awful lot like Santa Claus with his puff of white hair and long beard. His potbelly hung over his belt, jiggling when he laughed. "A few pops with my boys here ain't too much to ask before going home, now is it?"

Jack leaned over and whispered in her ear, "I think he's had more than a few pops, wouldn't you say?"

Alice smiled and remembered how her father used to stop here after the theater. It had always been a favorite haunt of the locals.

The hostess, dressed in an elf costume, came over to seat them. They followed her to the back of the tavern, where the flames from a large stone fireplace lent a cozy glow to the room. She led them to a small wooden table in front of the fire. Jack held Alice's chair while she sat.

Alice pulled off her leather gloves and tucked them into her jacket pocket. "What a lovely time I'm having. I can't thank you enough for this." Her lower lip quivered as she spoke, and she tried not to let emotion overcome her.

He moved the holly centerpiece and reached across the table to hold her hands. "You're a special person, and I'm only now learning just how special."

Guilt washed over her as she thought of how she'd deceived him. If he knew, would he still feel that way about her? For a moment she considered telling him everything—how a tin angel had granted her wish, how she was really Alice—but the craziness of it kept her from speaking. She couldn't risk spoiling this night. No, it was better to remain silent.

He let go of her hands and reached into his pocket, pulling out a red foil box. It was the same wrapping paper the sales clerk at Miller's had used to wrap the gift she'd purchased for him. He slid it across the table in front of her.

"I know it's not Christmas yet, but I just couldn't wait any longer to give it to you. I hope you don't mind." His face was illuminated in the flickering firelight, a handsome sculpting of darkness and light. The gleam in his eyes told her this gift was special.

She wanted to trace her fingers along the dark stubble shading his jaw. "Not at all," she said, ripping open the paper. "It was a tradition in my family to open one gift on Christmas Eve."

He lifted a brow slightly. "You don't follow that tradition any longer?"

She paused before opening the black-velvet box in her hands. "I'm sorry. I don't know what you mean."

"You spoke in the past tense. You said it *was* a tradition. I wondered what happened. Your family doesn't do that any longer?"

Now she realized her mistake. She'd spoken as Alice. It had been a very long time since she celebrated the holidays with her family, her parents having been dead for years. But Ally's father was supposed to be alive and well.

She was becoming too comfortable with Jack. Memories that popped into her head were slipping out of her mouth, and if she wasn't careful, she might say something she wouldn't be able to explain away.

"I was thinking of this year. That must be why I said that. We're not following tradition. I'm here, my family's not." Her fingers tightened on the box. She wished he would stop analyzing her words.

"Sorry. Go on, open your gift."

She flipped open the lid. Inside a beautiful gold piano sparkled. "Oh, Jack," she said, covering her mouth with her hands. Emotion bubbled up inside her, and her eyes grew misty. "A piano."

Despite her joy, worry swept through her. This was something she'd have thought he'd give to Alice, not Ally.

As if reading her mind, he smiled and slipped the charm from her hands. He let it dangle from his fingers. "I know what you're thinking. Why did I choose a piano for you?"

She nodded, and her chest tightened.

"You have an appreciation of music. It was evident the night I played for you. The way you touched the keys… You know, you don't have to play to have music be a part of your soul."

"Thank you. I love it. It's amazing how well you've gotten to know me already."

"I felt our connection the first time I laid eyes on you. You felt it too, didn't you?"

This was too good to be true. Jack did have feelings for her, and it was becoming clear that they were as strong as the ones she had for him. "Yes," she said softly, not wanting to break this magical spell.

He dropped the charm back in its box, then lifted her hand and brought it to his mouth. His lips lingered on her skin, and she thought her heart would burst right out of her chest. The waitress came by with their menus just in time to keep her from fainting. Happiness and love weren't emotions she was familiar with.

"Mr. Billings, how are you?" The young woman was tall, though not as tall as Alice. She had on brown stretch pants and a matching turtleneck. Her long auburn hair was swept back with an antler headband. When she moved, the tiny gold bells dangling from it tinkled. She made a very attractive reindeer.

Jack grinned. "Lena? Is that you?"

She laughed. "Hard to recognize me in this getup, huh?"

"You look great. Love the antlers."

Alice pulled her hand away from Jack's embrace and stuck it under the table. She could still feel the sizzle of his kiss on her skin. How did he know the waitress? Was she someone he'd dated? He did sometimes go out on a Saturday night.

From beneath her lashes, Alice studied the pretty young woman. Her coppery hair framed her face, and her vivid green eyes were locked on Jack in open admiration. Alice shifted her gaze to the paneled wall where a row of pictures hung, depicting the town as it had looked long ago. She belonged in that time period, not in this one. She knew nothing of this new world or of women who openly flirted with a man while he was on a date with someone else.

"Al, this is Lena Robbins."

It took her a moment to realize Jack was speaking to her. She'd thought he'd forgotten her presence. "A pleasure to meet you." She reached across the table to shake the woman's hand.

"This is Ally Hart, my landlady's niece," Jack said, completing the introduction. "She's here for the holidays."

"A beautiful time of year to visit our little town. Have you seen the lights on the green?" Lena asked.

The way she said, *"Our little town,"* made Alice feel like an outsider and sent her pulse racing. "Yes, they're lovely."

"We took the sleigh ride," Jack chimed in. "It was as if we'd gone back a hundred years, right, Ally?"

"Absolutely," she replied curtly.

He lifted a brow, and she knew he was wondering what was wrong. All her insecurities had resurfaced, and she wished she was home with Jasper curled on her lap.

"Lena works part time at the school's library," Jack informed her.

Ah, a librarian by day and a cocktail waitress by night. Alice gave her a tight smile.

"Her son's one of my music students. He plays the violin." Jack beamed as he always did when he spoke of his students. "Zack's got a lot of talent. You should be very proud of him."

Alice's pulse had slowed to normal again once she knew Lena was married and wasn't a threat, but her cheeks burned with shame. Jealousy was a strange new sensation, and she didn't like the feel of it one bit.

"I'm lucky to have him," Lena said, her voice full of pride. "Zack's crazy about you, Mr. Billings. He jumps right out of bed in the morning because he can't wait to get to your class."

"I know I've done my job when I hear things like that." His smile lit up his face.

"I'll give you two some time to look over the menu."

"We're here for the hot apple cider." Jack handed the menus back to her.

She tucked them under her arm and scribbled their order on her pad. "It's out of this world. Sally keeps the recipe hidden, and she won't let anyone in the kitchen when she's preparing it."

"A family secret." Jack laughed.

Alice had a few of those herself, but he wouldn't find hers amusing. She shifted her weight on the chair and crossed her legs at the ankles. The evening had lost its charm. She wished the waitress would get them their cider so she could go home.

Jack leaned his elbows on the table and caught her gaze. "I could go for some dessert. What do you say, Ally?"

Lena had her pen poised to write. "The gingerbread cake ala mode is fantastic. And it's huge."

"I'm really not hungry," Alice said, not wanting to prolong their stay any longer than necessary.

"Split one with me?" Jack's mesmerizing blue eyes implored her to say yes.

How could she let him down? "All right. I'll try a little."

"Great, I'll put your order right in." Lena headed toward the kitchen with the bells on her antlers jingling as she walked.

"She seems nice." Too nice, and too pretty. Lena might be married, but she still made Alice insecure by the way she looked at Jack.

He sat back in his chair and stretched his long legs out by the fire. He looked comfortable and relaxed and completely unaware of the turmoil raging inside her. Enjoy this night. Don't spoil it, she warned herself, but her emotions were running helter-skelter. Terrified that Jack would lose interest in her, every little thing put her into a tizzy. It had to be the guilt that was at the root of it. If he only knew the truth...

"Tell me about your life." He slid her chair across the hardwood floor so that she sat beside him, then draped his arm over her shoulders. "I want to know everything about you."

"Can't we just enjoy tonight? Why talk about the past?"

He ran his hand along the back of her neck. "We don't have to talk about past relationships. That's not what I'd meant. I sure don't want to talk about Bethany, and I know you don't want to discuss the old boyfriend you left back in New York. No, no, I want to know what you were like as a little girl. What are your dreams for the future?"

She stared down at the table, her gaze following the grain of the wood. "There's not much to tell. I was very shy. Didn't have many friends or boyfriends."

"I find it hard to believe your parents weren't beating boys off with a stick."

She looked up at him. "I didn't always look like this." Now was her chance to tell him the truth. She wouldn't get a better lead-in than this. "There's something you don't know about me."

He studied her carefully, the sparkle in his eyes hardening into something she couldn't define.

Her courage evaporated, and she dropped her gaze back down to the table. "I was really unattractive when I was younger."

She could almost feel him exhale with relief. What did he think she was going to say? That she had a criminal record or something?

"I doubt that. What teenage girl doesn't go through that awkward stage?"

Ninety years was a bit longer than a stage. She tried to steer the conversation to him, but he wouldn't have it.

"Were you born in New York?" he asked.

Here we go. She was about to spin another tale. "Yes."

"Where about?"

She'd known that question was coming, and her mind struggled for a town in upstate New York. She spouted the first one that came to mind. "Syracuse."

"Never been there. What's it like?"

"Just a regular town, like any other," she said. "I really don't want to talk about me. I've lived a very boring life. I'd much rather talk about you."

This time he didn't fuss. He told her stories about his youth, and she listened with great interest. She'd heard most of them before, but Jack could tell her the same story a hundred times and she wouldn't grow tired of it.

Lena returned, carrying their dessert. She'd been right about it being huge. She set the glass bowl in the center of the table and handed them each a spoon.

"Sally will be right out with your cider." Lena must have noticed Alice's shocked expression, because she patted her arm. "Don't worry, she might be old, but she doesn't bite. Sally always serves the cider herself. She loves to see the customers' reaction when they take their first sip."

Lena's explanation did little to alleviate Alice's fear. Although she hadn't seen Sally in years, she'd known her since she was a young woman. She must be eighty-something now. Maybe her memory wasn't as sharp as it used to be.

"I like that." Jack dipped his spoon in the bowl. "Most business owners couldn't be bothered. Sally realizes the importance of customer satisfaction," he said before taking a bite of gingerbread cake.

Lena left them to their dessert, and a few minutes later, Sally's familiar form headed toward their table. She carried a silver tray with two steaming mugs on top. She walked with a slight limp, and her varicose veins were evident even through the thick stockings she wore. Her short, curly hair was almost entirely gray, except for the dark patches around her temples. The smile she presented them made her round face appear even rounder. She'd always been a good-natured woman, and Alice could see that hadn't changed.

"Merry Christmas. You've come to try my cider." She balanced the tray on one hand while she served their drinks with the other. "I'm modest about most things, but when it comes to my cider, I'm not ashamed to brag. It's the best in all of New England," she said with a laugh.

Jack wasted no time in taking a sip. "You're right, Sally. I've never tasted better."

Alice realized all eyes were now on her.

"Blow on it a little, then take a sip," Jack advised.

She brought the cup to her lips while Sally studied her.

"You look very familiar."

Alice swallowed the steaming liquid, not caring that it burned going down her throat. "Really?" she squeaked, then set the cup down quickly.

Jack reached for her hand and squeezed. "She must be referring to your aunt." He turned to Sally, excitement glistening in his eyes. "You know Alice Hart?"

Sally slapped her thigh. "That's who you look like. Why, if my memory's not playing tricks with me, I'd say you're the spitting image of her." She narrowed her eyes while she stared at Alice.

"I guess there is quite a resemblance." She hoped no one noticed the nervous twitch at the side of her mouth.

"A resemblance, you say? Nah, you could be her twin. Well, that is if she were still twenty-five." Sally shook her head and chuckled. "Of course she don't look like that no more."

"She's still a very attractive woman," he said in quick defense.

Despite her nervousness, Alice's spirits rose that Jack would think so.

"I've wanted to know what she looked like as a young woman," he said. "She didn't keep any photographs of herself. Did you know that?"

Alice opened her mouth, but Sally spoke first. "I'm not surprised. She was always self-conscious about her looks, though Lord knows why. And a shy girl too. But after that young man of hers was killed…well, she shut herself up in that big old house, and none of us saw much of her after that."

Tears stung her eyes. Alice turned her head away and stared into the blue-tipped flames shooting up from the fireplace.

"Oh, I'm sorry, miss," Sally apologized, "I didn't mean nothing bad about your aunt."

"I know." Her voice cracked.

"I guess I'd better get back to the kitchen. You two enjoy yourselves." Sally left them, but not before Alice caught a glimpse of the embarrassed flush covering her face.

Jack squeezed her hand. "She didn't mean any harm."

A sad smile curved her lips. "To think of all those lonely, wasted years breaks my heart."

"Mine too." His gaze held hers in an unwavering stare as if he could see into her soul.

ℴℙℂℚ

"I'm almost done in the bedroom," Daryn yelled to Cassie, who was stationed in the living room as lookout. He'd waited until he saw Ally leave with the upstairs tenant before sneaking up to the front door to pick the lock. It had only taken him a second or two to get inside. And what a treasure trove. The place was filled with porcelain, silver, and fine Queen Anne-style furniture.

"Good, because we've been here awhile, and the longer you take, the more nervous I get," Cassie shouted back.

"Just hang on. I'll be through in a minute." What he didn't need was for Cassie to leave her post to join him in the bedroom. There was a gorgeous collection of jewelry that was kept in a wooden box on the dresser. Once she laid eyes on the gold rings, necklaces, and bracelets adorned with precious stones, he'd never be able to get her to keep her hands off them. And this wasn't the time to steal jewelry. There'd be plenty of time for that down the road. They were here to find the safe. The elderly he'd stolen from in the past had safes. He'd bet his life this one did too.

Daryn had searched the entire bedroom, except the closet. He shoved aside the rows of stretch pants and cardigan sweaters to expose the walls. Nothing. No hidden safe. Just bare walls. Shit! There had to be one somewhere in this place. Unless the old broad hid her money under her mattress. Anything was possible. He pushed the clothes back and walked over to the bed when Cassie appeared in the doorway.

"They're here," she said.

His hand froze on the bed. "What? I told you to keep watch."

"I did. How do you think I knew they were back? What do we do now?"

"Where exactly are they?"

"On the front porch."

Daryn took hold of Cassie's hand, and together they sprinted down the hall.

"What if they come in the front door right now?" she puffed.

"You'd better pray they don't, or be prepared to knock them down."

"I don't think I could do that," she said.

"Don't think. Just run." In a flash, they were in the kitchen and at the back door. As Daryn's hand turned the knob, the front door creaked open.

"I had a great time," Ally said.

"Me too." The man's voice was deep and rugged.

"How about a nightcap?" Ally asked. "Alice has some brandy in the cabinet."

Their voices were growing louder, as were their footsteps, and there was no doubt they were headed toward the kitchen. Daryn opened the door and pushed Cassie out.

"Run," he growled. She obeyed without hesitation, and they bolted to the car, arriving breathless but happy to have escaped.

Once they were settled in the Beemer, Daryn's tension began to melt away. "That was sooo close," he said with a chuckle. "I like a thrill every now and then, but that was pushing it, even for me."

"You don't think they'll notice this is missing?" Cassie pulled a porcelain sculpture of Venus from her handbag. It glistened a milky white in the moonlight.

A blood vessel popped in Daryn's eye. It took all his willpower to keep from wringing her neck. "What the hell were you thinking?" he yelled. "I told you not to touch anything. And that meant not to lift anything either." He slammed his hands on the steering wheel. "I thought you understood. We were there just to scope out the place, and you risked everything for one naked statue."

"I'm sorry. I didn't mean to take it. It's just so beautiful. Before I knew what I was doing, I'd put it in my purse, and then I heard voices outside. It all happened so fast. I barely had time to think."

"That's obvious." Daryn took out a pack of Pall Malls from his pocket and lit a cigarette. He took a deep drag, then blew out a long stream of smoke. "For someone who's supposed to be intelligent, you sure can be stupid sometimes."

"What do you want me to do now? I said I was sorry." Her voice cracked when she spoke.

Great. She was on the verge of tears. On top of everything else, he didn't need a weepy female. "Okay. Apology accepted. Let's go back to the hotel and figure out our next move." He patted her leg. "I'll bet Ally won't even notice the statue's missing."

೮೦೧೪

Jack watched Ally pour the brandy into two snifters. There were many nights he'd share a drink with Alice before going upstairs to his apartment. The similarities between her and Ally were uncanny. Even Sally had made a big deal of that. She'd said Ally was the spitting image of Alice as a young woman. He'd always wondered what she must have looked like, and now he knew. She'd been drop-dead gorgeous.

He glanced at Ally through hooded eyes. Every time he looked at her, his pulse raced. He put his arms around her waist and pulled her to him. Her hair brushed his neck, and her warm breath tickled his ear. After their romantic evening, he was very close to being putty in her hands. If he lost control and let his emotions take over, he might lose track of his objective—to find out if she was one of those grifters. What he should do was thank her for a wonderful night, then go home. But her lips parted slightly, and he brought his mouth down on hers. She returned his kiss with a fiery passion. Her hands clutched at him, and her eyes were wide yet innocent. A wave of arousal shot through him, and he wanted her more than he ever thought possible. With desire clouding common sense, he lifted her into his arms and carried to her the bedroom, then gently eased her down onto the bed.

She lay back against the comforter, her hair splayed out around her like a halo. He leaned over her, his breath mingling with hers and kissed the base of her neck, where her pulse thrummed. He unbuttoned her blouse and ran his finger over her black lace bra, then reached inside it to touch the soft skin of her breast, slowly tracing her nipple. It hardened beneath his touch.

He lowered his body onto hers, and she arched her back to meet him.

"I want you so much," she whispered against his ear, kneading her fingertips into the muscles along his back. When she reached the base of his spine, she held him to her.

His thigh pressed against her, and he savored the incredible feeling raging through him. "Are you sure you want to do this?"

"Positive."

He wasn't going to ask her twice. It was as if his body had taken control of his mind. He started to unbuckle his belt, never shifting his gaze off her beautiful face. Her eyes shone like those of a woman in love. Could Ally be in love with him? An inner pain ripped through him. What on earth was he doing? He couldn't use her that way. If she opened up to him after they made love, he'd have to bring whatever information he gleaned to the police. He wanted the truth, but he didn't want to break her heart.

"I'm sorry, but I can't do this tonight." He rolled onto his back and redid his belt buckle.

"It's not you," he said, knowing he owed her an explanation. "Believe me. I want to make love to you more than you can imagine. It's just not the right time."

She lay beside him unmoving, her blouse still open and the creamy skin of her chest exposed. It took all his willpower to keep from touching her. If he didn't leave now, no amount of guilt was going to keep him from her. "I'll be over tomorrow. I'll make Christmas dinner."

She didn't say a word as he left the room, yet he felt her indignation more than if she'd shouted a thousand angry words at him.

He strode to the front door. In his hurry to leave, he knocked against the hall table. It wobbled precariously, and he grabbed for the porcelain statue of Venus that Alice kept there. She'd never forgive him if he broke it. But it was gone. How strange. He could have sworn it was there yesterday. Would Ally have moved it? But why?

He went into the parlor and scanned the room. It wasn't there. His gaze settled on the Christmas tree with the missing tin angel. Anguish washed over him as he realized he had to face the truth about Ally. She might very well be Alice's niece, but it looked like she was also a thief. She'd stolen the tree topper, the statue, and who knew what else. He needed to do something and fast, before she completely cleaned out Alice's house.

His initial reaction was to storm back into the bedroom and

demand that she return the items, but he knew she'd deny taking anything. She was a pro. A grifter. No, he needed to outsmart her. Beat her at her own game.

Even if that meant breaking her heart.

CHAPTER SIX

*A*lice lay on the bed and wondered what just happened? Jack wanted to make love to her. She didn't doubt that, but something had made him withdraw. Could it be that he still didn't trust her? When was he going to move beyond all that?

Her lips still tingled from his kisses, and her skin burned from his touch. She wanted him so badly her body ached. *So this is love?* Agony and ecstasy all rolled into one. She'd never felt this part of love before…the physical part. After all, when she'd been engaged to Tom, good girls didn't do things like that. They saved themselves for marriage. And he'd been taken from her before… She stopped herself from traveling down that road again. It was Tom's doing that she'd been given this miracle. He wanted her to experience love again, so she'd better not dwell on the past, especially since she didn't have much time left.

She buttoned her blouse, then sat up, her hair falling around her shoulders in tangles. She must look a mess. As she went over to the dresser and grabbed a brush, the front door closed. Jack had left. Her ragged emotions turned to hurt…and anger. How dare he do that to her? Walk out like that, with little to no explanation, when she'd been ready to give herself to him. Well, next time, if there was one, it would take a lot more than a kiss to get her back into bed.

She brushed her hair into a ponytail, not caring that she yanked through the snarls as she did so. These feelings were foreign to her. She wished she had someone to talk to. Someone to help her sort them out. Her gaze scanned the room, hoping to see the flutter of gossamer wings, but the angel didn't appear, and she was left to simmer alone.

A short while later, she went into the kitchen and put the kettle on for tea, hoping a cup would help her relax. While she waited for the water to boil, the telephone rang. There was no one she wanted to talk to, unless it was Jack calling to apologize for his running out on her.

She picked up after four rings.

"Hi, Ally. It's Ross. I was wondering, if you don't have any plans for Christmas, would you have dinner with me? I really enjoyed your company this afternoon and would love to see you again."

She couldn't help but be flattered by his invitation. After all, he was a very attractive man. A man who didn't judge her like Jack did. It was just too bad she didn't get that tingle of excitement for Ross like she did for Jack. Her initial reaction was to turn him down, but then a wild thought occurred to her. Why not see if she could make Jack jealous? A little bit of competition just might be what was needed to make him realize how much he cared for her. "Why don't you come here, Ross? Christmas dinner is always better at home than in a restaurant."

"I'd love to. Thanks."

"It's the big blue Victorian at 117 Main Street. Be here at two thirty." Ally hung up the phone with a smile on her face. Tomorrow should prove very interesting.

ℰꙅ

"Baby, we're still in the game." Daryn picked Cassie up and swung her around the hotel room.

A smile of delight curved her full lips. "So she took the bait?"

"Hook, line, and sinker. Now all I have to do is reel her in."

"What's my part tomorrow?" she asked eagerly.

Her role was to stay far away from Ally. He couldn't run the risk that her temper would get the best of her and she'd say something she shouldn't. Or that she'd steal something else from the house. She'd nearly ruined everything as it was. He wasn't about to give her another chance to mess things up. "I think it's best if I do this phase alone." He put her down, and she dug her heels into the carpet.

"Really? You think so? And you came to that conclusion without consulting me?" There was no missing how her mood had veered sharply to anger.

"Look, I can see where this conversation is heading, and I'm not going there. I don't want to fight with you."

"Then maybe you should have talked to me first before *you* decided how things would work. I thought we were partners. And partners discuss everything," she spat.

"I do discuss everything with you. Most of the time."

"Well, most of the time isn't good enough. If you can't commit to me one hundred percent, I'm done." She left him standing in the middle of the room and snatched her purse from the bed. "I'm outta here. You can do this one alone and all the rest too, for all I care."

"Whoa." He grabbed her arm before she reached the door. "You're not going anywhere. I need you."

"Need isn't enough."

"I want you." He spun her around so that she faced him. "I love you." Before she could say a word, he brought his mouth down on hers.

She resisted at first but opened her mouth to his persistent kisses and relaxed against him. He ran his hands down her voluptuous body. A heat raged through him, but this wasn't the time to let his lower region do his thinking. No, he had to use his head. He had to make her understand why he needed to spend time alone with Ally. There had to be a large amount of money in that house, and he was going to do whatever it took to find it. If Cassie went with him, he'd never be able to do that.

"Listen, babe. This has to be done my way, not because I don't value your input, but this can be a big score, and we can't blow it. I can get the job done fast; then we can get out of this town. But you've got to trust me." He held her gaze and looked deep into her eyes.

"Ahhh, I don't know. You haven't given me many reasons to believe you, let alone trust you. And with another woman…a good-looking one too. I'm not stupid."

"I know that. But you have to let the past go and believe me when I tell you tomorrow is strictly business. I don't feel anything for Ally. She's just a means to an end. A very lucrative end. And one that could put some diamonds here." He touched her earlobe; then he lifted her ring finger on her left hand and kissed it.

A soft gasp escaped her. "A-are you sa-saying what I th-think you are?"

He hadn't planned to propose. It just sort of slipped out of his mouth, yet he wasn't sorry that he had. If it meant keeping Cassie, it'd be worth it. Besides, he wasn't getting any younger. He might have had his one-night stands, but Cassie had his heart. Always would. Why not take the plunge and make their relationship permanent?

He put his arms around her waist. "So whaddya say? Will you have me for your husband?"

Her vivid eyes opened wide and brimmed with emotion. "Are

you kidding? Yes! Yes! Of course. I can't believe you just asked me to marry you."

"Believe it, baby. We're partners in every way. And if things go according to plan, you'll have a ring by the New Year."

She held up her hand and studied her fingers. "A big round sparkly one that people will stare at with envy."

"Only the best for my girl." He walked her toward the bed. Tonight they had lots to celebrate.

ഗ്രൗ

Jack wrapped Alice's yellow-and-white-striped apron around his waist, then tied it snugly behind his back. He always wore it when he cooked dinner for her. Alice thought he looked cute, but after last night, he wasn't sure Ally would mimic her aunt's sentiments. He opened the oven door to peek at the turkey roasting inside.

"How's it look?"

He started when Ally came up behind him. She peered over his shoulder. Her hair brushed his neck, and her warm breath tickled his ear. A fire shot through him as hot as the oven, and it disgusted him that he still had such a hard time resisting her. After discovering the statue missing last night, he'd dialed the police three times but had hung up each time before getting an answer. He had no proof that she'd done anything wrong, so what would he say? That he suspected she was a grifter? Where was the evidence? He couldn't prove that she'd stolen the tin angel and the statue. He couldn't prove that Alice wasn't staying in upstate New York. All he could do for now was stay on guard, watch her closely, and hope that she would make a mistake that would give him the proof he needed. As long as his emotions didn't get the best of him.

"We should be ready to eat in about an hour." He closed the oven door and turned to face her.

She tugged on the apron. "I like this on you. You look cute."

Her choice of words made him raise his brows in surprise. If he didn't know better, he'd think it was Alice here in the kitchen with him. "Thank you. Alice always thought so too."

She looked away, and a warning signal shot through him. Had she done something she regretted?

"You should stick around here after Alice gets back. Get to know her better." He kissed the side of her neck, inhaling the citrus aroma of her perfume. "Get to know me better."

"That I'd like, but I'm afraid I'll have to get home. Work and all…" She still avoided his gaze.

There was more to her not wanting to extend her stay here than she was letting on. "Something's been bothering me since last night," he said, watching her closely.

Her cheeks reddened. "Obviously. You left just as we were about to make love…"

A painful knot twisted inside him. He'd hurt her…and owed her an explanation, but what was he going to say? *Last night I didn't want to break your heart. Now I'm willing to do whatever's necessary for Alice's sake.* Instead, he draped his arm across her shoulders and simply said, "I'm sorry. That'll never happen again."

He walked with her into the foyer, stopping at the marble table. "Alice kept a statue of Venus, right here." He pointed to the spot where the statue used to sit. "And now it's gone. Do you know what might have happened to it?"

"No." The color drained from her face, and her eyes glazed with tears.

A heaviness centered in his chest. She'd taken it, just as he'd feared. Guilt was written all over her, and the tears were because she'd been caught. He needed to press her. Get her to confess. "What do you suppose happened to it? It was here just the other day."

"I know. I don't know how it could be gone." Her lips trembled.

His instinct was to take her in his arms, but he couldn't do that. He had to remain detached. "Where could it be, then?"

She shrugged. "I have no idea. I need to find it, though. It was a gift from my moth—Alice's mother."

She ran into the parlor and stood in front of the Christmas tree, mumbling under her breath. Something weird was going on. She'd almost said it was a gift from her mother, before correcting herself and saying Alice's. And not too long ago, she'd almost referred to Jasper as her cat. On top of everything else, could she be delusional too?

He put his arms around her, letting her rest her head on his shoulder. "It's okay," he whispered against her hair. "Relax. We'll find it. A statue can't just disappear into thin air." He would deal with the missing Venus later. This obviously wasn't the time to press her.

She sucked in a deep breath, then said, "You're right. It's got to be around here somewhere. Besides, I'm not going to let it spoil the holiday." A slight smile curved her luscious lips as she left his arms and reached under the Christmas tree for a small red foil box, then pressed it into his palm.

She had to have gotten it at Miller's, where he'd gotten hers, and that could mean only one thing. Expensive. "Ally, you really shouldn't have—"

"Don't be silly," she interrupted. "As soon as I saw it, I knew I had to get it for you. Besides, we're friends, and friends exchange Christmas gifts."

He tore open the wrapping. Inside he found a black velvet box similar to the one he'd given her, only this one was larger, quite a bit so. He sighed inwardly. Just how much money had she spent? He opened the box. A glistening gold key chain with a treble clef charm shone brightly against the black satin lining.

For a moment he didn't know what to say. This had to have cost a lot more than the charm he'd given to her. It was so much larger. Guilt pressed hard against his chest. You didn't just give a gift like this unless the person meant something special. She really did care for him. But where did she get the money for such a gift? Was fashion merchandising that lucrative? Or maybe she'd come into money by some other means…by stealing from the unsuspecting elderly.

Oh no, Alice please don't tell me you kept your life's savings stuffed in shoeboxes in your closet. When she'd told him a few months ago that was where she hid her money, he'd made her promise to consider putting it in the bank, but he knew how stubborn she could be. Ally was watching him closely, so he forced a smile.

"What's wrong? You don't like it?" she asked

"No, no. I love it. It's beautiful, but way too expensive. I can't accept it." He held it out to her.

Her lovely gray eyes clouded over and turned dark with disappointment. She pushed his hand away. "Nonsense. Money doesn't matter to me. Besides, I haven't got much else to spend it on anyway."

What an odd thing to say! Especially coming from a beautiful young woman with a keen eye for fashion. She must have noticed his furrowed brow, for she offered up an explanation.

"I live at home with my parents, remember. I have very little in expenses, so I can be extravagant sometimes. Please don't make me feel bad about this."

The sincerity in her voice struck him. Boy, she was good. Much better than he'd thought. She could lie without batting an eye. Well, there was only one thing for him to do—up his game.

"Thank you." He spun her into his arms, crushing her to him, then he pressed his mouth to hers. Last night he'd gone home before things went too far, but he wasn't going to think twice about making love to her today. He wasn't above using sex as a weapon, if that would get her to tell him the truth. However, the loud buzz of the kitchen timer indicated it wasn't going to be now.

ഇ൦ര

Alice stood in the parlor and stared at the Christmas tree while Jack put the finishing touches on dinner. She didn't doubt that he was very attracted to her, but he was still suspicious of her—probably even more so since discovering her Venus statue missing. And rightly so. What in the world could have happened to it?

"I'm only waiting on you."

She spun around at the sound of his voice. He took hold of her hand and led her from the room. The aromas coming from the kitchen made her mouth water, but he pulled her past, stopping at the dining room.

"I hope you don't mind eating in here."

The table was set with her finest china. A bottle of wine served as the centerpiece, and, adding to the ambiance, "White Christmas" played on the stereo.

"Mind? You're amazing, Jack. I love it."

"Good. I did it all for you."

He took her in his arms and danced with her. She laid her head on his shoulder and closed her eyes, moving effortlessly to his lead. The telephone's ringing broke the magic.

"Maybe it's Alice calling to say Merry Christmas." There was no mistaking the hopeful gleam in his eyes.

"Maybe." She headed for the foyer with a feeling of dread. Whoever it was would no doubt put a damper on her day.

She lifted the receiver reluctantly, wishing she could just let the phone keep ringing. "Hello."

"Is this Alice's niece?"

She knew the caller immediately. Pastor Riley! Her heart thundered against the wall of her chest. "Yes."

"I hope I'm not interrupting your dinner, but I've been meaning to call, and it keeps slipping my mind, so I figured I'd better do it now before I forget again. How's Alice? Is she enjoying New York?"

"Yes."

"Good to hear... Good to hear... Every year she volunteers at our rummage sale at the church. It's the one time she gets out with people, and since she's not here, I was hoping you'd fill in."

Alice squeezed her eyes shut. They always held the rummage sale the Saturday after Christmas. That was tomorrow. No, no, no. She couldn't. Everyone at church knew her.

"I know it's short notice," the pastor continued, "but even just an hour or two would help us tremendously. We're shorthanded."

"I'm sorry, but I don't think—"

"Now don't say no. You're probably afraid you'll feel awkward not knowing anyone, but that's not the case. Jack'll be there. He signed up a while back."

"Jack?"

"What about me?" He came up from behind her and put his arms around her waist.

She wondered how long he'd been standing there. She hadn't heard him approach.

"Is that Alice?" he asked, putting his ear next to the phone. "Merry Christmas."

Alice clamped her hand over the receiver. "It's not Alice. It's Pastor Riley. He's calling about the rummage sale."

"Oh, that's right. It's tomorrow. You've got to come. It'll be fun, and you'll get to meet lots of great people."

"I-I wouldn't know what to do. I'd feel out of place."

"Don't be silly. I won't take no for an answer." He slipped the phone out of her hand and spoke into the mouthpiece. "Merry Christmas, Pastor. Ally will be there. She's coming with me."

Jack hung up the phone and spun her around to face him. "Good thing the pastor called. I'd forgotten I was scheduled to work. Guess I had other things on my mind." He grinned and kissed her cheek.

In spite of her misery, she forced a smile. It would only make matters worse if Jack knew how much she dreaded going. She wouldn't worry about the rummage sale now. She'd push those thoughts to the back of her mind and try to concentrate on having a wonderful day with Jack. She slipped her arms around his neck and pulled him close. She brought her mouth up to meet his, letting his intoxicating kisses erase her worry. She lost herself in his embrace and relaxed against him, savoring the feel of his strong arms around her waist and his thigh against hers. He undid the buttons on her blouse, and the soft material fell open, exposing her bra. He ran his fingers over the lacy material, and her nipples hardened at his touch. Forget dinner. And forget her hurt and anger from last night. She wouldn't mind at all if he wanted to make love to her right now.

As if reading her mind, he slipped her shirt off her shoulders. Goose bumps covered her skin as he let it drop to the floor. With trembling fingers, she undid his shirt, exposing his muscular chest. He pulled her closer so that she could feel the beating of his heart.

She ran her hands over his skin. Her breath hitched in her throat, and she let out a soft moan as he kissed the base of her neck, then moved his mouth down to the curve of her breasts. When the doorbell rang, she wanted to scream.

Jack leveled his gaze to meet hers. "Are you expecting someone?" he asked, his eyes full of disappointment.

Oh Lord! She'd lost all track of time. It must be Ross. "I'm so sorry," she said as she slipped on her blouse. "I meant to tell you earlier. I invited a friend over for dinner."

಄ದ಄

Jack could barely believe what he'd just heard. Ally had invited someone over for dinner? On Christmas. And she'd forgotten to tell him. Who could it possibly be? He didn't think she even knew anyone in Silvercreek. While he buttoned up his shirt, he tried to read her expression. There was no doubt she was embarrassed, but he wondered if there was more to it than just her omission of another dinner guest.

"Seems like we're not destined to make love," he said as he followed her into the foyer.

"You had your chance last night, and you blew it," she shot back sarcastically before swinging open the front door.

On the porch stood a man as good looking as Brad Pitt and as suave as George Clooney. He held a poinsettia plant whose leaves were curling, and Jack got the impression he'd just picked it up at a roadside stand on his way over.

"Merry Christmas," he said, handing the plant to Ally, but his gaze was fixed on Jack. It looked like he too was surprised to find he wasn't Ally's only dinner guest.

"Thank you. Please come in." Ally quickly stepped aside, letting him enter the foyer, then said, "Ross, this is Jack Billings. He lives upstairs. And Jack, this is Ross Saunders. We met the other day while I was shopping."

Jack raised a brow. Really? Come on, who invited a complete stranger over for Christmas dinner—a dinner that Jack was preparing—and then forgot to mention it? How big a fool did she take him for? No, he didn't buy one word of it. His guess was that Ally had known this joker for some time. He could even be her boyfriend from upstate New York. Or worse yet, Ross could be a grifter and her partner in crime. A terrible sense of bitterness swept over him. He was getting tired of playing this game with Ally. He wished, just once, she would tell him the truth. Instead, she continued to lie, bringing him close to his breaking point.

Jack bit back an angry retort and held out his hand. "Nice to meet you." Ross shook it but tightened his grip before letting go as if to say Ally was his, confirming Jack's suspicions.

"Let's go have dinner." Ally led the way down the hall and into the dining room.

Jack frowned as he looked at the beautiful table he'd languished over in the hopes of having a romantic dinner for two. Ross also stared at the table. He had to be wondering why there weren't three place settings. Talk about awkward moments. Jack was tempted to let Ally come up with an explanation, but when he saw her cheeks go pale, his heart softened. She would have a lot of making up to do later, that was for sure.

He took another place setting from the china cabinet and set it on the table. "I was just finishing up when the doorbell rang."

Ally smiled gratefully at him. "Thank you, Jack. The table looks lovely." She turned to Ross. "Why don't you two get to know each other while I serve dinner?" Before either of them could answer, she headed toward the kitchen.

After she left, an awkward silence fell over the room. Jack eyed Ross suspiciously and said, "So you just met Ally the other day?"

"Yes. At Miller's. She dropped some money, and I returned it to her."

"Really? That was very nice of you." Jack reached across the table for the bottle of wine, never shifting his gaze off the man.

Ross returned the stare with an icy glint in his eyes and said coolly, "I'm sure you would have done the same."

"Of course. Any *honest* man would." He studied Ross, waiting for a reaction, but his face was as expressionless as a mask. Why was this guy really here? Was it to help Ally steal more of Alice's belongings? Well, whatever they were up to, he was going to get to the bottom of it.

Jack popped the cork on the wine and poured them each a glass. He took a sip, then asked, "I don't recall ever seeing you around Silvercreek."

Ross pulled out a chair and sat across from him. "I don't live in town. Just here on business until after the New Year."

Of course. Just like Ally. "What's your line of work?" *Thief? Grifter?*

"Life insurance. Wills. I help people invest their money."

I'll bet you do. The guy was a shady character, no doubt about it. "Actually, I could use some insurance." Jack watched carefully for his response, hoping he could break the creep's poker face, but Ross didn't react.

"Sure. We'll talk later." He took a long drink of wine, then leaned back in the chair and stretched out his legs in front of him, looking way too comfortable for Jack's liking. "You know Ally a long time?"

Nice way of changing the subject. "Long enough to know she's a good person and deserves an equally good guy," Jack said smugly.

"And would that be you?" There was an edge to his voice, and his eyes darkened dangerously.

Jack wasn't intimidated. "If I have my way, yes." He smiled widely, knowing full well that he was inviting a challenge from someone who could be a formidable opponent.

೮೦೧೨

Alice loaded a silver tray with food. Everything looked delicious. Jack had worked so hard on the meal, thinking they were going to have a romantic dinner together. And she had ruined it by inviting Ross. How stupid could she be? Her plan to make Jack jealous would probably backfire and result in him not speaking to her. And she wouldn't blame him. He hadn't done anything wrong. She'd overreacted to his leaving last night, and now she was going to pay the price. Unless she could think of a way to make it up to him. The beginning of a smile tipped the corners of her mouth.

She carried the tray into the dining room. The first thing she noticed as she set it on the table was the silence in the room. The second was that both men were drinking wine. Things weren't going well already. "Jack, would you help me with the turkey?"

"Sure." He pushed back his chair and crossed the room in three long strides.

When they were in the kitchen, he said, "Something's off with that guy."

She raised her brows in surprise. "Really? In what way?" She'd hoped to make Jack jealous, but she'd never expected him to dislike Ross.

He leaned against the counter and folded his arms across his chest. "I don't know. He just seems dishonest to me."

She stared at him in disbelief. "How can you say that? You don't even know him."

He stared back at her. "You're right. And I have no desire to know him better. What I am wondering, however, is just how well you know him."

She couldn't help herself. Her mouth twitched with amusement. "Why, Jack Billings, are you jealous?"

"Is that what you think? Wow!" He drew his dark brows together in a straight line and pulled his lips tightly over his teeth. It was obvious he didn't find this funny.

"If that's not it, then what's the problem?" she asked, confused.

After a long pause, he said, "I don't trust him, and I get the feeling that you're not telling me the whole truth."

Alice planted her hands firmly on her hips. "About Ross?"

He nodded. "Yes."

"I don't know what you mean."

He leaned in toward her, and his voice was tinged with bitterness when he said, "You can play games with me all you want, Ally, but I will get to the bottom of what's going on between you two."

She was so startled by his accusation that she was at a loss for words. She'd never seen Jack this angry. He quickly carved the turkey, then picked up the platter and carried it into the dining room.

This day had not turned out at all as she'd hoped. And she was afraid it was about to get worse.

CHAPTER SEVEN

C assandra dropped her fork on the dinner plate and sent food flying. Maybe ordering room service hadn't been such a good idea. She'd had it with spending Christmas alone in her hotel room. What she needed was a drink. Or two. Or three. She picked up her purse and headed down to the Ginger House.

The bar was nearly empty. There was an elderly man with thinning hair and a long beard who looked like he was about to fall asleep in his beer, and a few stools down was a young couple who could have been newlyweds, judging from the way they were all over each other. Watching them only made Cassandra feel worse, and it reminded her that Daryn should be with her, not another woman. She'd believed him when he said he was doing this scam for her, but that didn't make the hollow feeling inside her go away.

She chose a seat at the far end of the bar and slid onto the stool.

The bartender, who looked to be barely over twenty-one, set a coaster in front of her. "What can I get for ya?"

"A martini," she said without hesitation.

"You got it."

A moment later, he returned with her drink. She guzzled down half of it. It wasn't long before she felt the effects of the alcohol and her mood brightened. "What's a good-looking guy like you doing working on Christmas? Shouldn't you be with your girlfriend?" she asked him.

"Workin' my way through college. And there's no girlfriend. Not one anyway." He smiled at her, exposing his perfect teeth. "What's a gorgeous woman like you doin' drinkin' alone?"

She shrugged and took another gulp of her drink. "My fiancé's working. I guess you could say he's a workaholic... Work, work, work. That's all he wants to do. Well, mostly." A slow smile curved her lips. She had no doubt the bartender knew what she meant.

"That's not right to leave you alone," he said sympathetically.

"Not right at all." She finished the martini, and before she set her glass down, he brought her another one.

Resting his elbows on the bar, he leaned in toward her. "I get off in about an hour, and we could... Um...celebrate the holiday together, if you get my meaning."

Cassie's cheeks grew warm but not from embarrassment. From anger. Did he think she was some cheap tramp? Was that the impression she gave people? Was that the way Daryn viewed her?

"I'm not like that. I'm faithful to my man." She quickly downed her drink, after which she reached into her purse and pulled out two crinkled bills. She slapped the money on the bar, not bothering to see how much she'd left, then stormed out.

As she walked back to her hotel room, she tried concentrating on each step so that she wouldn't stumble, but that only worked until her heel caught on a tear in the hall carpet, and she fell on her hands and knees. Thankfully, no one witnessed her embarrassing tumble. She pulled herself up and made it the rest of the way without another incident. Before she opened her door, she prayed that Daryn would be inside waiting for her. But her room was empty. Damn! What was taking him so long? She flopped down on the bed, and a war of emotions raged within her. She hated this part of her life. The part that left her lonely, angry, and confused. She wanted to scream, or, better yet, break something. The statue of Venus sat on the nightstand next to the bed. She reached over and grabbed it, desperately wanting to hurl it against the wall and see it shatter into a million pieces. But she fought for self-control. Her temper combined with alcohol was a deadly combination. If she crossed the line and let her feelings overcome common sense, she would surely regret it.

She set the statue back on the nightstand and then went into the bathroom for a glass of water. As she took a sip, she stared at herself in the mirror over the sink. She looked pretty good. She'd expected her eyes to be bloodshot, but they were bright and clear. No one would even know that she'd been drinking, except maybe Daryn. And he wasn't here. *What the hell is taking him so long anyway?* Her temper flared again. Well, she would just have to pay him a little visit.

৪৩৫৫

Daryn pushed his food around his plate. It wasn't that he didn't like it. He just didn't like being a third wheel. He hadn't anticipated there would be another man at dinner. Talk about a big surprise. And to top it off, the connection Ally had with Jack had the same high voltage as a live wire in a lightning storm. He was going to have to come up with a plan to get her alone, or this dinner date would have been for nothing. When the doorbell rang, he balled his hands into fists under the table. Shit. Another guest.

Ally excused herself but returned alone a few minutes later. "Ross, there's someone here to see you."

"What the—" He caught himself before he used an expletive. He took the napkin off his lap and placed it next to his plate. Who could want to see him? His mind raced while his body stiffened with dread. The police? Could they be on to him?

Jack was staring at him with a smug look of satisfaction, almost as if he had the same thought.

"I'm so sorry," Ally said.

Damn. It looked like he was about to spend the rest of the holiday in a jail cell.

"I had no idea you had a sister," she continued. "I feel so bad that Taryn wasn't invited to dinner. But at least she's in time for dessert."

His relief that he wasn't about to be taken away in handcuffs soon turned to rage. He gripped the table as he stood, his knuckles turning white. "Where is she?"

"She's in the foyer. I asked her to come back here, but she said she needed to speak with you in private first."

"Excuse me." He ground his teeth as he walked. This was turning into a nightmare. How dare Cassie not follow his orders?

When he reached the foyer, he grabbed her by the arm and pulled her outside. "What's wrong with you? You could have blown everything by coming here."

"Is that all you care about, another scam? I thought I was important to you. It's Christmas, and I've been alone long enough." She swayed and grabbed the post on the front porch to steady herself.

"You've been drinking," he hissed.

"No kidding."

"Don't push me, Cass, or you'll regret it."

"I'm so tired of you telling me what I can and can't do. I'm here because I missed you." Her full lips turned down in a pout, and her shoulders sagged against the pole.

He shouldn't have left her alone. "Look, I know it's tough on you. I'm sorry." He tilted her chin up so that she met his gaze. "Am I forgiven?"

A small tight smile began to form on her mouth. "I guess."

"Why don't you come inside and have some dessert?"

Cassie shrugged. "You sure?"

"Yeah, just promise me one thing."

"Anything."

"Be on your best behavior. I mean it. No messing up," he said sternly.

She looked up at him, her gorgeous eyes wide. "I promise."

"And one more thing," he went on.

"What is it?"

"Ally has another dinner guest over. That tenant. I need you to turn on the charm. Keep him preoccupied so I can get her alone, or this will have been a waste of time."

Cassie groaned. "Oh no. I don't want to do that."

"Come on, baby. You said you'd do anything. And it's not like I asked you to sleep with him. I just want you to flirt a little. You can do it. I know you can. Think of the payoff. Imagine that beautiful glittering diamond on your finger." He turned away from her without waiting for a reply and opened the front door.

She came up behind him and whispered, "The things I have to do for you."

"For us," he corrected. "Now come on. Act happy."

ഒരു

Alice had been trying to make light conversation with Jack while Ross was gone, but it hadn't been easy. He was still upset with her for inviting Ross over, and now he was going to have to contend with Ross's sister as well. No doubt that was adding to his displeasure. This day had turned into a disaster, and she couldn't wait for it to end. She wanted them all to leave so that she could be alone. Yesterday, she couldn't have imagined ever wanting that, as she'd spent most of her adult life alone. However, the way she felt now, it would be a huge relief. But she had to finish playing hostess first.

"Are you looking forward to the rummage sale tomorrow?" she asked Jack, again trying to engage him in small talk.

It took a moment for him to respond. "Actually I am. It's for a good cause. I think you'll enjoy it too."

"I'm a little nervous. All those strange people. I hope I don't feel out of place."

He leaned back in his chair and looked at her quizzically. "You sounded just like Alice—afraid to go out in public and meet new people."

She shrugged. "I guess we have more in common than I knew."

"Don't worry. I'll introduce you to everyone."

That's exactly what she feared—that he'd parade her around. She'd have to explain a million times that she was Alice's niece and deal with all those skeptical glances.

She was grateful when Ross and his sister entered the dining room, until Taryn sat across from Jack. The way she smiled at him and batted her eyelashes spiked Alice's blood pressure.

"I could use some help in the kitchen." She took hold of Jack's hand and pulled him to his feet. After they left the room, she said, "Taryn's awfully pretty, don't you think?"

"If you like that kind of woman."

She'd hoped he'd say something like that. "Not your type?"

"What do you think?"

"I don't know."

He tugged on her hair. "You're my type."

Her cheeks warmed. Jack could be such a charmer. She just hoped he really meant that. She didn't need to compete with another woman for his affection. Her time to find love was so limited. "I hope so," she said under her breath.

He pulled her into his arms. "You don't have anything to worry about."

She looked up into his clear blue eyes and saw that he was telling the truth. A big weight lifted from her heart. Perhaps she would find love in time, after all. To answer him, she stood on tiptoe and kissed him. When their lips parted she said, "Thank you. I'm glad you're not mad at me anymore."

"If you want to thank me, get rid of those two."

She laughed and handed him a stack of plates from the cabinet. She grabbed the apple pie. "I'll do my best. After dessert, I'll show them the door."

"You better, or I'll tell them we have business to attend to…in the bedroom."

Alice threw a towel at him. "I'll handle the guests."

Ross and Taryn were talking softly when they entered the dining room. Alice couldn't make out their words, but it seemed like whatever they were discussing was serious since neither one was smiling. They changed their facial expressions, however, when they realized they were no longer alone. She wondered why Ross hadn't mentioned that his sister was traveling with him.

As if sensing her concern, he said, "Taryn's my business partner. We had a little work emergency, but everything's fine now."

"Yes, I'm sorry to have barged in on you," Taryn apologized.

"That's quite all right. I'm glad you're here." Alice cut and served the pie. There was a long silence while they ate.

Taryn set down her fork and directed her attention to Jack. "So did you grow up in town?"

He shook his head. "No. My work brought me here. I teach music over at the elementary school."

"Really? I sing a little myself."

"My passion's the piano," Jack replied.

"Didn't I see one in the parlor?" Ross chimed in. "Maybe you two could offer up some entertainment?"

"That's a great idea." Taryn jumped out of her chair. "What do you say, Jack? Come on, let's give it a shot."

Alice expected Jack to resist, but he went along easily, and a second later, she was alone with Ross. "Your sister seems nice."

"Talented too. Wait until you hear her sing."

Wonderful. If Jack wasn't attracted to her before, he would be now. "I can hardly wait," she said, trying to put on a happy face.

"Your aunt has a lovely home," Ross said, changing the subject. "Did she grow up here?"

"Yes. It's the only home she's lived in."

"There must be lots of memories here."

Her mind drifted back to when she was young and engaged to Tom. The sense of loss brought a heaviness to her chest, and despair seared her heart. She closed her eyes, trying to hide her misery from his probing stare.

"Did I say something wrong? I didn't mean to make you sad."

Alice opened her eyes and answered him thickly. "No, no. It's okay. I was just thinking back, and it made me a little sentimental. That's all."

"Are you her only niece?"

"Yes. We don't have much family left. She's ninety, and I'm pretty much all she has. I mean, other than my dad—her brother." Alice hated to tell another lie.

Ross glanced around the room. "This place is historic. I love it. And all those antiques must be worth a small fortune. I sure hope she has them insured."

Alice shrugged. Her belongings weren't insured. She was an old woman who was going to die soon, and she had no relatives to leave them to. So what did it matter?

"I could write up a small policy for her. Wouldn't cost much per month, but she'll be well protected. That is if she doesn't already have one. Maybe you could check?"

Alice stared at him. She didn't like all his probing. She needed to think of a quick response, but before she could come up with one, he was asking more questions.

"Do you know where she might keep her paperwork? A safe, maybe?"

This conversation had headed in the wrong direction. Thankfully, Jack began to play the piano—just the diversion she needed. "We should join the others."

When they entered the parlor, Alice noticed that Jack shared the piano bench with Taryn. And she was sitting way too close to him. She flipped the music sheet and began to sing. Ross had been right. Taryn did have a beautiful voice.

Alice listened while they performed two more songs together, then pasted on a pretend smile. "That was lovely."

The gorgeous redhead looked at her through veiled lashes. "Thanks. My mom always thought I should be a singer. But fate had something different in mind." She shifted her gaze over to Ross. "Isn't that right?"

"Yeah, but you've done okay for yourself...so far."

Something was going on between those two that she couldn't quite put her finger on, and it made her uneasy.

Taryn ignored Ross's remark and asked Alice, "Would you mind if I use your bathroom?"

"Not at all," she replied. "Go down the hall; first door on the right."

After Taryn left, Alice sat on the bench beside Jack. "Play Rachmaninoff for me."

He looked at her and grinned, letting his fingers fly effortlessly over the keys.

Ross settled into the big overstuffed armchair and stared at the Christmas tree, but every now and then his gaze would scan the room, giving Alice the impression he was taking note of her belongings. She hoped he wasn't going to put more pressure on her to take out an insurance policy.

℘℃

Cassandra looked at her reflection in the bathroom mirror. Her pale skin had a yellowish cast. She hadn't felt well since eating dessert. She leaned over the sink and splashed her face with cool water. She wanted to go back to the hotel. Daryn could scope out the house another time. He didn't need to do it tonight. She would tell him they needed to leave. He might be angry, but he'd get over it.

She dried her face and hands, then left the bathroom. She walked down the hall, stopping when she came to the bedroom. A lovely canopy bed covered in a rich tapestry bedspread was too inviting to resist. What could it hurt to lie down for just a minute?

As she sank into the soft down mattress, she noticed the dressing table across the room. It held a lavish jewelry box. Her fingers itched to go through it. Common sense told her it would be insane do so. Ally could come in at any time. But the temptation was too great, and she gave in to her desire.

When she opened the box, her jaw dropped. Inside were strands of pearls and gold, along with rings containing a variety of stones. She picked out one with rubies and diamonds and tried it on her left hand. It fit perfectly. This could serve as her engagement ring. At least until Daryn presented her with the real one.

She slipped it off her finger, then dropped it into the pocket of her pants. Next, she selected a beautiful gold necklace with an oval locket and dropped it into her pocket too. She would have loved to help herself to more, but that would have been stupid. She mustn't be greedy. Chances were good that one ring and one necklace wouldn't be missed, not until after she was gone from this town.

Cassandra smiled as she entered the parlor. Jack was still playing the piano. Ally was sitting beside him, and Daryn was across the room, looking extremely bored. She walked up to him, trying to conceal her excitement. Stealing gave her almost as big a thrill as fabulous sex.

"Everything okay?" he asked. "You were gone awhile."

"I'm not feeling that great."

"Probably all the booze you consumed earlier," he said dryly.

"I don't think it mixed well with the dessert. Do you mind if we get going?"

"Sure. I'm done here anyway. At least for tonight."

They went over to the piano, and Daryn said to Ally, "We're going to head out. Thank you for a great evening."

"I'm glad you could make it. Both of you."

Cassandra gave Ally a quick hug, then a wave to Jack, who had just begun to play another song.

"I'm so glad that's over," she said to Daryn when they were outside.

He looked at her with distrust. "What's going on?"

"What do you mean?"

"You're not really sick, are you?"

That was just like him. He always thought the worst of her. "I told you the truth. I'm not feeling well. That's why I went to the bathroom."

"That's it? That's all you did?"

Damn! She couldn't hide a thing from him. But she wasn't about to let him know that she'd stolen some jewelry. At least not yet. "Of course. I'm so tired of you accusing me of things."

"Okay, babe. Just checking. I know you, that's all."

Daryn had parked the car across the street. When Cassie reached the BMW, she didn't wait for him to open the door. She slid into the seat and stared out the window. They drove back to the hotel in silence.

Once inside the room, her stomach started to gurgle and her mouth filled with saliva. She ran for the bathroom, making it to the toilet just in time. She hung her head over the bowl and vomited. It served her right, she thought glumly. Maybe this was payback for all her lies.

A few minutes later, Daryn came in with her bathrobe. "Here, babe. Put this on. You'll be much more comfortable."

"Thanks." She took it from him and began to unbutton her shirt, but the room started spinning, so she grabbed hold of the sink for support.

"Here, let me help you." He got her undressed in no time and had the robe draped around her shoulders and a cool washrag on her forehead. "Anything else I can do?" he asked.

"Maybe get me a glass of ginger ale?"

"You going to be okay while I run down the hall to the vending machine?"

"I'll be fine." But shortly after he left, another wave of nausea hit, and she was back crouched over the toilet. She wished she hadn't gone into that bar. Martinis never agreed with her. What had she been thinking? When her stomach finally finished revolting, she washed her face and brushed her teeth, then left the bathroom.

Daryn was sitting on the bed. Beside him, on the nightstand, was a glass of ginger ale. And the jewelry she'd stolen.

She swallowed hard. "You went through my things?"

"That's all you have to say? You could have jeopardized everything, and you have the nerve to accuse me of going through your things. Well, for your information, the necklace fell out of your pocket when I was putting away your pants. After that, I thought it might be wise to see if you'd taken anything else. And what do you know? I found a ring." His tone was flat.

She could hardly lift her voice above a whisper. "I…um… I don't know what's wrong with me." She crossed the room, then sat next to him. Her shoulders sagged as she hung her head. "I can't help myself. I don't want to take things, but I can't stop. I'm sorry."

To her surprise, he put his arm around her. "I'm sorry too."

She looked at him, her eyes open wide. "Why?"

"Because we're quite a pair, aren't we?" He pulled her closer. "How can I be mad at you for taking some trinkets? The game I got you involved in is so much more dangerous. I should have thought of that before letting you get sucked into it."

She kissed his cheek. "I haven't regretted one moment. I'd do it all over again. You're everything to me."

"What do you say if we make this our last scam? We have enough money to live a good life. Not extravagant, but good." His gaze was riveted on her face.

She stared back at him. "You mean give up our work altogether? What would we do?"

"We could go legit. I could get a real job—really sell insurance. I'd be good at it. And you, well, you're a great singer. You should pursue your dream."

A delightful shiver ran through her. "You mean that? You'd do that for me?"

He kissed her softly in answer.

"You wouldn't get bored with that life?" She wanted to be sure he'd thought it through.

He grinned widely. "Baby, I'd never be bored with you."

She smiled back at him. "Okay. It's a deal."

"Only thing is, I'm gonna finish this up myself. I can't let you put yourself in more danger."

Suddenly, all pleasure left her. "W-what do you mean?"

"You can stay with my cousin in Jersey until I come get you."

"No. Are you crazy? I'm not leaving you." She wrapped her arms around his neck and clung to him.

"Listen to me. It's for your own good. If anything goes wrong, I'll be the one going to jail. Not you."

Her stomach churned with fear. What if she never saw him again? "No, no, no. Absolutely not. We're partners, remember? I'm with you all the way."

He unlaced her fingers from his neck. "Baby, this isn't negotiable. I'm calling to make the arrangements in the morning."

Her throat ached with defeat. Once Daryn made up his mind, there was no changing it. Tears filled her eyes and spilled over onto her cheeks. She hated to cry, especially in front of him. "How long will it take you to wrap things up here?"

"I don't know. Not long, I hope."

She stared at him.

"Now don't look at me like that. You don't have anything to worry about. Didn't you see the way those two love birds were acting? Jack's crazy about Ally, and she feels the same about him. I'm not even going to try to get alone-time with her."

"How are you going to get to the money, then?"

"Remember that rummage sale we'd heard them talking about?"

She shrugged. "Yeah, so?"

"Well, when she goes out tomorrow, I'll slip inside the house. The money's got to be stashed under the mattress. I've looked pretty much everywhere else. And besides, if it turns out there's no money after all, there's plenty of stuff to fence. It's one shot. In and out, babe. That's it; then I'm done, and we'll get married. I'll make an honest woman out of you." He kissed the tears from her cheeks.

"Promise you'll be careful?" she whispered.

"Promise."

Jack glanced at Ally, who sat beside him on the piano bench, as he played one last song. The evening had been a farce, but he was happy now that those two characters had left. They were like something out of a spy novel. He didn't trust Ross for a second, and he didn't believe Taryn was his sister. There was something fishy going on. For all he knew, they were all grifters, plotting to steal from Alice. One way or another, he would get Ally to open up to him, bringing this charade to an end…and then he could go to the police.

When he finished playing, he took hold of Ally's hand and pulled her to her feet. He put his arms around her waist, then bent his head and pressed his lips to hers, caressing her mouth rather than just kissing it. He teased her until a fire grew in him that he could barely control. He ran a hand up the back of her head and tangled his fingers in her hair, pulling her head back so that he could run his mouth down along the soft curves of her neck. Her pulse throbbed under the pressure of his mouth. She dug her nails into his back and let out a small moan of delight.

He wanted her now. Right now. And nothing was going to interrupt this time. He ran his other hand over the curves of her butt and pressed her against him so that her thigh rubbed against his erection. With both his hands on her hips, he rocked her back and forth. She moved with him in a steady rhythm. "Do you want me as much as I want you?"

She curled her arms around his neck and whispered in his ear, "You know I do."

His mouth found hers, and he kissed her again until the pounding in her chest was as fierce as a drumbeat. He ran his fingers along the hem of her blouse and, not bothering to unbutton it, he pulled it up over her breasts, exposing her bra. He moved his hands across the delicate fabric, watching her nipples harden at his touch; then he gently slipped each strap off her shoulders. Her body tensed as he unhooked her bra and let it drop to the floor, leaving her partially naked.

To his surprise, she used her hands to cover herself. She had no reason to be embarrassed. Ally was a splendid goddess. "Don't." He lifted her arms and tugged the blouse over her head. "You don't need to be shy around me."

She closed her eyes. "It's just that—"

"Shhh." He put a finger up to her lips to silence her protests. "You're beautiful, and I want to see you. All of you." With that said, he ran his finger down her chin, along the base of her neck, and then between the swell of her perfect breasts. He watched them rise and fall with each quivering breath she took. He outlined her nipples with his fingers, then ran his hands over her breasts. He took one in his mouth, careful not to hurt her with his teeth.

He slid his hand down the front of her jeans and along the inside of her thigh, where she was moist and warm and delicious. Her legs went limp, and she held on to his shoulders for support. He slipped a finger inside her and moved it in and out while stroking just the right spot to make her explode. She arched her back, her body responding to him, and let out little gasps of delight.

He withdrew his hand from between her legs and gently laid her down on the floor. It took him only a moment before he had her completely naked: jeans off, panties tossed across the room. And just as quickly, he stripped off his own clothes. His gaze took in every inch of her luscious body, her skin flushed with a rosy glow. He kneeled over her with one leg on either side of her thighs; then he brushed her hair back from her forehead and kissed her brow before covering her with his body.

෴

A dangerous, dizzying heat flooded Alice, leaving her breathless. She'd never been with a man before. When Tom had been alive, doing things like…well, like this, were frowned upon before marriage. Yet making love to Jack seemed so natural, it was as if they'd done it a thousand times before.

He stroked her from head to toe, and she moved in perfect sync with him. His bare skin rubbed against her breast, stomach, and thighs, leaving her aching to feel more of him. When he pushed her legs apart to enter her, she rose to meet him. The initial thrust ripped through her in a tearing, burning surge of pain and ecstasy. After that, all she felt was pure joy. His musky male scent filled her lungs, and she wrapped her legs around his hips, surging and arching until her entire body trembled along with his.

She was in heaven. *So this is what it's like to make love to a man.* All these long years, this was what she'd missed. What a fool she'd been. She should have put herself out there and met someone years ago. But there was no going back, and at least she'd found Jack now. And if he felt the way she did—if he loved her—then she'd have a lifetime to spend with him. She stroked his muscular chest. "You're amazing. I never knew I could feel like this."

He rolled onto his side and smiled. "What about your ex back in upstate New York? He didn't make you feel this good?"

She paused before replying. This was her chance to tell him the truth…that she was Alice. She tried to find the right words to begin her tale, but they wouldn't come. Her mind went blank and her throat went dry. All she could think of was that Jack wouldn't believe her. He'd think she was insane. Or worse. He'd go back to thinking that she was a criminal. She wanted so badly to tell him that she'd never made love before, that he was her first and only lover, but that would sound unbelievable too. Instead, all she said was, "He never ever made me feel like you do."

Jack grinned and slowly moved his hands downward, skimming her thighs. "Good. I'll bet he never did this either."

His fingers burned into her tingling skin as he ran them across her stomach, then down between her legs. She was on fire. Wave after wave of pure ecstasy throbbed through her.

She drew herself closer to him, and he took her hands, encouraging her to explore him. His hardness aroused her even more, awakening her long-repressed sexuality. And then he was on top of her again, her breasts crushed against his chest. She welcomed him inside her, and skin to skin, they moved as one. She matched his urgency with her own salacious needs.

He kissed the tip of her nose, her eyes, and then her mouth. When she kissed him back, he thrust into her. Her body began to vibrate, sending a hot tide of passion raging through her. She soared with him, and together they shuddered in an explosive euphoria. Afterwards she lay in his arms, exhausted but content.

He ran his finger from the base of her neck all the way down her stomach. "Do you think your aunt would approve of us?" he asked with a chuckle.

"As a couple, or doing this in her house?"

"Both."

She wrinkled her brow. "I don't know. You certainly know her better than I. What do you think?"

He hesitated a moment before answering. "I think she'd be very pleased that we liked each other, but as for making love, ah, that I'm afraid she might frown on. After all, she's old-fashioned, grew up in a different era."

Alice couldn't help but smile. Little did he know, not only did she approve, but she was giddy with joy. This was her chance to open up to him. "I have something to tell you."

He stroked her hair. "You can tell me anything. Anything at all."

Awkwardly, she cleared her throat. "I...um, I'm not who you think. I...um, well, I'm..." Her voice trailed off. He stared at her as if he thought she was going to confess to some terrible crime.

"Go on," he coaxed. "Who are you? You can trust me. Tell me your secret. You'll feel so much better. I promise."

As casually as she could manage, she said, "I know I can trust you, and that's why I did what I did."

His body stiffened. "What did you do?"

"I'm really not that different from Alice." To her dismay, her voice broke slightly.

"You're not?"

"No." She paused, swallowed hard, then continued to explain. "We're both old-fashioned. We both have high moral values. And we both believe in waiting until we're married to make love."

Jack gaped at her. "What? But—"

"I know," she said, cutting him off. "I just broke that rule with you. I don't regret it for one moment, though."

He had a baffled expression on his face. "You mean...you mean you were a virgin?"

Alice nodded.

"What about your ex-boyfriend?" His blue eyes still showed disbelief.

She shook her head. "We never..." She let her voice trail off, not quite knowing what more to say.

"You never—"

"No." She cut him off before he could ask more questions.

"Wow!" He wrapped his hand around the back of her neck and pulled her close. "I'm so flattered that you care enough...think enough of me to have let me make love to you. Thank you."

She hoped her disappointment didn't show on her face, but she'd expected a different response from him. Not that she'd thought he'd say, *I love you*, those magic words she needed to hear, but she had thought he'd express more romantic feelings for her.

Then, almost as if he knew he hadn't said enough, he whispered, "I'll never forget this night. You're very special to me."

She felt an instant's squeezing hurt, but then realized she might be expecting too much too soon. Jack had no idea how desperate she was for him to fall in love with her. What she should do was enjoy the moment. She might never have another night like this.

Swallowing the lump that lingered in her throat, she said, "You mean a lot to me too."

He kissed her gently; then she snuggled against him, resting her head on his chest. At some point, she fell asleep in his arms, and when she woke, his breath softly fanned her cheek. A lock of hair lay across his brow, and she lightly brushed it back, careful not to wake him. *So this is what it's like to have a man beside you.* Her heart filled with joy, and she thought she might suffocate with the happiness of it. She closed her eyes and must have dozed again, because she was reawakened by Jack's warm hands stroking her back.

"Good morning," he said. "How did you sleep?"

She smiled up at him. "Never better."

He ran his hands down her hips and then over her thighs. "We should do this again."

Aching to feel him inside her, she said, "I think I might be able to arrange that."

With his fingers, he caressed her skin. "Tonight too soon?"

A delicious shiver ran through her, and she said playfully, "Did you forget the rummage sale? After that, you might rescind your offer and be glad to get rid of me."

"Never. However, speaking of rummage sales"—Jack glanced at his watch—"we better get a move on, or we'll be late."

She watched him climb out of bed and stroll naked across the bedroom, his taut muscles rippling as he moved. He must have noticed her admiring him, because before he reached the bathroom, he raked his gaze over her slowly and seductively, sending a wave of hungry desire through her. She had to fight the overwhelming need to be back in his arms.

When he came out of the bathroom, he slipped on his clothes, then kissed her softly. "I'll be back to get you in an hour."

"I'll be ready."

After he left, she took a shower. As the hot water ran over her body, her skin tingled, and she was pretty sure it wasn't just from the water temperature. Thinking back over last night sent a scorching heat over her body. Her only regret was that her fear had kept her from telling Jack that she was Alice. But if she had, she might never have had the opportunity to make love to him. And she wouldn't have given up that for anything. However, if she didn't tell him soon, it would be too late.

CHAPTER EIGHT

As Jack dressed for the rummage sale, he thought back over last night and still couldn't believe he was the only man Ally had ever slept with. And not just because she was a fabulous lover, but to still be a virgin in this day and age... Guilt washed over him as he thought of how he'd deceived her. Not that he hadn't wanted to make love to her, but if she had opened up to him about Alice, he would have had to go to the police with the information. And Ally could have wound up in jail.

He knew he shouldn't care about that. He should only be concerned with Alice's welfare, but he couldn't help it. He'd grown so fond of Ally. And if he wasn't careful, he could find himself head over heels in love with her, if he wasn't already. He remembered the softness of her skin, the sweet smell of her hair, and the way her warm body felt pressed against him as she slept. There was a bond between them he couldn't explain.

All the months he'd spent with Bethany, he'd never felt that way. Sure, he'd been physically attracted to her, but that had pretty much been the extent of it. Emotionally, they were worlds apart. With Ally, though, it was different. And now that he'd made love to her, he was more connected to her than ever before. And she had to feel the same way about him. After all, she'd been a virgin. To give herself to him was huge. He prayed Pastor Riley was wrong about her, because then they'd have a chance for a future together. These doubts were driving him crazy. He had to find out the truth soon. The more time he spent with her, the more he fell, and if she was a grifter, it would tear him up inside. It would be impossible to forget her.

With a heavy heart Jack buttoned up his shirt, slipped on his boots, and ran a comb through his hair before heading out the door and down the back stairs to get Ally.

ဆဝဗ

Alice studied her reflection in the vanity mirror. Overall, she was happy with her appearance. The blueberry-colored sweater made her gray eyes appear brighter than usual, or maybe it was due to her cheeks' rosy glow. Whatever the reason, she was happy, despite the headache that pounded behind her temples. Stress, no doubt…at going to the rummage sale. And stress at how her feelings for Jack had developed. She'd made love to him, yet she wasn't able to tell him the truth about herself. If she didn't find the courage soon, it would be too late, and her life would be over without her ever having lived it.

Her head began to throb again. Hopefully, the pain medication she'd taken would begin to kick in. She pulled her hair back in a loose ponytail. All she needed now was a pair of earrings and she'd be ready to go. Looking through her jewelry box, she found her favorite gold hoops, but her oval locket was missing, as was her ruby-and-diamond ring.

She searched through the box again, but no luck. They were gone, just like the Venus statue. Granted, she hadn't worn them in years, but they had been in there. No doubt about it.

Panic took hold. What could have happened to them? No one

had been in her bedroom except Jack, and he certainly wouldn't take anything that didn't belong to him. Ross's sister had used the bathroom the other night. Could Taryn have taken the jewelry? She hated to think badly of anyone, but what else could have happened to her things?

Should she confront Ross? That would be so awkward. But she had to do something. Those pieces had been given to her by her mother. They were family heirlooms. Tears pricked at her lids. Don't panic. You'll get them back, she told herself. But how? She'd talk to Jack. He'd help her figure out what to do. The only problem was she'd have to tell him she was Alice. Otherwise, how would she know the ring and necklace were missing? What a dilemma!

She paced the floor while she thought. If she went to the police, they'd ask her birth date and want to see identification. She couldn't provide that to anyone, let alone the police. "I don't know what to do." She ran her hands through her hair and tugged at it in frustration.

A thud came from inside her closet. She raced over to it and opened the door. A shoebox had fallen off the shelf. Beside it, the tin angel fluttered. "What are you doing in here? Another miscalculation?"

The angel laughed. "Yes. I'm sorry."

"No need to apologize." Alice placed the shoebox back on the shelf. "I'm just glad you're here."

The angel's wings ruffled Alice's clothes as she left the closet. "Some of your jewelry is missing?"

"I'm pretty sure I know who took it, but I don't know what to do about it. If I go to Jack or the police for help, they'll find out I'm ninety years old."

"How are things going with Jack?"

"Last night we…well, let's just say we had a wonderful night together. He stayed over." Her cheeks warmed with the memory.

"Did you tell him?"

She bit her bottom lip.

"When are you going to?" The angel floated nearer. "You're running out of time."

Alice wrung her hands. "I know. I know… I keep trying, and I keep chickening out."

"You need to find the strength, or it will be too late, and then it won't matter what happened to your jewelry, will it?"

Fear at what fate had in store shook her. "I don't need to be reminded that I'll be dead soon."

The angel's usually cheery face darkened. "I'm afraid you do."

Alice sank onto the bed and buried her face in her hands. "What should I do?"

"Take a leap of faith."

She spread her fingers out and looked straight into the angel's eyes. "I'll tell him today. After the rummage sale."

Golden curls danced around the tin angel's shoulders as she swirled through the air. "I hope so. You have to trust…in yourself, and in others. Especially Jack. That's if you want to find love."

"You know I do." But she spoke to herself. The tin angel had disappeared.

She slipped on her earrings and checked her reflection in the mirror one last time before the doorbell rang. Butterflies churned in her stomach, not only in anticipation of seeing Jack again, but of going to the rummage sale and facing all those people who would question her about Alice. This charade had really taken its toll on her.

When she opened the door and saw Jack's smiling face, her worries began to evaporate, and when he took her in his arms, everything in the world seemed right again.

"Ready to go?" he asked, his warm breath caressing her cheek.

"As ready as I'll ever be." She turned off the foyer light and then was pulled back into his arms. He covered her mouth with his, and what she thought would be a quick peck turned into a long, smoldering kiss. Maybe they wouldn't make the rummage sale after all.

He must have had the same thought, because he ended their kiss and said, "If we don't go now, we won't go at all." With his arm around her shoulders, he led her out the door.

When they reached the car, Alice noticed the engine running. She slid onto the heated leather seat and was struck by the fact that Jack had prewarmed it for her. He was the most thoughtful man she'd ever known. Aside from Tom. For a moment, she was taken back in time, and a feeling of melancholy took hold, but she pushed it aside and brought her thoughts back to the present and to the man she'd come to love. Jack slid onto the seat beside her, reached over and took hold of her hand, then backed the car out of the driveway.

A few minutes later they pulled into the nearly full church parking lot. As Jack drove around looking for a space, her nerves kicked into overdrive. Her clammy hands and racing heart were signs that she needed to go home, but she couldn't... What in the world would she say to Jack? No, she had to be brave and deal with her anxiety. Besides, maybe the day wouldn't turn out as bad as she anticipated.

Ω℥

Daryn watched Cassie leave the bathroom wrapped in a towel, her skin still dewy from the shower, her hair wet and slicked back from her face. He adjusted his pants to make room for his arousal. It took all his self-control to keep from yanking that towel off her and making love to her, but he had to get her in a taxi and safely on her way to his cousin's place before he could head over to Ally's to find that safe. Both she and Jack would be at the rummage sale. In and out. That was his plan, then he could join Cassie in Jersey, and they could start fresh.

She sashayed across the hotel room, her hips swaying as they always did when she walked; then she sat in the straight-backed chair in front of the desk, pointing to the purple shadows beneath her eyes. "See these. They're your fault."

"Here we go. I know I get blamed for everything, but how is it my fault that you have dark rings? Last night was one of the rare occasions when I didn't keep you up."

She snorted and began to comb through her hair. "Sex isn't the only reason you're able to keep me from sleeping. I'm worried sick about today."

"Why?" He walked up behind her and began to rub her shoulders. "I'll be fine."

She shook her head. "I have a bad feeling. I don't like that you're doing this heist alone. You need me."

"You're right, I do." He bent down and kissed the side of her neck. "I need you to be safe."

"I'm safe with you."

He turned her toward him and cupped her chin in his hand so that she looked him straight in the eyes. "Babe, I'm not going to argue with you. This is a done deal. You're going to Jersey this morning."

"But—"

He silenced her words with a kiss. When their lips parted, he said, "You're too damn distracting. When you're around, I have trouble concentrating, for more reasons than one."

She glared at him. "What other reasons?"

"Well, this habit, for example." He reached across the desk and picked up the necklace and ring she'd stolen from Ally.

"You're kidding, right? This is what we do. We steal." She took the ring from him and slipped it on her finger, then reached for the necklace, but he fastened it around her neck instead.

"Yeah, baby, but you take things that we haven't planned on taking, and it puts us in greater jeopardy. That's exactly why you're leaving town. So hurry up. Get dressed." He walked over to the bed and tossed the clothes that she had laid out at her. She was silent as she dressed, a sure sign she was angry, but better upset with him and safe than making a mistake that could land them both in jail.

A short while later, they were both packed and ready to go. Cassie still wasn't speaking to him when he ushered her into a taxi and gave the driver instructions on where to take her. He kissed her good-bye, unfazed at her lack of response. He had to do what was best for them. She would come to realize that. Besides, his cousin's wife would keep Cassie occupied until he arrived. She loved shopping almost as much as Cass did.

He watched the cab drive away until it disappeared from sight; then he walked to the parking garage, suitcase in hand, and quickly found his Beemer. He tossed his bag in the trunk, slid into the soft leather seat, and started the engine. An unexpected twang tugged at his heart as he drove down Main Street and toward Ally's old Victorian house. He missed Cassie already.

ജ്ഞ

As the taxi sped along the highway, Cassandra had a hard time relaxing. That unsettled feeling was back and stronger than ever. She knew it was a mistake for Daryn to be at Ally's alone. Who would be his lookout? What if Ally came home while he was still in her house? A number of terrible scenes flooded her mind. Her life wouldn't be worth living if Daryn wasn't in it, and he wouldn't be if he was serving time in jail. As she thought, she drummed her nails on the taxi's armrest. She needed to do something. Daryn was wrong to send her away. He wasn't protecting her. He was ruining their lives.

In that instant, she knew what she had to do.

"Driver," she said through the plexiglass partition, "take me back."

"What?" He turned the knob on the radio to lower the blasting music. "What you say?"

"I need to go back to Silvercreek. Take me to 117 Main Street." She could see his startled expression in the rearview mirror.

"But the mister, he already paid for the trip to Jersey."

"That's okay. You can keep the money. Just take me back and quickly."

He chewed his bottom lip as he debated what to do. "I don't know, miss."

She clenched her hands in her lap. "There's a big tip for you, if you do as I ask."

The driver got off the next exit, then got back on the highway headed north. Daryn would be furious at her for coming back, and she started to doubt her decision, but she pushed those thoughts away, knowing she was doing what was best for them.

As the taxi drove through the narrow streets of Silvercreek, she took some money from her wallet, ready to tip the driver, then send him away before Daryn knew that she'd returned. When the driver pulled the cab in front of the old Victorian, she handed him the money, grabbed her suitcase, opened the door, and jumped out.

Daryn's black BMW was parked a few houses down. She raced over to it, tossed her suitcase onto the backseat, then surveyed the area, making sure no nosy neighbors saw her approach the old Victorian. She hesitated at the front door, her fingers resting on the knob while she fought back the nervous butterflies in her stomach. You're doing the right thing, she told herself as she opened the door. She listened for a sound to indicate where Daryn was, but only silence greeted her. She took a few careful steps across the foyer, when her heart nearly stopped beating.

A hand covered her mouth, while an arm clamped around her waist. "What are you doing here?" Daryn's voice was cold as ice. "Are you out of your mind?"

His hold on her relaxed, and she wriggled free. "That's not exactly the reception I'd hoped for."

"What did you expect? I sent you away for a reason," he snapped.

"And I came back for a reason—to keep you out of jail."

"You think being here in Ally's house, arguing with me, will do that? You must have lost your mind."

"I didn't come here to argue with you. I came here to do what I do best—be your partner."

"I sure hope we don't live to regret it, Cass."

She kissed the side of his cheek. "Lighten up, hon. How are things going? Find any money?"

He shook his head. "I checked under the mattress. Nothing. I thought for sure that's where she'd have stashed it. I was just about to do another check of the rest of the house when you snuck in and nearly scared the shit out of me."

"You did a pretty good job of that on me."

"Well, babe, you deserved it."

"What now?" she asked, ignoring his jabs.

"I thought I'd do a quick search of her closet again."

Cassie settled into an armchair by the front window. "I'll keep watch."

Daryn kissed the top of her head. "For what it's worth, I'm glad you're back."

CHAPTER NINE

*A*lice wanted to hide under the folding table. Every time someone stopped to look at the lace doilies or purchase a potholder, she held her breath, afraid they might ask her about Alice. She hated the phony smiles and made-up stories. These ten days were supposed to be life's best. What they'd become were the most stressful.

A glance at the wall clock across the room indicated she had more than an hour left to go. She leaned back in the chair and hoped the time would go by quickly.

The room was getting stuffy. More people kept parading down the stairs to the basement, where the church held its many functions.

"Look here, Mom, maybe I can find a tablecloth." A petite young woman with spiky red hair and a booming voice pulled the older woman alongside her through the crowd to get to Alice's table. She rifled through the piles Alice had so neatly arranged, putting everything into disarray.

"See anything you like?" Alice smiled sweetly, while inwardly she seethed.

"No, nothing seems to match my room." She jerked her head around looking for another table to ransack. "Ooo, oh, Mom, over here." She grabbed the woman's arm and dragged her away.

As Alice began to straighten up the mess, she noticed Jack grinning at her from his table across the room.

She planted her hands on her hips and scowled at him. *It's not funny*, she mouthed, knowing he wouldn't be able to hear her.

He laughed, spoke briefly to the man beside him, then headed her way.

"Having fun yet?" he asked.

"Way more than I could ever have imagined."

"Aw, come on. It's not so bad. The people are nice." He looked at the potholders spread across the table. "Most are, anyway, and it makes you feel good to volunteer, doesn't it?"

"Yes, of course." For more than fifty years, she'd helped out. The proceeds were used to help local projects such as the Silvercreek Emergency Center, providing food and shelter for the homeless. She was well aware their work today was for a good cause. It was the questions she hated. But she had to admit that so far the day hadn't been as bad as she'd expected. Very few people had brought up Alice. She hadn't let her guard down, but she was beginning to relax.

"I'm headed to the kitchen for coffee. Would you like a cup?"

Jack must have read her mind. That was exactly what she needed—caffeine to keep her going. "I'd love some. Just cream, no sugar."

"You've got it. I won't be long."

Alice watched Jack make his way through the crowded room out into the hall, and she noticed she wasn't the only woman with her eyes on him. She wasn't surprised. He was so handsome. But instead of feeling insecure, she was proud that such an attractive man was interested in her.

Wait a minute. Should she pinch herself to be sure she was awake? Not long ago, she was worried about a waitress flirting with him and Taryn sitting too close on the piano bench. When had she blossomed into this self-assured woman? One who wasn't worried about getting hurt. She didn't know when the change occurred, and she didn't care. All that mattered was she trusted Jack and felt good when she was with him.

∎∏

"We need to talk."

Jack finished pouring the cream in Ally's coffee, stirred it twice, then popped on a lid. He grabbed his coffee along with hers and turned to face Pastor Riley. "Sure. You have somewhere in mind?"

"My office."

He'd had a feeling the pastor was going to say that. What he wanted to discuss with Jack was private.

They skirted around people eating hot dogs and fries and left the kitchen, heading for the steps that would lead them upstairs.

One would never know the noise and chaos of the rummage sale was only one floor below, for the sanctuary lay quiet. Jack followed the pastor down the center aisle, their footsteps muffled by the plush red carpet. To the left of the altar, the pastor unlocked the door to his office. He ushered Jack inside, closing the door behind them.

The pastor rounded a large wooden desk. Behind it, built-in bookcases lined the wall. The room smelled of old leather and parchment.

"Have a seat." The pastor sank into a swivel chair, while Jack sat on a red leather armchair across from him. He set the coffee cups on the desk and waited for the pastor to bring up the topic of the grifters.

Pastor Riley leaned forward to place his arms on the desk and fold his hands together. "Are you as concerned about Alice as I am?"

"Of course." Jack knew exactly where this conversation was headed. "But Ally would never harm anyone."

The pastor raised a bushy brow. "How can you be sure? Have you spoken to Alice recently?"

"No, but—"

"Has Ally? If that's even her name."

Jack had the same doubts about her as the pastor, but to hear someone else voice them didn't sit well. "I can't know for sure whether she has or hasn't."

"You've been spending a lot of time with her. What have you come up with? Anything we can take to the police?"

Jack sat back in the chair and shook his head. He thought of the missing tin angel and the Venus statue, but he had no proof Ally had taken them. "Nothing that would make them suspect her of anything criminal. Maybe she really is just here for the holidays, and Alice will be back after the New Year."

"I'd feel a lot better if I thought you really believed that. I know your head doesn't, but your heart...well, that might be another story."

"I gave you my word I'd get to the truth, and I have every intention of doing just that." His words came out sounding harsher than he'd intended. "I'm sorry. I'm on edge. I want to know Alice is okay as much as you."

"I know you do. But she's not the only one I'm worried about. You might be in too deep, Jack. Be careful. I don't want to see you get hurt."

"I appreciate your concern, but everything's under control." Jack hoped that was really true. When he was with Ally, she had a way of making him think she was the most wonderful woman on earth, even when things about her didn't add up.

"If there's anything I can do to help, please let me know."

"Don't worry. I can handle her." Despite his words, he knew he hadn't fooled the pastor...or himself.

Alice scanned the room for Jack. He'd been gone awhile. How long could it take to get two cups of coffee? The crowd had thinned a little, and she was able to see across to his table without any difficulty. She was beginning to think maybe he'd forgotten her and had gone back to his post selling sweaters, but he wasn't there. Maybe one of those women who'd been admiring him earlier had him cornered somewhere. She smiled when she thought of him trying to make a polite getaway. He might need rescuing.

Alice glanced over at the elderly woman seated at the table beside her, who was eating a doughnut. She cleared her throat. "Excuse me, since we're not real busy now, would you mind watching my table while I go grab something to drink?"

The woman wiped the corners of her mouth with a paper napkin. "Sure, honey, you go on."

Alice grabbed her handbag, slipping the leather strap over her shoulder. "Thank you so much. I won't be long."

"Take your time," the woman said between bites.

She hurried past the more than thirty tables of miscellaneous new and used items on her way to the kitchen. Her heart sank when she discovered Jack wasn't there. Where could he be? And what could he be doing? It wasn't like him to keep her waiting. Something must have happened. But would he leave without telling her?

Her steps were leaden as she walked upstairs. Jack had parked his Acura on the street in front of the church. She would know in a minute if his car was still there. Pushing open one of the heavy front doors, she peered outside and spotted the silver coupe immediately. Thank goodness. That meant he was around somewhere, and she was bound to find him sooner rather than later. The church wasn't that large.

Alice pulled the door shut, then turned to go back downstairs, but her attention was drawn to the sanctuary. Its elegant harmony invited her in. She stepped through the center doorway. Spacious stained glass windows reflected the sunlight in a rainbow-like pattern, illuminating the alter. A memory of long ago staggered her, and she clasped the back of a pew for support. She'd planned to marry Tom here. It seemed like only yesterday that they'd anticipated spending their lives together, when in fact more than half a century had passed.

She'd be joining him soon, though, she thought, but it wouldn't be in matrimony. A deep sadness tightened her chest, and she was surprised at the feeling. She should be joyful at the prospect of reuniting with her beloved. Her life had been long and lonely. It was time for her to move on. Besides, she wasn't leaving a family behind.

Through the blinding sunlight, a figure emerged from the side of the altar. She blinked back the tears blurring her vision. Tom?

She took a step forward. His mane of raven hair glistened in the light, and his dazzling blue eyes held hers in an unwavering stare. Jack! She nearly choked on her joy-filled sob.

He smiled as he walked toward her. "I'm sorry to have taken so long, but I didn't forget your coffee." He held up a Styrofoam cup.

It took all her willpower to keep from racing into his arms. "I came here to clear my head." She wasn't about to tell him she'd searched the building looking for him.

"Time slipped away from me," he said, glancing at his watch. "And our shifts are up."

"But I didn't get to drink my coffee," she joked.

"Aw, I'm sorry. It's probably cold anyway." He looped his arm across her shoulders. "Come on, I'll make you a fresh cup at home."

∞∝

The sun beat through the window, warming Cassandra's face. She closed her eyes. Now that she was back with Daryn and content, it was easy to fall asleep. She wasn't sure how long she dozed, but the footsteps on the front porch and Ally's voice jolted her awake. In a flash, she crossed the room. At the end of the hallway, she called, "Daryn, she's home. Come on. We have to get out of here."

Daryn charged down the hall. "Where is she?" he hissed.

"On the front porch. And she's not alone. I think Jack's with her."

"Great. Is there time to get out the back door?"

"I—" As Cassandra was about to respond, the front door burst open.

Daryn looped his arm around her waist and pulled her into a coat closet. He closed the door silently as if he'd done this a thousand times before. "Not a word. Not a noise," he whispered.

She nodded her agreement, but this was close. Way too close for comfort. All she had to do was sneeze and it was all over for them. She sucked in her breath and wondered how Daryn planned to get them out of this. She listened for voices and footsteps, hoping for a clue as to where Jack and Ally might be. A few minutes later, she heard noises in the kitchen. Dishes rattled, and then the loud wail of the teakettle.

"This is it," he whispered. "We're outta here." His fingers curled around her arm and tightened like a vise as he pulled her out of the closet and toward the front door. Her heart pounded against her chest, and it felt like it would burst right through. It was only when they were outside and making their way down the porch steps that she was able to breathe normally.

Suddenly, Daryn spun her around. It happened so quickly it nearly knocked the wind out of her, and the next thing she knew, they were headed back up the steps and onto the porch. Ally stood in the doorway, a silver tray in her hands. She stared at them through the storm door.

This was Cassandra's worst nightmare. Caught red-handed. Her mind went blank. She had no idea how they were going to get out of this mess. Her life flashed before her eyes and ended with a picture of a jail cell.

"Hello. I wasn't sure if you were home," Daryn said to Ally. His voice echoed in Cassandra's ears. The porch began to spin, and everything started to go black. As her knees buckled, Daryn caught her in his arms, holding her steady on her feet.

"Are you okay?" Ally set the tray on the hall table and came outside.

"I—I'm fine," Cassandra stuttered, but her parched throat felt like she hadn't had anything to drink in days.

"Well, you don't look well. Come in and sit down," Ally said, placing her hand on Cassandra's arm.

She looked at Daryn for reassurance, and he nodded. "Okay. Thanks," she croaked.

Ally led them through the foyer and into the parlor. Daryn helped Cassandra sit in a big overstuffed chair while Ally poured a cup of tea from the silver service. She began to relax. It appeared that Ally hadn't seen them leave the house. Thank goodness Daryn was such a fast thinker and was able to make it look like they'd just arrived.

As Cassandra took a sip of tea, she realized that Ally's eyes were focused on her neck—specifically on the locket she wore. *Ally's aunt's locket.* And then to make matters worse, she lowered her gaze to Cassandra's hand—to the ruby-and-diamond ring. Cassandra nearly choked on the tea. "I—um…"

Daryn patted her arm. "Let me explain. I know how upset you are." Then he turned his attention to Ally. "I don't know how to say this. The reason we came here today, and the reason my sister nearly fainted a moment ago, is because she's so embarrassed and so sorry for taking your jewelry. She has this problem—she takes things. She can't help herself. We don't expect you to understand or forgive her, but she wanted to return the jewelry."

Cassandra sucked in a deep breath when she realized what he'd just said. She shifted her gaze to meet his, wondering if he was throwing her to the wolves in an attempt to save himself. No matter what his motive, she had no option but to go along with him. Tears filled her eyes and ran down her cheeks. Her chin trembled when she spoke. "Yes, I'm so sorry. I don't know what's wrong with me. I'm so ashamed." She slipped the ring off her finger and handed it to Ally; then she undid the chain around her neck and handed her the locket as well.

It dangled in Ally's long, thin fingers, but she never took her gaze off Cassandra's face. Her gray eyes bore into her like a knife. "I don't know what to say. I thought you were my friends, but you stole from me—from my aunt. How do I know that you haven't taken more from her? There's a statue. A statue of Venus that's missing. Somehow you must have gotten into the house and taken that too."

Cassandra looked at Daryn, expecting him to answer, yet he remained silent. "I swear to you, Ally, I haven't stolen anything else. Please believe me." She twisted her hands in her lap and pleaded with her eyes for Daryn to help her out.

His face was expressionless, and when he opened his mouth, Cassandra couldn't believe what she heard. "What are you going to do?"

Cassandra's cheeks burned. *That's it. That's all he has to say.* He didn't plead her case to Ally. What the hell did he think she was going to do? Of course she'd call the police. She rubbed her sweaty palms together and was once again overcome with dizziness. "Please forgive me. I know I need help. Why, just this morning, I was telling Da— Ross that after I returned the jewelry to you, I was going to find someone to talk to…"

Ally held up her hand, silencing her. "Do you really expect me to believe a word you say?"

"I was hop—"

"You're a thief, and no doubt a liar," Ally said, cutting off her words.

Cassandra set the teacup down and gripped the arms of the chair. That was it. Her life as she knew it was over. She closed her eyes and waited for her world to come crashing down.

"I should call the police," Ally went on, "but you returned the jewelry, and for that, I'm grateful."

Cassandra's lids flew open, and she sucked in a giant gulp of air. From the corner of her eye, she saw Daryn's stiff posture relax a bit.

"So this is what you're going to do," Ally said. "You're going to promise me that you'll never take another thing from anyone again, that you'll get the help you spoke of, and you'll leave town immediately. If I see or hear that you two are still in Silvercreek, I won't hesitate to contact the police. Do you understand?"

Cassandra couldn't believe her good luck. "Yes, yes. I promise."

Jack entered the parlor, balancing two plates of food, and when he saw them, he stopped dead in his tracks. "Why, hello." He raised his brows in surprise.

Ally dropped the jewelry into the pocket of her pants. "Ross and Taryn just stopped by to say good-bye. They're leaving Silvercreek."

Daryn gripped Cassandra's elbow and helped her out of the chair. "Yes. Business calls. It was so nice meeting you both."

"You're leaving now?" Jack didn't hide his pleasure.

"Yes." Daryn kept a tight hold on Cassandra's arm and led her toward the front door. He must be thinking the same thing as she. They had to get out of there while they still could. Ally might change her mind at any moment or tell Jack and he might convince her to call the police, and then they could have the entire force after them.

"Good-bye."

They left the house and raced along the sidewalk toward the BMW. It wasn't until they were safely seated in the car and speeding down the road that Cassandra said, "Well, thanks for nothing. I can't believe you offered me up for sacrifice."

Daryn didn't take his eyes from the road, but she could tell he was seething. "You should be thanking me that you're sitting here and not in a jail cell."

Had he lost his mind? "Really?" she groused. "Thank you?"

"Yeah. Do you think it was just your good fortune that Ally didn't turn you in?"

She shrugged, not quite sure where he was heading with this conversation.

"Do you really think I'd set you up to take the fall?"

"If you'd asked me that yesterday, I would have said no. But after that little episode, I don't know what else to think."

He reached over and squeezed her knee. "I'd never set you up, babe. I was setting up Ally. I knew if I spoke in your defense, it wouldn't be anywhere near as convincing than if you were fighting for your life. Like you'd done the other day when I found the jewelry in your pockets."

She stared at him. "You were that sure Ally would let us go?"

"Yeah, I was betting on it. But if she hadn't, I would have had to resort to Plan B."

"And that was?" Cassandra asked.

"Let's just say I would have had to take a more drastic approach."

She arched her brows at him in shock. "Like what? We've never hurt anyone before. You know how much I hate violence."

He chuckled. "I didn't mean I'd hurt Ally, but I would have restrained her if needed, to give you time to get away."

"Well, I'm glad things turned out the way they did."

He ran his hand up her leg. "Me too." He pressed his foot on the accelerator, and the car shot forward with a jolt. A few minutes later, she saw the sign for I-91 up ahead. Cassandra leaned back in the seat and closed her eyes. Soon they'd leave this small town behind for the bright lights of Atlantic City and a whole new life. An honest life.

ಬಂಡ

Ally stuck her fork in the delicious-looking omelet Jack had made for her, and her hand shook. She was still upset with Taryn. Lucky for her, Jack was devouring his meal and hadn't noticed the tremor. However, he looked at her uneaten food.

"Not hungry?" he asked.

"No, I am." She took a quick bite.

"Quite a surprise to find Ross and Taryn here, wasn't it?"

She studied his face. Was he fishing to see whether she knew if there was more to their leaving town than just business or was he simply looking to make polite conversation? Either way, that was one subject she wanted to stay away from. It was bad enough that she couldn't stop thinking about it and wondering if she should have had Taryn arrested. Who knew how many other people she might have stolen from? But how could Alice have called the police? They would have asked her a million questions. Questions she wasn't prepared to answer. No, she had done the right thing. The only thing. Besides, Taryn had promised never to steal again. She just hoped they'd left town and that she'd seen the last of them.

"I'm just glad they didn't stay long," she said, answering Jack's question. "So I can spend my time with you." She smiled at him. "Only you."

He pulled his chair closer to her and draped his arm across her shoulders. "Me too. There was something about those characters that bothered me. Something was off that I couldn't quite put my finger on."

She wished she had Jack's intuition, but she'd been completely taken in by them. Especially Ross. She wondered if he was really as honest as he'd appeared when he returned her fifty dollars. She hated to think he might have set her up to be a sucker.

"They seemed nice enough to me." She stuck her fork back in her food and took a bite.

Jack pressed on. "I got the feeling Ross wasn't being truthful with us about his business. I wouldn't be surprised if he never sold a thing in his life other than a pack of lies. I sure would have liked to have found out more about them."

Alice didn't want to discuss Ross and Taryn any further, and she certainly didn't want to have to lie to Jack more either. "Don't be so cynical. I'm sure they're just as they seemed."

He looked straight at her. "I know you're not that naïve. People can do a good job at hiding things."

There it was again. His suspicion. What was it going to take to get him to trust her? She knew the answer. It would take her telling him the truth about her transformation. She should tell him now. She'd promised the tin angel she would. But she still hadn't worked up the courage. "I'm sure there are people in the world who are good at being deceptive, but I don't know any."

ଚୌଡ

Jack studied Ally's face to see if she was lying. She knew more about Ross and Taryn than she was letting on. It had been quite obvious when he'd arrived in the parlor earlier that he'd interrupted something. Ally had been angry and trying hard to hide it. And the other two were nervous wrecks. After saying good-bye, they practically ran to the car. Today had done a lot to confirm his suspicions that they were all up to no good and probably working on some scheme. A scheme to swindle Alice.

Sooner or later, Ally would open up to him. He just had to make her believe she could trust him. Last night, she'd almost been there. Especially after he'd learned she'd never made love before. She had to have strong feelings for him—might even be in love with him. He didn't want to break her heart, but until Alice was back safe and sound, he couldn't worry about that. And if he was being honest with himself, he'd admit he cared deeply for her. Maybe even loved her. But he couldn't let himself go there. Not now.

He could tell Ally no longer wanted to discuss Ross and Taryn, so he changed the subject. "I hope you enjoyed the rummage sale. You fit right in, but then I knew you would."

Her face brightened at his compliment. "Thank you. And yes, I did have a nice time. The people were so friendly; they made me feel at ease right away."

"What are the chances I can persuade you to stay here and make this charming little town your home?"

It took her a moment to respond. "I guess that depends on what you had in mind."

Jack left the table and stood behind her chair. He reached over her shoulders and stroked her arms, letting his hands slide down farther until he reached the swell of her firm, round breasts. "How about this?" he whispered against her hair.

She rested her head against his chest. "Is that all you have to offer?"

He slid his hands down lower, slipping them inside her pants. "What about this?"

She melted against him. "You're doing better."

"This should make you commit." He gently lifted her into his arms and carried her to the bedroom.

౸౸౸

"Hey, babe. I need a bathroom," Cassie whined.

Daryn glanced at her briefly, then focused his full attention back on the highway. "We've only been on the road a half hour."

She fidgeted in her seat. "Tell that to my bladder, hon."

He wanted to put as much distance between them and Silvercreek as possible before stopping anywhere. "If you're that desperate, I can pull over to the side of the road."

She jabbed her finger into his side. "Very funny. No, I'll wait for a toilet, thank you."

A few minutes later, he pulled into a rest area and maneuvered the Beemer into a parking space between two large trucks. In the event Ally had changed her mind and called the police, he wanted to stay as inconspicuous as possible. Cassie could make that difficult, however. She stood out where ever she went. With her fiery red hair and Marilyn Monroe-like face and figure, Cass was one hell of a good-looking woman.

He reached into the backseat and popped open one of her suitcases, rifling through her belongings until he found what he was looking for—a thick, gray wool hat that she'd used for one of their scams. "Here, put this on," he said, tossing it at her.

She raised her brows in surprise, but then understanding registered in her fabulous green eyes. "Good thinking." She tucked her hair inside the hat, then reached into her purse and took out a silk scarf, which she draped around her neck and décolletage before buttoning up her coat. "Am I okay now?"

"Perfect." Despite her faults, and she definitely had a few whoppers, he was lucky to have her in his life.

He walked with her to the rest room, then went into a convenience store for a bag of chips. A few minutes later, she was back by his side. "Hungry? Go grab something."

She glanced over her shoulder at the food aisle. "Okay. Be right back."

When she walked away, he picked up a bag of barbeque chips and headed over to the cooler to get something to drink. The bell above the store's door tinkled as a customer entered.

Daryn barely took notice of the tall, stocky man until he heard Cassie say, "What do you think you're doing? Take your hands off me."

Instincts took over, and without thinking, he was at her side. A blinding rage consumed him when he saw the man's hand on her upper arm. "Hey, creep. Don't touch her."

The next thing he knew, he curled his fingers into a fist, pulled his arm back, and connected his hand with the man's chin. What happened after that was a blur. Daryn's arms were held in a steel grip behind his back, and handcuffs had been slapped around his wrists.

Cassie watched in horror. The blood seemed to have drained from her face, even her lips. She clasped her hands over her mouth, but they couldn't stifle her cries of dismay.

The man pulled a radio from his pocket and called for backup.

Shit. He'd slugged a cop.

"Hand it over, miss," said the plainclothes officer.

"I don't know what you're talking about," she protested.

Daryn starred at Cassie in disbelief. "Oh, Cass. What have you done?"

"Nothing," she sobbed, but she couldn't lie to him. The awful truth was there in her eyes.

He shook his head sadly. "Give it up, baby. Game's over."

She stared at him for a moment, then reached into her handbag and pulled out a package of yogurt-covered pretzels.

Daryn's shoulders sagged. He was a pro. His mother's son, after all. Master of deceit. He'd scammed so many people he'd lost count, yet everything had come crashing down around him over something that cost less than five dollars. They'd been so close to living a new life too. By this time tomorrow, they'd have been in Jersey looking for real jobs. But it was too late now. Everything was over. He wondered what was going to happen to them.

Outside, red lights swirled and sirens blared. Seemed like too much activity for such a minor crime. Would he ever see Cass again? No matter what, he'd never forget her. She was the love of his life.

CHAPTER TEN

With Ally curled against him, Jack found it difficult to focus on the old Bing Crosby movie they were watching. Especially since every now and then she would move her hand up and down the back of his neck, gently stroking his hair.

He'd spent the last four days with her, making love and getting to know her better. He was beginning to think he might have misjudged her. She was sweet and wonderful—far from the monster Pastor Riley believed her to be.

The squeal of tires and the roar of an engine—a sports car engine—shifted his thoughts away from the woman in his arms to another woman—one he hoped would stay in his past. Bethany! Though he couldn't fathom why she'd come here. He hadn't returned her calls about spending the holiday together. Would she be so bold as to come anyway…uninvited? His chest tightened as an uncomfortable thought sprang to mind. He hoped she hadn't come to resurrect their relationship.

When he rose from the sofa, Ally looked up at him, her gorgeous eyes questioning. "I think Bethany's here." The words were like poison on his tongue. He hated to think what his ex-fiancée's arrival would do to his cozy evening with Ally.

"What?" Her shock was apparent in her voice and the chalky color of her skin. "Did you invite her?"

He was stupefied that she'd think that. "Of course not."

"Then what's she doing here?"

"I have no idea, but I'm sure we're about to find out." The second he uttered those words, a loud rapping sounded on the door. "I'll get it. You stay put," Jack said, heading toward the foyer.

"The heck I will." Ally sprang off the sofa and was on his heels. "I want to know why she'd drive from Boston, fighting traffic, to see you. I mean, if things are over between you two…"

Jack looked over his shoulder at her. He hated that she doubted him. "I haven't lied to you. My relationship with Bethany is over." Relief crossed her beautiful face. He patted her shoulder. "Don't worry. Everything's okay. I promise." He opened the door to a burst of wintry air.

"Surprise and happy New Year, Jack." Bethany's smile turned into a frown as she stared past him to Ally.

"I thought your landlady was ninety." She pushed by him, not bothering to remove the snow packed around the stiletto heels of her black leather boots. Her gaze swept Ally from head to toe. "I might not be the best at guessing someone's age, but I'm sure this girl can't be more than twenty-something." Her usually controlled tone was high-pitched, and her voice quivered slightly when she spoke.

Jack draped an arm across her shoulders, careful not to muss the fox-fur collar on her coat. Bethany hated to have a hair out of place, even if it wasn't her own. "This is Ally, my landlady's niece."

She kept her hands firmly planted on her hips, making no attempt to shake Ally's outstretched hand. "Under different circumstances I'd say, 'It's a pleasure to meet you,' but seeing as I've interrupted your…" She let the words fade, as if finishing the sentence was distasteful.

Ally moved around them to shut the door, but not before a burst of snow blew in. "Bethany, please come inside and have a seat," she said, shooting Jack a curious gaze. "How about a cup of tea? You must be exhausted from the drive."

The tightness around Bethany's mouth started to subside. Flicking a snowflake from her coat as if it were a speck of dirt, she strolled into the parlor. "That would be lovely."

"Great. Make yourself at home, and I'll go put the kettle on."

Jack watched as Ally hurried toward the kitchen before he followed Bethany into the parlor. He admired Ally's tact in handling what could have been an explosive situation.

Bethany was lounging comfortably on the sofa. She patted the cushion next to her. "Come here and sit with me, love. The girl's quite charming I have to admit, although a bit old fashioned, don't you think? I've never heard anyone use the word 'kettle' before."

Jack was used to Bethany's sharp tongue, but he wouldn't let her belittle Ally. He sent her a warning look and sat beside her.

She smiled seductively and wrapped her fingers around his hand. "She's lovely, really."

He knew she only said that to placate him. Anyone who threatened her spotlight became her prey, and with Ally's classic features, she was sure to be a victim. Bethany's icy looks were the complete opposite to Ally's dark smoldering beauty. With champagne hair and pale blue eyes, Bethany turned heads wherever she went, but there was a hardness to her that kept her from being truly beautiful.

"Beth, what's up? Why are you here?"

She leaned in so that her lips brushed his ear. "I've missed you," she whispered, then with teeth as perfect as a strand of pearls, she began to nibble his lobe.

He pulled back, and she looked up.

"What's wrong, love, you don't desire me?"

"What's wrong with you? It's over between us. I thought that was made perfectly clear when I moved away."

"Oh, darling, you know the phrase, 'Distance makes the heart grow fonder.' Well, that's certainly been true for me. Hasn't it been for you?"

Before he could answer, she pressed her lips against his and wrapped her arms around his neck.

The clatter of dishes enabled him to break free from the she-devil who'd held him captive.

Ally stood in the doorway clenching a tea tray. Her face was as white as her knuckles. At her feet lay shards of glass from a broken cup. "I-I'm sorry,' she stammered, "I didn't mean to interrupt, but the cup…well, it fell and…oh, never mind. I'll clean it up later." She set the tray down on a side table and raced from the room.

"Ally, wait." Before Jack got up, Bethany grabbed his arm, keeping him firmly seated on the sofa.

"Let her go. Don't go running after her like you're her lover who's just been caught cheating." She raised one thinly penciled brow at him. "Unless, of course, there's something I don't know?"

Jack looked hard at her. "Why are you here, Bethany? What exactly do you want from me?"

"That's simple. I want you, of course."

"But why? We were over a long time ago."

"You don't really believe that. If that were true, you wouldn't have kissed me back just now."

"Kissed you back? Are you insane? I certainly did not!"

She looked at him coyly through a fringe of artificial lashes. "You don't need to play hard to get. I know what I felt, and that kiss didn't come from a cold fish. You want me, and I know it."

Jack simmered. The woman had always been intolerable.

ഇൻൽ

Bethany was everything Alice wasn't. Worldly…elegant. She could have stepped off the pages of any fashion magazine. Next to her, Alice felt like a church mouse—drab and boring. How could she ever expect to compete with someone like that? Was it any wonder she'd found Bethany in Jack's arms?

She leaned against the kitchen counter and blinked back the tears that burned beneath her lids. Despite Jack's protests, it was evident he wasn't over Bethany. How could she have been so stupid as to think Jack might fall in love with her? Beneath this young, attractive exterior, she was still the same old Alice—a pitifully shy, self-conscious recluse.

"You're not giving up, are you?"

"What?" Her startled gaze scanned the kitchen, but the voice seemed to come out of nowhere.

"You don't have much time left. You should use it wisely."

She recognized the tin angel's lilting voice. "Where are you?"

"Over here."

The sound came from the direction of the pantry. She ran across the room and yanked open the door.

"I must have overshot the kitchen," the angel said with a chuckle. "Why are you in here when Jack is in the other room with that woman?"

Ally shrugged. "I can't compete with someone like that."

The angel floated nearer. "Of course you can."

She shook her head sadly. "Jack seemed to like me, but now…now that his ex-girlfriend is here…well, it looks like she won't be his ex much longer."

"Then what are you waiting for? You've been given a second chance. A chance to experience all the things you missed the first time around. Go after what you want. You've nothing to lose."

She paused for a moment. "But how can I compete with Bethany?"

"You don't have to. Just be yourself."

"If I could only figure out who that is."

"I have faith in you. Now don't waste any more time wallowing in self-doubt."

Alice looked toward the parlor, where Jack and Bethany were probably locked in each other's arms. "I don't know how to get him to want me more than her." She turned back to the angel, but she spoke to an empty room. The tin angel was gone.

"Why do you always leave like that, with no warning, and when I still have so many things to ask you?"

Alice thought back over her life, past the decades of loneliness to a time when she'd been filled with love and happiness…to those few short years she'd spent with Tom. She'd forgotten those feelings, having buried them long ago in an attempt to relieve her grief, but she was starting to remember… Jack was making her remember, and she liked that feeling. She recalled the tin angel's words: *"Go after what you want."* Maybe she was right. Maybe it wouldn't hurt to fight for love. Besides, how else would she know what Jack's real feelings were?

When she entered the parlor, she was surprised to see Jack standing by the window, staring out at the snow-covered lawn. Bethany sat on the sofa, scowling at Jasper as he attempted to rub against her black wool pants. Hardly the picture of a loving couple.

She crossed the room to stand beside Jack, pretending not to see Bethany's pointed stare. "What's up?"

He gritted his teeth. "I'm going to show Bethany my apartment, then get rid of her."

"Really?"

"Of course. What you saw…well, it's not what you think."

Bethany sashayed over, placing a possessive arm about Jack's waist. "Come on, love, I'm ever so anxious to see that apartment of yours."

Jack glared at Bethany, then turned to Alice. "I better get going. I'll talk to you later."

Sure you will. The thought of what Bethany would do once she got Jack alone made her wrinkle her nose in distaste. What could she do, though? Jack needed to handle this situation in his own way.

She heard the front door open, then footsteps out on the porch.

Well, Alice, you certainly lost that round.

ℝ℞

Jack needed a miracle. One that would send Bethany back to Boston. No matter how many times he told her things were over between them, she refused to believe it. As warped as it might be, his disinterest turned her on. There was nothing Bethany liked better than a challenge. But no matter how hard she tried to seduce him, he was not going to give in. She turned him on about as much as a can of split-pea soup.

"Nice place. A little small, but nice." Bethany stood in the center of his living room, surveying her surroundings.

Although warm and homey, his apartment was by no means her taste. Most of his furniture had come from Alice's attic: a couple of overstuffed chairs, a few small tables, a wooden rocker, and an old sofa. By the look on her face, she wasn't impressed. No surprise there. He didn't own a leather sectional or a piece of chrome.

"Have a seat," he said.

She hesitated a moment, then perched on the edge of the rocker, as if its age alone might dirty her clothes.

"Beth, I appreciate you making the drive here…and with the snow and all—"

"How sweet of you, but you don't have to thank me."

175

Thank you? I wish you hadn't come. He raked his fingers through his hair in frustration.

She prowled across the room to stand in front of him, then curled her arms around his back, pressing her body close to his. "I wanted to be with you," she purred. "I've missed you. We were good together. I want that back."

How differently she remembered things. He couldn't think of a time when he wasn't miserable, but then he wasn't the one doing the nagging and complaining and trying to turn her into something she wasn't. No, she'd been the one doing that to him, and there was no way he was going to get sucked back into her manipulative trap.

He disengaged himself from her embrace, and, keeping her at arm's length, looked her straight in the eyes. "This is not going to work. I don't love you."

She stared back at him, disbelief written all over her face. She opened her mouth, but the ringing of her cell phone delayed her reply. Grabbing the phone from her purse, she looked like she wanted to hurl it across the room.

"Hello," she growled into the mouthpiece. "Randolph, this is really bad timing." She was silent for a moment while listening to what her boss had to say. The only sound that came from her was the drumming of her perfectly manicured nails against his table.

Jack hoped this phone call meant she had to go back to Boston. He leaned against the doorframe and crossed his arms over his chest while he waited for her to finish her conversation.

"Are you crazy? I only just got here." Her voice was high-pitched and very close to a screech.

A few more seconds went by while she listened to Randolph. She chewed her bottom lip, twisting her mouth to the side in an unattractive shape. "But I'd planned to ring in the New Year with Jack." Her tone had changed to a spoiled-child whine.

He hated to get too hopeful, but it was beginning to look like he just might get his wish.

"Yes, Randolph, I'll be careful driving." She dropped the iPhone back into her purse and looked up at him. Her eyes glistened with tears. He wasn't sure if that was due to disappointment or annoyance at not getting her way.

"I'm so sorry, Jack, but I'm not going to be able to spend the holiday with you after all. Randolph needs me back at the station. I've got to fill in for *my* replacement who's suddenly come down with the flu. How ridiculous is that?"

Looked like someone did hear his prayer. "When are you leaving?"

"Now," she said flatly, straightening the coat she hadn't bothered to remove. "Maybe this has worked out for the best." She took both his hands in hers and squeezed. "I think you need to take some more time to think about us; then maybe you'll realize how much I really do mean to you."

It didn't even occur to her that she might not be what he wanted, he thought dryly. He kissed her cheek with the same amount of passion a brother would a sister, then walked her out to her car. When he turned back toward the house, he caught a glimpse of a lace curtain falling across Alice's parlor window. Had Ally been watching?

He climbed the steps to the front porch and rapped on her door. She opened it immediately, almost as if she'd been expecting him.

"Where's your girlfriend going?" Sarcasm laced her words.

"Home. And she's not my girlfriend."

Ally raised a brow. "Does she know that?"

Jack shivered without his coat and folded his arms across his chest. "Can I come in please, or are you going to let me freeze out here while we play games?"

"I'm not the one playing games. You're the one who kissed the peroxide queen—" Ally slapped her hand over her mouth, obviously embarrassed by her outburst.

A smile twitched the corners of Jack's mouth. He liked that spunky side of her. Sidestepping her, he walked into the house. "I can explain—"

"No, no. You don't have to." The fire had left her eyes, and her shoulders sagged. "I had no right to behave that way. No right to care who you kiss or where."

He wiped his boots on the doormat. "Of course you do, and it's not what you think."

"I know what I saw," she said flatly.

"No, you know what you think you saw." He moved into the parlor and flopped down on the sofa. "Bethany's tough, and she doesn't give up easily. She comes on strong and is really good at catching me before I can defend myself."

She eyed him suspiciously. "So you're trying to say that you were just an unwilling victim?"

Jack leaned his elbow on the arm of the sofa and rested his chin in his hand. "Yes." He watched Ally's defensive pose, her arms across her chest, her eyes narrowed ever so slightly. "I care about Bethany, and I don't enjoy having to hurt her," he continued, "but I don't have romantic feelings for her."

"I see." Ally's eyes sparkled again. "So then I'd be correct if I were to assume you'd let Bethany or any woman kiss *you* in order to spare her feelings?" She moved across the room and sat down next to him. She leaned in closely. "You wouldn't want her to feel rejected."

Her lips were full and moist and just inches away...

"Is that what you're saying Jack?"

His mind whirled...the scent of her cologne...her hair tickling his neck... "No, well, not exactly," he sputtered, not knowing quite how to respond or exactly what she was up to, but he did know he wanted her to kiss him. Now!

"Maybe, maybe. Yes," he said, playing along with her, hoping he'd feel her soft body pressed against his.

"Okay. I'll remember that if I ever need a quick boost to my ego," she said smartly as a big, smug smile spread across her face.

Touché, Ally. Before she could say anything else, he pulled her into his arms. "You're the only woman *I* want to kiss," he said, bringing his mouth down on hers.

ഇരു

Alice had wanted desperately to initiate the kiss, but that would've been too bold. She was only just learning to flirt. And doing a darn good job at it, too, she had to admit. So when Jack kissed her, she didn't resist. A tingle of excitement ran through her. Maybe New Year's wouldn't be so bad, after all.

"Is all forgiven?" he whispered against her hair.

She rolled her eyes and snuggled against his chest. "Only if you can forgive me for acting like a jealous girlfriend."

"I liked that."

She wrinkled her brow. "What? The jealous part or the girlfriend part?"

"Both."

Her insides jangled with excitement. Had she heard him correctly? Could he possibly mean he wanted her to be his girlfriend? "I don't understand—"

He silenced her with another kiss. She melted against him, momentarily forgetting her worries. All that mattered was that she was in his arms. His kiss deepened, arousing such passion that she thought she might explode with desire.

But her happiness was bittersweet. She had just a little over twenty-four hours left; then her miracle transformation would end. She'd had a wonderful taste of youth, the way it should be lived, and she'd found love again. But in order to have a real second chance at life, she had to tell Jack the truth. True love wasn't based on secrets and lies.

She opened her mouth to speak. No words came out. Her courage evaporated with one thunderous beat of her heart. If she told him now, she could ruin the time they had left together. He might not believe her, or worse, he might think she was nuts. A chill raced up her spine.

"You're shivering," he said, holding her closer.

"No, I'm fine."

"You can't fool me." He drew back to study her. "I can see that you're cold. I'll get you a blanket if you'll save my spot." He rose from the sofa.

"Only if you're back before Jasper takes it," she teased. The cat sat by the Christmas tree ready to pounce onto the sofa so he could curl up next to her.

"I won't be long."

Jack left the parlor, returning a few minutes later, carrying a winter coat and a pair of boots. Alice's coat and boots! *Oh Lord, he must have found them at the back of her closet while he was looking for a blanket.*

He stared at her in confusion; then his blue eyes darkened into cold, hard rage.

A long, uncomfortable silence stretched between them. She turned her gaze away, unable to bear the look of wounded fury burning in his eyes.

"What are these?" he demanded.

She stared back at him, digging her nails into her palm until it hurt. "Alice's clothes." Her shaky voice betrayed her distress.

"Exactly! Why are they here and not with her? I would think she'd be awfully cold traveling without them." His voice was cool, but it was his expression that bothered her the most. Gone was the loving way he looked at her. His mouth was taut with disapproval, and in that moment, she believed he hated her.

Her heart thudded wildly against her chest, making it difficult to breathe. She inhaled small gulps of air while she tried to think of a reasonable explanation to offer him. "I-I think Alice was wearing a parka when she left."

He unclenched his jaw and spoke with forced civility. "Her suitcases are in the closet, and so is her purse. I don't think she'd go anywhere without those."

She plucked at the armrest, pulling loose the old threads that barely held the worn fabric together. A horrible pounding beat against her head. "I'm sure there's an explanation," she said wearily.

"No more stalling. I want the truth, and I want it now." He leaned against the doorframe as if using it for support.

She closed her eyes against the terrible feeling of dread that washed over her. There was no way out of it this time. She would have to tell him the truth. He would either believe her or not. She opened her eyes slowly and took a deep, steadying breath. "I'm afraid I haven't been completely honest with you."

His brow furrowed, and his skin paled. She looked away, afraid if she saw the pain in his eyes for a second longer, she wouldn't be able to go on.

"I'm not who you think I am," she blurted. She wanted to run to him, throw her arms around him, and tell him she wasn't the evil, despicable person he must think her to be. She knew he wouldn't accept her embrace, though, and she couldn't bear it if he pushed her away.

"I'm Alice." She sat on the edge of the sofa, her hands clenched tightly together. She didn't know how she got the words out, but she had, and then the whole incredible story bubbled from her lips.

"A miracle's happened. I've been given another chance to live my life… The one I should have lived after Tom died. In fact, this was all his idea." She paused a moment, half expecting him to say something…anything…but he stood there rigidly as if he'd been turned to stone.

She ran her tongue over her dry lips and cleared her throat, then pressed on. "The tin angel, the tree topper Tom gave me, is a real angel." She knew she sounded insane, but it was too late to worry about that now. She had no choice. She had to tell him the entire story and hope when she was done, she'd made him believe her. "I don't know if you've noticed, but it's missing. Well, not missing as in stolen; missing as in it only appears when I need advice."

Jack still hadn't moved. In fact, she was getting worried that he might keel over—his skin was such a sickly shade of gray—but she had to finish. "This miracle has a condition. I've only been given until the New Year to find true love or…" Her voice trailed off. This was the toughest part—telling him that she might only have one more day to live; however, she gathered her strength. "If by tomorrow night at midnight, I haven't found true love, I'll be transformed back to ninety…" She lowered her voice to barely more than a whisper, "And I'll die."

She was surprised at the relief she felt at having finally told him everything. "I know it sounds incredible, but I swear to you, it's the truth." She waited expectantly for his response.

He blinked, then narrowed his eyes as if trying to get a better look at her. She couldn't read his expression, his emotions were so guarded. Slowly he moved toward her, until he came to stand before her. He placed his hands on her knees and leaned into her, staring directly into her eyes.

"See, Jack, it really is me."

"Just how big a fool do you think I am?" His tone was as cold as the wind whistling through the windowpanes. He backed away from her, never taking his eyes from her face.

"You're no fool."

He spoke over her. "I asked for the truth. I prayed that you'd open up to me, trust me enough. But instead you tell me some crazy fairy tale that a five-year-old would have trouble believing."

By the time he reached the doorway, his voice had risen enough to send Jasper scurrying from the room.

"Wait, please!" Alice sprang from the sofa and rushed over to the piano. "At least let me prove to you that I am telling the truth." Her fingers flew over the keys, flawlessly playing Rachmaninoff's "Rhapsody." He knew that piece was Alice's favorite.

His eyes were veiled with what appeared to be regret. "The only thing that proves is that I really was a fool…to have fallen in love with you."

The quiet stillness he left her with was far more final than if he'd slammed the door on his way out. She laid her hands flat against the cool ivory keys and wished she could take back every word. Was this how her life was to end? Miserable and alone?

She glanced up at the top of the Christmas tree, her vision blurred by tears, to where the tin angel used to sit. "Why did you grant me this miracle, give me this short taste of happiness and love, only to have it ripped so cruelly from me?" she sobbed.

She sat there till her body and mind went numb, but she didn't get an answer to her plea. The tin angel never appeared.

CHAPTER ELEVEN

*J*ack leaned against the headboard. He hadn't even bothered to remove his boots before climbing onto the bed. The snow packed on his soles from the trek around the house started to melt, dripping onto his comforter. He didn't care. He didn't care about anything.

How could he have been so stupid as to fall in love with Ally? He'd kept telling himself over and over, be careful. *Don't lose your heart.* Well, a lot of good that had done. He closed his eyes, trying to shut out the picture of her that haunted him, but he couldn't erase the memory of her touch or the intoxicating fragrance of her perfume. In that moment, he wanted to feel her soft body next to his and to drink the sweet nectar of her kisses.

"Damn you," he spat, "not only are you dishonest, but you're a witch too. I fell under your spell, and now I'm paying for it with my heart."

The telephone's ringing interrupted his thoughts. He was in no mood to talk to anyone, but he strained to hear the caller's message. Despite everything, he half hoped it was Ally.

"Jack, love, are you there?" Bethany's smooth voice flowed from the answering machine. "I hope you are and that you're listening to this. Forget what I said about needing more time. I've got a fabulous idea. Since I can't be there with you, why don't you come to Boston and be with me? I'll give you a New Year's Eve you won't forget." She made a noise that sounded like a growl, then hung up.

If he was smart, that was exactly what he'd do—leave this town and that woman downstairs, whoever she might be, far behind. He should spend a night with Bethany having wild, incredible sex and forget about Ally and love. Both brought nothing but trouble.

He rolled onto his side and turned off the Tiffany-style lamp on his nightstand. The streetlight shining in through his window kept the room aglow. He squeezed his eyes shut, too drained to even pull the window shade.

After what seemed like hours, he drifted into an uneasy sleep and woke at six a.m. still wearing his clothes from the night before. He undressed and padded toward the shower.

As the water ran over him, his thoughts drifted back to Ally. His plan had failed miserably. She not only didn't confide in him, she must think him an idiot to have fed him that crazy tin angel story.

He wanted to hate her, but he couldn't. How could he have fallen so hard for a woman he knew nothing about? He didn't even know her real name. Suddenly a thought occurred to him. What if that part of her story had been true? What if Ally Hart really was her name, and what if she really was from Syracuse? Then maybe that was where he'd find Alice.

He knew he was probably grasping at straws. He should call Pastor Riley and the police, but he was going to get to the bottom of this once and for all, and the only way to do that was to go to New York.

ωα

Alice hung up the phone when Jack's answering machine picked up.

She'd already left three messages. If he would just talk to her, she'd find a way to make him believe her.

Tired and cranky from a night spent tossing and turning, she was in no mood to be ignored. She slipped on her coat, then took the spare key from the hall table. If Jack wouldn't pick up his phone, he'd darn better answer his door, or she'd have no choice but to let herself in.

I'm not giving up on you, Jack Billings, even if you have given up on me.

She stomped through the snow to the back of the house and raced up the stairs to his apartment. She banged on the door. "Open up, Jack, or I'm coming in." She waited a few moments, then put her ear to the door, hoping to hear the sound of his footsteps. But all was quiet. She knocked again, waited, then stuck her key in the lock.

"I've given you fair warning. Now I'm coming in." In case he'd been in the shower and not able to hear her banging, she opened the door slowly. An image of him wearing nothing but a towel filtered behind her eyelids.

"Hello," she called, before entering the dark apartment. The lingering scent of deodorant soap hung in the air. He couldn't have left that long ago, but for where?

She walked into the living room and sank onto the sofa. Defeat sagged her shoulders. She buried her face in her hands and sobbed quietly. The telephone's ringing broke through her misery, and she looked up, her cheeks wet with tears. Jack's sexy voice pierced her heart as she listened to his greeting play from the answering machine. After the beep, she heard a woman's voice.

"Jack, I hope you took my advice and decided to spend the New Year with me. If you're not here soon, though, I'll have to make other plans." The annoying drone that was Bethany's call disconnecting seemed to go on forever before the answering machine clicked off.

Alice wanted to scream in frustration. He couldn't do that. He couldn't go back with that woman. Not out of anger. Not when he loved her… And she loved him. She might only have one day left, but, by golly, she was going to tell him what he meant to her before it was too late. She grabbed the phone and dialed Silvercreek Cab Company.

೩೦೮

Alice paid the taxi driver, offering him a hefty tip. She'd been a nervous wreck the entire trip to Boston. A wet snow was falling, glazing the road, and her trip had taken a lot longer than expected. But she wasn't complaining. She was thankful she'd gotten to Chesterfield Hall safely.

She stared at the large brick buildings in front of her, having no idea which one housed the dean's office. As she walked toward the closest one, a student with an armful of books passed through its front doors.

"Excuse me," Alice said, "do you know where I can find Dr. Snow?"

The girl held her stack steady by resting her chin on the top book. "Next building over to your left. His is the first office. You can't miss it."

"Thank you." Alice hurried along the sidewalk. She shivered as the cold wet snowflakes hit her face. She walked up the four concrete steps, taking care not to slip. Once inside, she blew into her frozen hands, then rubbed them warm.

She was taking a chance coming here. Dr. Snow might not be in his office, and, even if he was, there was no guarantee he'd give her Bethany's address, but it was the only hope she had of finding Jack. Getting this far hadn't been hard. Jack had mentioned his former employer many times, but finding Bethany's house was the tough part.

She checked her appearance in the reflection of a large glass showcase. Using her fingers like a comb, she smoothed the snarls from her windblown hair, then straightened the waistband on her pants.

Her heels clicked loudly over the highly polished floor as she walked toward the office. Her fingers trembled slightly, and she clasped them together. What was she doing here? This was crazy, chasing after Jack like some lovesick fool. She never would have had the courage to do this before. Part of her was proud that she'd overcome her fear to go after what she wanted, and the other part wanted to go home.

Nervously, she knocked on the dean's office door. At first she thought no one was in there, but as she was about to leave, a man's deep baritone voice said, "Come in."

She took small, tentative steps forward, her gaze scanning the room for the man who'd spoken. When she reached the dean's desk, his huge leather chair spun around. A distinguished gentleman with shiny silver hair and the same pale blue eyes as Bethany eyed her from head to toe.

Taken back by the intensity of his gaze, she squared her shoulders, pulling herself up to her full imposing height. "Dr. Snow?"

"Have we met befah?" he asked, his Boston accent pronounced.

"I'm Ally Hart."

He reached across the desk to shake her hand, then said, "Have a seat and tell me what I can do for you."

She sank into the chair behind her and returned his attentive gaze. "I'm not a student here. I'm looking for your daughter. I was hoping you'd give me her address."

"And why should I do that?" His friendly demeanor was replaced with a suspicious gleam in his eyes. He tapped a silver pencil on the desk while he watched her.

She should have known this wasn't going to be easy. She thought for a moment, trying to figure out her best approach. In crossing her leg she kicked over her handbag, spilling its contents out onto the floor. Not that she carried much with her: a wallet, mirror, some face powder and lipstick, but it still took her a few moments to gather her things and shove them back into her bag.

"Sorry," she said looking up, her face burning with embarrassment. She followed the direction of the dean's gaze and realized her scoop-neck sweater had slipped down enough to expose the lace trim on her bra.

"I-I've come a long way," she said, adjusting her neckline and sitting straight in the chair. "From Connecticut," she continued, "and if I don't find her..."

He gave his pencil one more loud rap, then sprang from his chair to come stand beside her. "You're one of Bethany's old college chummies, come to ring in the New Year. I thought you looked a tad familiar." He scribbled an address on a piece of notepaper and pressed it into her palm. "It's not far from here. Just one block north."

"Thank you." She shook his hand again, then quickly left the office.

Once outside, she took a deep breath, inhaling the frigid air. She pulled up her jacket collar tightly around her neck, then headed across the school campus toward the lovely tree-lined road. She stepped onto the cobblestone street and followed Dr. Snow's directions to Bethany's house, a beautiful brownstone.

Was she doing the right thing coming here? What if Jack wouldn't see her? Or worse, slammed the door in her face. The temptation to turn around and go home was growing stronger by the minute. Her knees began to shake, not only out of fear, but from the raw winter cold. She needed to do something. She couldn't just stand there or she'd freeze to death. *Don't chicken out now, Alice. Go do what you came here to do. It's your one and only chance. If you don't, you'll never see Jack again, and he'll never know that you loved him.*

With courage she didn't know she possessed, she walked up to the front door and gave it a strong knock. The door opened, revealing a muscular, bare-chested man…and it wasn't Jack. Tanned and gorgeous, with ripples in places she hadn't known existed, the statuesque man stepped aside so she could come in.

Perspiration glistened like liquid gold on his flawless skin. She felt awkward and uncomfortable by his raw sensuality. Her cheeks burned. "Is Bethany home?"

"I haven't been working up this sweat alone," he said with a wink.

At that moment, Bethany came up behind him. She wrapped her arms around his waist and kissed the back of his neck before she spotted Alice standing in the doorway. "Isn't this a surprise? What are you doing here?"

"I'm looking for Jack. I thought he might be with you, but I can see that's not the case." Her gaze quickly flicked over Adonis, then back to Bethany.

"That's right," Bethany said coldly. "I'm through throwing myself at him. As you can see, I've moved on." She tilted her head and kissed her new lover's eager mouth. "I suggest you do the same. Why, if you don't know where Jack is, maybe you should take the hint and go home. He might not want to be found."

Alice's back stiffened, and she could feel the blood drain from her face. "I need a cab."

"Come on, I'll call you one." Bethany stepped around her to close the door, then headed into a large room on the right. "You can wait in here by the fire until your ride arrives."

The room was an elegant mix of old and new. Sleek leather

furniture paired with centuries old antiques. Alice sank onto a chair close to the marble fireplace, but the warmth of the flames couldn't melt her chilled heart. Hope of ever seeing Jack again had died. Her time was almost up and she was alone, just as she'd been before her miracle transformation. There was nothing for her to do now, but take Bethany's advice and go home. A flicker of hope emerged. Could that be where Jack was? Could he be home now?

80C03

Jack left city hall with a heavy heart. This trip to Syracuse had been a waste of time. He hadn't discovered a speck of information on any member of the Hart family. He'd been lucky enough to engage the help of a clerk, but there was nothing showing that Ally had ever lived there. So that had been a lie. Everything she'd told him had been a lie. She wasn't from Syracuse. Who knew where she was from or who she really was. She might not even be related to Alice. And just where the heck was Alice?

How could he have been such a poor judge of character? The girl had completely conned him. The thought that he could be one of many who had fallen victim to her made his stomach churn, and for a second, he thought he might be sick.

The only thing left to do was to call the police and tell them everything he knew. The thought of Ally in handcuffs presented a depressing picture, though. He couldn't shake free the memory of her kisses...or the way her eyes deepened to a smoldering smoky gray when he touched her. Had her desire for him been a lie too? She couldn't fake that, could she? No, her feelings for him had to have been real. At least he wanted to believe they were.

He stepped carefully over a patch of ice as he headed toward his car. Against all logic, he found himself thinking of a good criminal defense attorney for Ally. John Gregory came to mind. He was one of the best around.

Jack caught himself before those kinds of thoughts went any further. This craziness had to stop. He pulled his cell phone from his jacket pocket and started to dial the Silvercreek police, but the bitter taste of betrayal came into his mouth. He couldn't make that call. He couldn't do that to Ally. Not yet.

Jack hung up, disgusted with himself. He shoved the phone back in his pocket and continued across the parking lot. When he reached his Acura, he realized he didn't know where he was going. Dusk had settled in. He was hungry and tired, and it was New Year's Eve. The long trip back to Connecticut would have to wait until morning. What he needed was a hotel room and a bottle of scotch.

He plopped into the driver seat of his car and started the engine. A few minutes later, he was on the highway, leaving Syracuse behind. He drove awhile before spotting a sign for food and lodging. The economy hotel was just off the exit ramp. He was given a typical room with a double bed, a desk, and an overstuffed chair.

While stretched out on the bed, he used the remote to turn on the television. He hoped to find something to take his mind off Ally, but Bing Crosby crooning "White Christmas" was not what he had in mind.

For a fleeting moment, he wished he hadn't found Alice's things in the closet. He'd so hoped his future would include Ally—beautiful, intelligent Ally. She intoxicated him like a bottle of the finest wine.

Suddenly, the room seemed stifling. He snatched his car keys from the bedside table. The sparkle of the gold treble clef dangling from his key ring was yet another reminder of what would never be. He remembered the look of anticipation in Ally's eyes while she waited for him to open the little red foil box. He'd been right when he wondered how she could afford such an expensive gift. She'd stolen the money from Alice. One thing was for sure, he'd return the key chain to Miller's and give Alice her money back.

He left the hotel, taking the back stairs down to his car. He wound through the streets, not knowing where he was going or even the name of the town. His stomach's rumbling called to him for food.

It wasn't long before he spotted the look-at-me neon sign for Chick's Diner. Its stainless-steel exterior served as a time capsule of the 1950s. He pulled onto the gravel lot and swung into the first parking space. Only a few cars were peppered about. He hoped nostalgia didn't take precedence over the food when it came to the menu selection.

Upon entering the vestibule, he half expected to be greeted by someone dressed as "the Fonz" from the television show, "Happy Days." The floor was checkered with black-and-white tiles, and the walls were a scallop-shaped stainless steel. Rounding off the time warp was a jukebox, playing tunes from the golden-oldies.

"Sit where ever ye like," yelled a robust woman with bleached blonde hair piled high on her head in a beehive hairstyle. She wore a tight pink dress with a ruffled apron tied around her waist, and her bright blue eye shadow was visible from where she stood behind the counter, a good twenty feet away.

She poured coffee for a couple of guys slumped on their stools, who looked like they'd been celebrating the New Year for some time, before leading him to a red vinyl booth at the rear of the diner. She plopped a menu down in front of him.

"Will anyone be joinin' ye tonight, sugar?" she asked, snapping the wad of gum she chewed.

"No," he answered, keeping his eyes glued to the menu.

"What a shame, good lookin' guy such as yerself, spendin' New Year's alone."

His thoughts were punctuated with Ally, and the force of his loneliness sent a sharp pain to his chest. He made a mental note to stop at a package store for a bottle of Johnny Walker before heading back to his room. "I'll have the beef stew and—"

"I'm sorry, sugar," she interrupted, "I ain't yer waitress. Suzie'll be right with ye." She left him with a heavy dose of cheap perfume.

Could this night get any worse? All he wanted was some food and something to numb his misery...

"What can I get for you?"

Her voice was soft and smooth, and when he looked up, he swallowed hard. The waitress had the same shiny chestnut hair and pale alabaster skin as Ally. He blinked a few times before he realized that was where the similarity ended. Her eyes were brown, the color of coffee, not the smoky gray he so loved. Her lips were thinner, and she was a good six inches shorter than Ally. "Beef stew and a glass of water. That'll do it." He handed her the menu and watched as she walked toward the kitchen. What was wrong with him? What was it going to take to get Ally off his mind?

When the food arrived, he barely tasted it. Everything felt like sawdust going down his throat. He was only able to eat half his dinner.

"What's the matter? You didn't like it?" The waitress picked up his plate and placed it on her tray.

"No, no. It was fine. I guess I wasn't as hungry as I'd thought."

"Can I tempt you with a piece of homemade cheese cake?"

"No, thanks. Just the check please."

"Not even a cup of hot apple cider, before you go back out in the cold."

He shook his head. The memory of Christmas Eve and Ally by the fire at Gilly's flooded his mind.

When he left the diner, his spirits were lower than when he'd arrived. He sat in his car for a long while, wondering how things between them could have gone so terribly wrong.

He drove through town, looking for a package store. Tiny white lights hung in the windows of the storefronts. The trees lining the streets wore the same lights too. It reminded him of Silvercreek. The memory of holding Ally in the moonlight was almost too much to bear. *Enough already. You're driving yourself crazy.* He reached in his pocket for his cell phone, intent on calling the police. Maybe that would remove her from his mind once and for all, but to his annoyance, the phone wasn't there. He must have left it in the room. Well, when he got back to the hotel, the first thing he was going to do was make that call.

So he didn't have actual evidence to prove Ally was a grifter, but she'd lied about everything, and that had to mean something. Let the police come up with the evidence. He needed to get his life back to normal. Whatever that was.

Yet, he wasn't so sure he was better off before. He'd been disenchanted by love. The women he'd known were selfish and self-indulgent—with two exceptions, Aunt Stacy and Alice. He imagined Alice as a young woman...a woman just like Ally. If he didn't know better, they could be one and the same. He raked his fingers through his hair. He must be losing his mind. The story of an angel tree topper granting her a miracle was crazy.

Jack found a liquor store and got that bottle of scotch he so badly needed. When he arrived back at the hotel, he tried the same back door he'd left from, only now it was locked. He had no choice but to go through the lobby. Hopefully, it would be empty. Encountering happy couples celebrating the New Year would only add to his foul mood.

He entered the front door with his package tucked under his arm. Two hotel employees stood like guards by the entrance, handing out noisemakers to each arriving guest.

A young woman offered him one, but he shook his head no. She put it back in her basket, and he accidentally bumped her arm, sending noisemakers flying across the room. Most landed around the large Christmas tree.

"I'm so sorry," he muttered, stooping under pine branches to retrieve them. When he stood up, he noticed the angel tree topper. His mind whirled with memories of Ally.

"Sir." The woman tapped his arm. "I'll take those from you."

"What?" He shifted his gaze from the tree onto her. She held her basket out, waiting for him to drop the noisemakers inside.

"Oh, I'm sorry. Here you go." He stuffed them in, then raced to the elevator, taking it up to the third floor.

He couldn't get to his room quick enough. Once inside, he took a swig of scotch, then slammed the bottle down on the table. Everywhere he went, everything he did, Ally was there, invading his thoughts. No matter how hard he tried, he couldn't get her off his mind.

Across the room, he spotted his cell phone on the bed. He needed to call the police. Now! He'd tell them the whole rotten story and then be done with her. He took another sip of scotch. With the bottle poised in midair, the angel tree topper in the hotel lobby sprang to mind, reminding him of the missing tin angel from Alice's Christmas tree. He put the bottle down slowly.

What if Ally had been telling the truth about that? What if she hadn't stolen the tree topper but really had been given a miracle transformation by an angel. Ridiculous. Don't even go there, he told himself. Maybe he'd had more to drink than he thought. He checked the bottle. Only a few sips were gone.

Be honest with yourself. You want to believe her so badly you're grasping at any story, even one so incredible it's laughable.

A nagging doubt remained, though. If she was telling the truth about the angel, that would explain everything—Alice's disappearance, Ally's remarkable resemblance, her knowledge of music, the cat... The list went on and on.

What a fool he'd been! Why hadn't he believed in her? Miracles happened every day. Just because he'd never witnessed one didn't mean they didn't exist. And what better time for one than at Christmas.

His breath caught in his chest. If Ally was indeed Alice, then that meant at midnight she'd be transformed back to ninety...and if that happened, then the rest of her story had to be true too, and that meant not only would she become Alice again, she was going to die! Jack's wrist shook as he looked at his watch. He had just over four hours to get back to Silvercreek.

CHAPTER TWELVE

*P*lease let Jack be home. Please let Jack be home, Alice prayed. She watched as another car zoomed past the taxi. She checked her watch for the time. 10:45 p.m. In a little more than an hour, her life would be over. Ally would disappear forever, and Alice would be there in her place—an old woman. A dying old woman.

Tears welled in her eyes, and a lump formed in her throat. It wasn't the thought of dying that saddened her so much as the possibility that she might never see Jack again, never have the chance to tell him she loved him...had always loved him from the first moment she'd set eyes on him. She wasn't a criminal. She hadn't done anything awful to Alice. In fact, she *was* Alice. Believe it or not, she was that old-fashioned woman he'd always dreamed of meeting.

"Oh, don't let me die without Jack knowing the truth," she whispered into the night. "I couldn't bear that." The thought that he might be left thinking of her as a liar and a thief sent a shiver down her back. Her hands went cold and her mouth dry.

She leaned forward and spoke through the opening in the taxi's plexiglass partition. "Please, if you could just drive a little faster."

The man nodded and swung left to pass a slow-moving pickup

with a load of furniture. "Don't worry, miss, I get you there fast." He spoke with a heavy Jamaican accent.

She didn't doubt that, the way he was weaving in and out of traffic. She only hoped he'd get her there in one piece. Soon they left the city lights behind and were traveling through the streets of Silvercreek. She pulled some money from her wallet as they neared Main Street. From the taxi's back window, she caught a glimpse of her old blue Victorian.

As soon as the taxi pulled up to the curb, she handed the man his fare along with a hefty tip, then nearly sprang from the cab to bound up the stairs to Jack's apartment. Her heart was pounding so fast she was left breathless.

"Jack? Are you in there?" She banged on the door. The silence was almost deafening. "Please, open up. I need to talk with you."

Where could he be? She wanted to sink to her knees and sob, but she remembered she still had his spare key. With fingers shaking, she pulled the key from her pocket and put it in the lock. Hopefully, she'd find something inside that would give a clue as to his whereabouts.

Her eyes took a few seconds to adjust to the dark apartment. She located the light switch on the wall, and the room was soon bathed in light. She looked for anything unusual, but everything was as it had been before. From the corner of her eye, she caught a flash of red. The answering machine. Her hesitation to play Jack's messages lasted no more than half a second. After all, they might be able to shed some light on his whereabouts.

It didn't take her long to zip through his messages. The one that caught her interest was from Pastor Riley.

"Jack, I've got good news and bad news," he said in his thick New Hampshire accent. "The police picked up the grifters. A male suspect in his early thirties. And a female, maybe a few years younger.

They're not talking, though. Looks like Ally could be a part of their crime ring. Have you come up with any evidence? Anything at all that could help the police. Thanks, Jack. Let me know."

"Grifters?" Alice shrank away from the answering machine. "Jack thinks I'm a grifter. Oh Lord, this is worse than I thought." Tears streamed down her cheeks and into her mouth. The salty taste on her tongue mixed with the bitter acid coming up from her stomach. This whole time he'd been playing games with her, wanting her to believe he cared for her so he could gather information for Pastor Riley…and the police.

Her chest tightened. He didn't love her. He probably didn't even like her. Oh, what a fool she'd been. She'd fallen for his whole act. Thank goodness this transformation was nearly over. Far from giving her a second chance at love, it only proved love was not meant for her. Empty and drained, she headed downstairs. At least she had Jasper, and he truly cared for her. When she was back in her parlor, she collapsed onto her favorite overstuffed chair. She shivered and pulled the wool throw over her lap.

From the top of her head to the tips of her toes, a cold like she'd never felt before shook her. She glanced at the grandfather clock. 11:45 p.m. The hand of death had come to claim her. She leaned back in the chair and let Jasper jump onto her lap. There was nothing to do now but wait for the clock to chime midnight. She clenched her jaw tightly to keep her teeth from chattering and stared at the comforting lights of the Christmas tree.

ഇോരു

Jack pressed hard on the accelerator. The Acura fishtailed over a patch of ice. He'd made it to Silvercreek safely. He didn't need an accident now, just a few blocks from Alice's house. He glanced at his watch. Almost midnight. He hoped Ally's tale of the tin angel was just another lie. He'd rather she be a grifter than dead.

When he pulled down the driveway, at first glance the old Victorian appeared dark, but with a closer look he spotted the lights on the Christmas tree twinkling through the parlor window. He said a silent prayer for Ally to be alive and well.

He parked quickly, not bothering to pull the car inside the carriage house. He sprinted across the lawn and up the porch steps, pounding loudly on the thick wood door. When Ally didn't answer, he tried the knob. The door opened.

Something was wrong. The house was still, eerily so. Only the grandfather clock's chiming midnight broke the silence. "Ally? Where are you?"

Crossing the foyer, he stepped into the parlor. He wasn't sure if it was Jasper's purring or the sound of labored breathing that shifted his gaze to the overstuffed chair. In the darkened shadows of the room, he saw a slumped form motionless in the chair. Strands of long gray hair covered her face.

"Alice!" He fell to his knees in front of her and took hold of her wrist, feeling for a pulse. If there was one, he couldn't find it. Her skin was unnaturally cold and clammy.

Jasper opened one ochre eye and stretched contentedly on her lap, unaware of his owner's condition.

"Hang on, Alice. Just hang on." He pulled his cell phone from his pocket and dialed 911. "Hurry," he shouted into the phone. "You've got to hurry. She can't die. She just can't." The operator assured him an ambulance would be there shortly. Beads of perspiration lined his brow, and a drop ran down the side of his face.

He heard a vehicle pull down the driveway and raced to the window. Pastor Riley? Jack met him at the front door. He was holding Alice's statue of Venus. "What the— Where did you get that?"

"The police have the grifters in custody—a young couple. The woman—a gorgeous redhead with an angelic face—must've had the elderly eating out of her hand. She had the statue in her suitcase."

Pastor Riley had to be talking about Taryn. She and Ross were grifters. Just as he'd suspected. "You can tell me the rest later. Come quick. It's Alice." Jack ushered him into the parlor.

"What's happened here?" The pastor set the statue on a table next to Alice's overstuffed chair and looked down at her still body.

Jack laid his palm against her cheek. "I only just arrived home myself. This is how I found her."

"It doesn't look good." The pastor took hold of Alice's hands. "Where have you been? You never should have left your home or your friends." He blessed her forehead with the sign of the cross. "I'm afraid the ambulance won't get here in time, Jack."

He didn't need the pastor to tell him that. He'd known it the moment he saw her, but hearing those words spoken aloud somehow made it more real.

The ache in his heart made it difficult to speak. "Please, I'd like some time alone with her, if you don't mind," he managed to sputter.

"Of course. Oh, I almost forgot. Ally's no longer a suspect. The grifters confessed to everything and assured the police that she had no part in their crime spree."

"I know." His voice sounded unfamiliar.

"That's a bit of good news, at least. I could tell you had soft spot for her."

Good news? He wished she was a grifter. At least she'd still be alive, but Ally and Alice were one in the same, and he'd lost them both.

He waited until the pastor left the room, then closed the door behind him before getting down on one knee and taking both of Alice's ice-cold hands between his own.

"Please don't leave me," he said, his voice husky with emotion.

"I know you're old and tired, but you've got a lot of life left. I know you do. Besides, if you leave me, who'll play Rachmaninoff?"

A tear ran slowly down his cheek, and he didn't bother to brush it away. He stared into her old, withered face, relaxed and peaceful now. If it weren't for the occasional rattle in her chest with each shallow breath, he would think she was merely asleep.

"I'm sorry I didn't believe you." He squeezed her hands. "If only we could have spent a lifetime together instead of just ten short days."

Off in the distance, the wail of a siren alerted Jack that the ambulance was near. He leaned over and kissed her cheek. "Twenty-five or ninety, you're the most wonderful woman I've ever known."

His throat tightened, but he managed to get out the words he'd been longing to say. "I love you."

ഉ൦ര

Alice was afraid to open her eyes. The last thing she remembered was Jack's kiss. She'd wanted to tell him she loved him, but she couldn't speak. Not only that, she couldn't feel anything. Not that that was necessarily a bad thing. Her ninety-year-old body was full of aches, and feeling no pain was a relief, but something wasn't right. She risked lifting one lid slightly. A thick fog surrounded her. Where in the world was she? This wasn't any place she'd ever been before.

Fighting her rising panic, she opened her eyes wide. Clouds of white drifted past her. A sinking feeling took hold. She must be dead!

Slowly, she scanned the area. This couldn't be hell; it wasn't hot enough. But if it was heaven, then where were all the other souls? Maybe she was in purgatory? It wouldn't surprise her if the tin angel had gotten it wrong. She took a small, weightless step forward. Through the mist, a familiar figure emerged. The sparkle of his medals stood out sharply against his uniform.

"Tom?" she gasped.

He opened his arms to her, and she accepted his embrace. He looked just as she remembered, although maybe a bit younger, but then it could be that she was just so much older.

"Oh, how I've missed you," she whispered against his chest.

"Too much, I suspect."

She looked up at him in surprise, and he cupped her chin in his hand.

"I loved you." His voice was deep and rich. "We should have had a life together, but it didn't work out that way. My journey was short and yours...well, look at you, you're an old woman. You were blessed, given many years to live a long full life, yet you shut yourself away and did nothing but grieve for a love that could never be."

She bit back a sob. "It was easier that way. I couldn't bear to let you go. Besides, no one could ever take your place."

He held her gaze with deep chocolate eyes. "And I wouldn't have wanted anyone to, but that didn't mean you couldn't have loved another. I think there's more to it than that. I think you were afraid."

She pulled back slightly from his embrace. "I couldn't go through that again. The pain...was just too much."

"Everyone suffers loss, different degrees of it, but it hurts just the same. It's part of life, but you shouldn't stop living to avoid it."

Alice took a deep, ragged breath. Tom was right. If only she'd met Jack sooner, then she could have had the life she was meant to have—with him—but it was too late now.

Her lips quivered, and her eyes filled with tears. She'd felt Jack's love and his grief when he'd spoken to her as she lay dying, and she hoped he wouldn't make the same mistake she had. He mustn't give up on life.

"You're worried about that young man," Tom stated, seeming to know her thoughts.

Alice nodded.

With a wave of his arm, he parted the fog, and as if she were watching a movie, the scene at her home unfolded.

Sirens cut through the silence of the night. Flashing lights swirled in her driveway. Two men jumped from the back of an ambulance and pulled out a stretcher. A uniformed police officer was talking to Pastor Riley. All of this was as she'd expected. What looked to be chaos was the systematic procedure used when someone reported a death. But where was Jack? Was he still inside? Her stomach contorted into a knot.

She shifted her gaze and was shown her parlor. Jack was on his knees, holding Alice's hands. His usually ruddy complexion, drained of color, was now a pasty shade quite similar to Alice's in death. His hair was ruffled as if he'd pulled at it in frustration. A faraway look glazed his eyes.

"I waited my whole life to meet you, and then I blew it. I didn't trust you." His tone was flat. "I treated you like a criminal. If I'd believed in you, I wouldn't have gone on that wild-goose chase to Syracuse. I would have been here with you, where I should have been. Maybe then you'd still be alive. Maybe I could have saved you." His voice cracked.

Alice wasn't sure she wanted to listen to any more.

"It's my fault, and now you're gone," he said. Maybe you were right to live your life as you did. You'd found your soul mate, and no matter how short-lived, you carried your love with you your entire life. Best to live alone with your memories than to settle for something less."

"No, you're wrong," she shouted. "Don't do that. Don't waste your life. You've got so much to offer…so much love to give…"

She turned to Tom. "It's my fault. It's all my fault." Tears streamed down her cheeks. "Please, do something. Don't let him give up on life."

His dark eyes were remorseful. "There's nothing I can do. People were given free will. You know that. I can't change the law."

She grabbed his hands and squeezed tightly. "Then let me go back."

He shook his head. "I can't do that. It's too late. You've left your mortal body."

"No one knows that. Look!" She pointed down to where the authorities stood waiting for the E.M.T.'s to carry the stretcher across the lawn. "They haven't pronounced me dead yet. Only Jack's in the room."

Tom cocked a brow at her. "Why now? Wasn't ninety years enough?"

"No, not nearly. I need ninety more…to be with Jack," she pleaded.

"Alice, I—"

"Please, help me. I know you can do this. You gave me ten days—promised me a lifetime if I found true love."

Her breath caught in her throat as she watched the procession of people outside move toward the front door. "Hurry, Tom, hurry. There's not much time. They'll be inside any minute now." She twisted her hands in front of her. "Give me a chance at happiness. Give Jack a chance at happiness. I love him."

A deafening whirl thundered in her head, and her lungs filled with oxygen. She felt as if she was being sucked from the window of an airplane at ten thousand feet. She spun through an abyss of colors more beautiful than a rainbow.

Then the world went black.

୫୦୦ଓ

The old grandfather clock chimed midnight…again. How could that be? It had to be close to one a.m. Jack stroked the back of Alice's hands with his thumbs, then watched with amazement as her old, withered skin changed into that of a young woman. *I must be dreaming.* He shook his head, trying to bring himself back to reality. The skin beneath his fingers felt warm and smooth, though.

"Get a hold of yourself, man, or you're destined for the loony bin." He watched, transfixed, as strands of long gray hair become a glistening rich, chestnut. While only a moment ago her lips had been the odd pale color that only death could bring, now they were rosy.

Gently, he touched her mouth, and her soft, even breath caressed his finger. "Ally?" A tear rolled slowly from the corner of his eye. He didn't care if he had lost his mind; he wanted this hallucination to last forever. "You're back."

She was more beautiful than he'd ever seen her. He covered her lips with his own and kissed her with all the passion of a man deeply in love. As if he'd willed her to life, she kissed him back. Her intensity matched his own, and she curved her arms around his neck, holding him close.

He watched her marvelous gray eyes open. "Jack, I..." she murmured.

"Shhh." He silenced her with another kiss, then drew back and said, "Don't talk; I don't want this dream to go away."

She moved her lips across the side of his face to whisper in his ear, "It's no dream, my love. I'm real, very real, and here to spend my life with you."

He widened his gaze, staring at her gorgeous face. "But I don't understand... How?"

She kissed his neck. "It doesn't matter. We were destined to be together." She turned her gaze upward and whispered, "Thank you, Tom." Before directing her stare back to Jack, it settled on the Venus statue, glistening on the table beside her. "Where did you find it?" she asked, tears filling her eyes.

"Taryn and Ross—I doubt those are even their real names—are

grifters."

She shook her head sadly. "I was so easy to fool, having shut myself away for so long. I'm going to need your help, Jack, navigating this new world." Just as she finished speaking, the front door burst open, and an onslaught of people flooded inside.

When Pastor Riley entered the parlor, his jaw dropped open. "What the heck?" Where's Alice?"

Jack winked at her and then turned to the pastor. "Do you believe in miracles?"

Pastor Riley stared at the young woman in Jack's arms. "Of course."

"Then you know Alice is right where she belongs," Jack said with a huge grin.

As if he knew their secret, Pastor Riley turned to the group waiting in the foyer. "Looks like it's a false alarm, folks."

When the front door closed and they were once again alone, Jack covered her mouth with a long lingering kiss. After their lips parted, he held her out at arm's length. "I don't plan on letting you out of my sight."

Her smile radiated more warmth than the sun on a bright summer day. "You'd better not. Not now or ever."

EPILOGUE

Christmas Eve, one year later

Alice hung the silver bell on the Christmas tree. She stood back and admired the shiny ornament engraved with her wedding date.

"I can't believe we were married this morning."

"Believe it, Mrs. Billings, it's true." Jack wrapped his arms around her, pushing aside the strap of her silk nightgown.

It hung loosely on her arm. With his finger, he lifted the other one. The bodice clung to her breasts. Any movement would have it falling around her feet.

"And you were an absolutely beautiful bride." He kissed the side of her neck. A tingle ran all the way down to her toes.

They'd taken a year to plan the wedding, sparing no detail. They were married by Pastor Riley, and the entire congregation attended their ceremony. Everyone assumed Alice had decided to stay in Syracuse with her brother, eliminating the need for any more tales. Only the pastor knew the truth.

Jack brushed her hair away from her face. He touched her

trembling lips with a soft kiss. Her legs went weak, and she curled her arms around his neck, pressing her body against his. His kiss deepened, his tongue flicking over hers. She was hungry for love, hungry for her husband. His hands slipped slowly over her body, with a promise of things to come.

She couldn't be happier, and she owed it all to a tin angel. Alice looked to the top of the Christmas tree where the special tree topper gleamed. She'd never forget the miracle she'd been granted.

"Do you know how much I love you?" she asked Jack softly.

"Why don't you show me?"

She took his hand and led him to the bedroom. "Oh, I plan to. Every day for the rest of our lives."

Also by Raine English

The Tempted Series

Book One

DATE WITH A VAMPIRE

She gave him her heart, but he wanted her soul...

Melody Johnson, a shy bookworm with a secret yearning for romance and love, dreams of meeting a man as dashing and wonderful as the heroes in the books she reads. But being a realist, she knows that's highly unlikely. Besides, men always leave her for someone more exciting—until she wins the lottery, that is. Pursued by scores of men happy to help spend her fortune, Melody longs to have her quiet life back. When a network executive calls her about appearing on a reality show, she seizes the opportunity to show the world she's off the single's market. Melody leaves her quaint hometown in New York for a sunny island in the Pacific where twenty gorgeous bachelors will vie for her heart and where she can stage a phony engagement. What she never expects, though, is to fall in love with a vampire.

Guystof LeBreque is a four-hundred-year-old Romanian vampire who hates the taste of blood. He's roamed the earth for centuries, feeding on criminals of the worst degree and loathing the monster trapped inside him. When his father gives him an ultimatum to marry a rich woman in sixty days or lose his legacy to his evil bloodthirsty brother, Guystof resorts to drastic measures. He becomes a bachelor on a hit reality show. What he doesn't anticipate is losing his heart to the woman whose mortal life he must end.

Please enjoy the following excerpt for DATE
WITH A VAMPIRE...

CHAPTER ONE

*M*elody Johnson's heart pounded. Her fingers trembled. She stared at the lottery ticket clenched in her hand, then glanced over the rim of her reading glasses to check for the umpteenth time the numbers shown on the television screen.

Yup. They all matched. She swallowed hard. Holy cow! She was a multimillionaire. Rich beyond her wildest dreams. One-hundred-million dollars rich. If she held the only winning lottery ticket, that was. But she wasn't greedy. Even if there were other winners, she'd be happy with whatever her share came to. She was about to have a lot more money than she'd ever dreamed of having.

She could even quit her job. Think of that—never having to shelve another book again. Although she loved working at the Reader's Den, the tiny bookstore paid only slightly more than minimum wage, and it could be years till a position opened at the library. Mrs. Smith had commanded the front desk for as long as Melody could remember yet showed no signs of retiring any time soon. Melody had always wanted to be a librarian, but she didn't want to leave her small hometown of Hope, New York, to do so. She'd grown up there. Her friends and family all lived there. And it was only an hour outside of New York City. Everything she could ever want was in Hope.

Besides, money had never mattered much. She shared the two-story townhouse apartment with her three best friends. They paid their bills on time and had a few bucks left each month for a night on the town—usually spent at Chucky's Bar and Grill sucking down margaritas and splitting an order of nachos supreme. What more could a girl want? She'd always figured she had plenty of time to worry about her financial future. Yet, it looked like that had all been taken care of for her, and it had only taken a trip to the convenience store for a box of dog biscuits for her little black pug, Gizmo.

She never bought lottery tickets, mainly because she just never thought to. Today had been different, though. When the clerk handed her the two dollars in change, it was as if someone stood beside her and whispered lottery numbers in her ear.

Melody stared at the paper in her hand. If this was an indication of the power of intuition, she'd make sure to listen to all her inner urgings from now on. Sliding the sleeping pug off her lap, Melody hoped her legs were now steady enough to support her. She rose from the couch and bolted upstairs to wake her childhood friends. Mags, short for Margaret, shared a room with Billy, aka Willamina, while she bunked with Ann, not short for anything.

As she ran down the hall, her gaze drifted to the lottery ticket in her hand. Just a few minutes ago she'd been your average twenty-four-year-old, and now… Well, her life would never be the same. What lay ahead, she couldn't even begin to imagine.

₧₧

Blood trickled from the corner of Guystof LeBreque's mouth. He grimaced and wiped at it with the back of his hand. The taste of his kill lingered on his tongue. He couldn't wait to get home to rinse his mouth. For nearly four hundred years, he'd scoured the earth, hunting unknowing victims to quell his hunger and hating himself for it. Why couldn't he have been more like his younger brother, Theo, who loved everything about being a vampire?

Guystof raced through the fog-filled streets of London, darting in and out of shadowy alleyways toward his flat on the outskirts of the city. The memory of the dead man with two perfect holes piercing his neck, his drained body abandoned to the shadows, turned his stomach. Why had Guystof been condemned to live this eternal nightmare? His only salvation lay in his choice of victims: criminals of the worst degree.

He skirted the piles of garbage lining the streets. A horrible stench permeated the air, adding to his nausea. The sun had begun to crest the horizon, and he shielded his eyes with his hand. If he didn't hurry, he'd burn. Only once in his life had he experienced the dreadful bubbling—nearly two hundred years ago—yet the memory was as fresh as if it had happened yesterday. The pain had been almost intolerable, for not only his skin was affected. He'd begun to boil internally too, and if Theo hadn't dragged him inside, he would have been reduced to nothing more than a melted puddle of flesh. The sun was his enemy, more powerful than any vampire-hunting assassin.

Guystof dashed over the cobblestone street, his black cape billowing behind him like the wings of a bat. He spotted his flat up ahead and heaved a sigh of relief. His muscles ached with exhaustion. He longed for sleep. When he slid his key in the lock, his fingers started to tingle. He'd made it home just in time.

Inside the safety of his flat, he leaned against the thick wood door. Beads of sweat lined his brow, and a drop rolled onto his cheek.

"Still living on the edge, I see."

Guystof froze. What was his brother doing here? There was no mistaking Theo's thick Romanian accent. He never tried to conceal it, thinking it added to his charm. Guystof scanned the darkened room for him. The squeak of the rocking chair and the glow of a cigarette gave away his location.

Guystof left the foyer and crossed into the parlor, pointing his finger at the stone hearth. A fire exploded, and flames shot through the iron grating. The sudden light waved across the old Victorian parlor, touched on the dark oak furniture and Aubusson carpeting. He rarely used his powers, and almost never to do something he could just as easily do manually, but he needed to see his brother's face to decipher the real reason he'd come to call. Guystof knew him well enough to know his words alone might not provide the truth. Though he cared deeply for Theo, and owed him his life, he was not fool enough to trust him completely, for there was a side to him that no one knew. He'd betray his family, if it served his purpose.

"A few more minutes out in the light and I fear I'd be treating you again, brother. Stirs up memories, doesn't it? Only this time might have proved more difficult. We're not in our country. These Brits don't look so kindly on our type."

Guystof studied Theo, outlined by the flickering orange flames. Although it had been more than a century since he'd seen him, his brother looked unchanged—shorter and stockier than he, with a face and body women adored. His blond curls were the complete opposite to Guystof's straight dark locks. Theo's boyish good looks were a tool he used to his advantage, but beneath his handsome facade lay a heart as dark as the devil's own.

Guystof leaned against the mantle, crossing one polished black shoe in front of the other. "What brings you to these parts? I know you haven't come merely to save my neck."

"That hurts. Why assume I don't care about your well-being?" The faintest hint of a smile graced his full lips, making him look oddly effeminate.

Guystof narrowed his eyes. Theo was toying with him and enjoying it. "You're fully aware no offense was meant, so let's cut to the chase, shall we?"

"All right, old boy, we'll save the small talk for later. You were right. I haven't come of my own accord. Father sent me." Theo leaned forward in the chair and reached into his back pocket, drawing out a crumpled piece of parchment. "I'm to give you this." He handed over the paper, with a look Guystof couldn't decipher.

After unfolding the letter, he began to read. His brow furrowed and he waved the paper out in front of him. "How long have you had this?"

Theo took a drag on his cigarette and exhaled a long line of smoke. "You're not an easy man to find. I traveled Europe for weeks before finding your quaint little London abode."

"Nonsense. Tessa knows my whereabouts," Guystof said harshly, aggravated by this game.

"You don't know?" Theo's eyes glistened. Were those tears?

His fingers tensed on the paper. Something had happened. "Know what?" His voice cracked when he spoke.

"Tessa's gone. Killed by an assassin."

Guystof squeezed his eyes shut and clenched his jaw. It had happened again… Memories of another time and place whirled through his mind. His own mother had been killed by assassins, when he was only sixteen. Her death had been so painful that he'd never forgotten the agony on her face. After that tragedy, he'd vowed to never turn a woman into a vampire. He'd travel through eternity alone, rather than risk losing someone he loved that way again. Yet it had happened…this time to his beloved Tessa… And she'd always been so careful too. That didn't seem to matter, though. A woman turned as an adult never acquired the skills necessary to protect herself from her enemies. It had only been a matter of time before she faced an excruciating death.

He crossed the room and stood beside Theo, placing his hand on his brother's shoulder. "I'm so sorry. I loved her too." Although she hadn't been his natural mother, he'd cared for her as such, and she'd returned his love by treating him as her own. She'd never showed Theo preferential treatment. Both boys had been raised under her careful tutelage.

"Is that the reason for this?" Guystof's gaze filtered down to the letter he held limply in his hand.

Theo shook his head. "Father's devastated. He'll not marry again. He's barely able to hunt for food, let alone raise enough money to keep Dragesa afloat. The castle needs repairs, to say nothing of the state of ruin the grounds have fallen into."

"But I can't marry. I took a vow."

Sneering scorn crossed Theo's handsome face. "That was no vow. Merely a silly promise you made to yourself as a boy. Now it's up to you to carry on the family legacy. You must choose a bride, and select wisely. You'll need one with a fortune," he said with a snicker. "Oh, and remember, you've only sixty days."

Guystof reread the letter, more carefully this time. When he finished, he directed his gaze back to Theo. "Father says nothing about the reason for the rush."

"Why prolong the inevitable? We all know you won't come through."

"And if I don't?"

Theo's eyes glittered dangerously, and a smug smile curved his mouth. "Then you'll no longer be a LeBreque. Father will disown you, and I shall become the family heir. We've ruled for centuries, and I'm not about to let the LeBreques lose that honor. Besides, I'll have no problem finding a mate. Of that, you can be sure."

The impact of Theo's words was not lost on Guystof. If he failed, not only did he face disgrace, but the kingdom would become a much more dangerous place. Theo loved nothing better than the taste of blood, and with him in control, there'd be nothing to stop him and his twisted desires.

℀℀

"Don't answer it," Melody shouted from the living room, wishing the phone would stop ringing. Her roommates chattered in the kitchen, preparing dinner. Just a week had passed since she'd gone to lottery headquarters and learned she held the only winning ticket, making her New York's latest most-eligible female, yet the word had spread like wildfire. It seemed everyone wanted a part of her.

"I want my old life back," she said wistfully while sinking onto the couch. She scooped up the pile of messages the girls had taken for her and fanned through them.

"Sorry, Mel, that'll never happen." Ann entered the room, carrying a tray filled with chips and dip. She set it down on the coffee table in front of Melody, then snatched the papers from her hands. "I'm afraid these are just the beginning. Not only are you rich, but you're single. And being gorgeous doesn't hurt, either. You're one hot commodity, babe."

Melody groaned. "I don't want to be a hot commodity. I just want to be me, unknown old Melody from Hope."

Ann dropped the messages on the table, took hold of Melody's hand and pulled her to her feet. She dragged her over to the wall mirror. "Look, Mel, with a face and figure like yours, there's no way the media's going to keep you from the spotlight."

Big blue eyes stared back at her as she studied her reflection. A nice straight nose and full lips rounded out her heart-shaped face, while long strands of honey colored hair draped her shoulders.

"Face it. You're America's new sweetheart."

Melody rolled her eyes.

"Get used to it. This is only the beginning."

"How am I going to live my life? How are we going to live? The phone never stops ringing." Her gaze scanned over the roses, carnations, and various other flowers spilling out from the vases sent to her by an endless stream of gold-digging men. "Seems like everyone in town now knows where I live." She turned to face her friend. "It's not fair to you…to any of you guys…but where can I go and not be found? What can I do to change all this?"

She crossed the room and plopped back onto the couch. Picking up a handful of messages from the table, she began to read. " 'I'm a single white male, thirty-five, who would love to love you.' " She made a face and tossed the paper onto the floor. "Here's another one. 'Although I'm fifty-seven, don't let my age scare you. I can teach you things that young guys don't even know exist.' Yuck." She crumpled the message and threw it on the floor along with the other one. "And the list of Hope's single men goes on and on," she said, fanning the rest of the letters.

Ann's eyes grew wide and her jaw dropped open. "I've got it, I've got it," she shrieked, jumping up and down.

Melody scowled. "Oh, not you too. Don't tell me there's someone you want to fix me up with."

"Not someone. Twenty someones."

"What?"

Ann spread the papers over the coffee table. "Oh, where is it? I only just took the message this morning."

Melody patted her friend's arm. "Calm down. Where's what?"

"The message from the producers of *Dream Girl.*"

Melody groaned, and her fingers tightened around Ann's upper arm. "You're not going to tell me what I think you are, are you?"

Ann's eyes sparkled with excitement. "Well, if you think they want you to be the next Dream Girl, then yes, that's what I'm telling you."

She took a deep breath and coaxed Ann onto the couch. "Sit here and listen very carefully. I am not going to be the next anything. I don't want any TV appearances or interviews of any kind. I want to live a quiet life. Got it?"

Ann drew her brows together into a deep scowl. "I know that's what you want, but I'm afraid the media doesn't give a fig about your wishes. That's why this idea is so fantastic. Don't say no. As a matter of fact, don't say anything until you've heard me out and given it some thought."

She leaned back against the couch and folded her arms across her chest. "Okay, I'll listen, but that's all. You're not going to convince me to do anything."

Ann grinned, exposing the gap between her two front teeth. "Fair enough." She tucked one leg up under her and faced Melody. "I was skeptical too when I took the call. I mean, who would want to star in a reality show? Especially one where twenty gorgeous guys are vying for your love? But think about it, Mel. The producers screen these guys. They do extensive background checks. We're not talking average Joes here. These guys are the crème de la crème. So aside from having a fabulous time with twenty hunks wining and dining you, we'll put an end to these." Ann held up the pile of messages from the litany of men wishing to meet Melody.

"I'm afraid I'm not getting it. How is my going on *Dream Girl* going to put an end to all this?"

Ann rolled her eyes as if Melody was dense. "It's simple, really. The purpose of the show is for you to find your soul mate, and that's exactly what you're going to do."

"Have you lost your mind? You know how I feel about those shows. They might be fun to watch, but I don't believe anyone there really finds a lasting love."

Ann took hold of her hands and squeezed. "No, silly. I don't believe that either. You only have to give the appearance of falling in love. Whichever man you choose, you announce your engagement to the world. A very long engagement," she said with a wink.

Melody's eyes widened. "I get you now. It's all for show, but as far as the public is concerned, I'm off the market."

"Precisely."

"Oh, Ann. I don't know. It sounds good in theory, but what about the poor man? The one I choose. It's not fair to deceive him."

"Mel, you're such a softy. You're worried about the feelings of a man you don't even know. Toughen up, girl, and worry about yourself."

She shook her head. "Even if I agreed to do it, I don't think I could carry it off. He'd see right through me and know my feelings weren't real. You know I'm a terrible actress."

Ann opened her mouth, then snapped it shut as Mags and Billy entered the room, carrying trays filled with food and drinks.

"Hey guys, what's up?" Billy asked, pushing the papers aside to set her tray down next to the chips and dip. "I've got a bunch of messages for you too, Mel." She reached into her pocket and pulled out a handful.

Mags laughed, though she sounded uneasy. "I do too. Looks like we're going to have to get an unlisted number."

Melody looked at each of her friends. Despite their joking, her newfound celebrity had become quite an imposition. They couldn't continue to live this way. Something had to be done and soon.

She took a deep breath and let it out slowly. Ann's solution was the only one she had. Spending a few weeks with twenty handsome bachelors sure beat disappearing into anonymity, or losing her friends because of this annoying, unwanted celebrity. If she was going to be a media darling, she might as well play the game and get the media to work for her. An island vacation. Fun times with guys who were undoubtedly searching for their fifteen minutes of fame more than true love, anyhow. No one would get hurt, and she'd be off the hook. *Go for it*, that little voice of intuition whispered. Grinning, she said, "Ann, I think you may have come up with the answer after all."

₞℣

Guystof paced his bedroom floor. The clock was ticking, and as each day passed so did his chances of fulfilling his father's ultimatum. He had to find a bride, no matter how distasteful that might be. But how was he to find one with a huge fortune and do so in a short period of time?

He crossed the room and grabbed his father's letter, then tore it into tiny pieces, letting them flutter to the floor. Impossible. And not only did Father know that, but Theo did as well. The thought of his brother as head of the LeBreque family turned his stomach. Theo was cruel, even by vampire standards, and to have him running things sent a chill straight to Guystof's heart. There had to be a way for him to find a rich woman to marry...

The knock on his door turned his thoughts from his dilemma, at least temporarily. The heavy wooden door opened, and Blakesley, his butler and confidant, strolled in carrying a silver tray topped with a tea set and the morning newspaper. "I thought you might like something warm to drink before you retire for the day, sir."

"That's very thoughtful of you," he replied, offering up a woeful smile. "But sleep is not something I've had much of lately."

"I know that, sir. It shows on your face, especially in the dark rings beneath your eyes. Perhaps if you read a bit, it will take your mind off your problems and help you to relax." Blakesley set the tray on the bedside table and poured a steaming cup of tea, then pulled down the bedspread and proceeded to shut the heavy velvet draperies surrounding the large mahogany four-poster.

Guystof watched as the elderly gentleman with his thinning crop of salt-and-pepper hair and faded hazel eyes, tried to make him comfortable. Blakesley's efforts were well appreciated.

He took a careful sip of tea, then picked up the newspaper. It was turned to the Entertainment section. The woman gracing the front page was a beauty. Even on cheap newsprint, there was no denying her classic good looks, but it was the heading, "Multi-Millionaire to be New Dream Girl," that caught his attention first.

"You sly devil." He laughed, slapping the newspaper on the edge of the table and shifting his gaze to Blakesley, who was trying to creep from the room unnoticed.

With a hand on the doorknob, his butler turned to face him. "Sir? Were you referring to me?"

Guystof let out a chuckle from deep in his belly. "I'm amazed at how clever you are."

Blakesley lifted a bushy white brow. "And how's that, sir?"

"Don't be coy, old man. You set me up to read this." Guystof waved the newspaper in front of him. "Though a splendid idea, it's a gamble. Even if the producers select me, there's no guarantee I'll win the Dream Girl's heart."

Blakesley crossed the room in his stilted gait to stand before him. "I've no doubt she'll fall in love with you, sir. None at all. For centuries women have been pursuing you. It's been you, sir, who has not been interested."

"But if this one was to select someone other than me, I'd have used up all my time, giving Theo control."

"You'll not let that happen, Count."

Guystof smiled and rubbed his square jaw line with his fingertips. "Ah, perhaps she will be impressed with the title. What American woman wouldn't love to become a countess, eh Blakes?"

"Indeed, sir. Indeed."

"It's settled then. Call the show's producers."

...Excerpt from *DATE WITH A VAMPIRE* by Raine English.

Available in ebook and print.

ABOUT THE AUTHOR

*A*ward-winning author Raine English always wanted to be a writer. She began her career as a journalist, but writing romance novels was her passion. Her stories have won many awards, including finalling in the Romance Writers of America® Golden Heart® and winning the Daphne du Maurier Award.

She enjoys writing both adult and young adult contemporary romance infused with elements of magic and the paranormal, along with eerie Gothic historical novels.

When not behind her computer, you can find her reading, usually something involving the supernatural. She lives in New England with her family, two dogs, and a mischievous cat.

Raine would love to hear from you! She can be reached at Raine@RaineEnglish.com.

Visit Raine's website at www.RaineEnglish.com
Follow Raine on Twitter at https://twitter.com/RaineEnglish
Join Raine on Facebook at www.facebook.com/RaineEnglish

www.ingramcontent.com/pod-product-compliance
Lightning Source LLC
Chambersburg PA
CBHW030303200626
46816CB00002BA/745